THE
FELLOWSHIP

an imprint of HarperCollins Publishers

To Annie, for all the miles so far,
and the new map yet to be discovered

Walden Pond Press is an imprint of HarperCollins Publishers.
Walden Pond Press and the skipping stone logo are trademarks
and registered trademarks of Walden Media, LLC.

The Fellowship for Alien Detection
Copyright © 2013 by Kevin Emerson
All rights reserved. Printed in the United States of America.
No part of this book may be used or reproduced in any manner whatsoever
without written permission except in the case of brief quotations embodied
in critical articles and reviews. For information address HarperCollins
Children's Books, a division of HarperCollins Publishers,
10 East 53rd Street, New York, NY 10022.
www.harpercollinschildrens.com

Library of Congress Cataloging-in-Publication Data
Emerson, Kevin.
The Fellowship for Alien Detection / Kevin Emerson. — First edition.
   pages   cm
   Summary: Thirteen-year-olds Haley and Dodger, winners of a fellowship,
set out to investigate a series of possible alien abductions on tortuous family
road trips that converge in a town that does not seem to exist.
   ISBN 978-0-06-207186-6 (pbk.)
   [1. Alien abduction—Fiction.   2. Missing persons—Fiction.
3. Extraterrestrial beings—Fiction.   4. Automobile travel—Fiction.   5. Family
life—Fiction.   6. Fathers and sons—Fiction.   7. Science fiction.]   I. Title.
PZ7.E5853Fel 2013   2012025498
[Fic]—dc23   CIP
                                                                             AC

Typography by Carla Weise
14 15 16 17 18   OPM   10 9 8 7 6 5 4 3 2 1
❖
First paperback edition, 2014

chapter

Juliette, AZ, April 25, 7:00 a.m.

Suza Raines was getting suspicious. As the screen
door slapped shut behind her, she paused on the front
porch thinking: *Mr. Davis. He'll come by in that maroon
jogging suit, walking MacDougals. . . .*

Sure enough, Mr. Davis promptly rounded the
corner, MacDougals straining at his leash and sniffing
the gutters. The big old golden retriever sounded like
a broom, the way his long nose swished the piles of
yellow pine needles around. Mr. Davis walked briskly,
his bald head, maroon jogging suit, and pristine white
sneakers gleaming in the pale dawn sun.

Suza shook her head and hopped down the stairs.

There was nothing weird about that. Mr. Davis and MacDougals walked by at seven every morning, just after Mr. Davis returned from his nighttime job at the town's power station. If there was anything out of the ordinary, it was that Suza was on time enough to actually see them pass. She was always late out the door because she hated morning, wanted nothing to do with it. And she only needed ten minutes to bike to school (even if it always took fifteen).

So why was she so early? Suza felt like it had something to do with her alarm clock. It had kinda freaked out this morning. Instead of waking her up like usual, with the bubbly voice of DJ Alpine and hit country music on KJPR, it had blasted a strange old-timey song with a deep voice singing in another language. And then she hadn't been able to read the time because the numbers were incomplete, like a few of the red digital bars were on the fritz. So, instead of hitting SNOOZE a few times until her father, Matt, would come in to roust her, she just got up, only now here she was: early.

Or was she? She pushed up the sleeve of her denim jacket and looked at her bare wrist. Where was her black and purple watch? With that weird old cartoon character named Thundarr that she'd seen on Cartoon Remix? He was all shirtless and silly looking and had a dinosaur for a pet, and the watch was cool because behind him, the moon hung in the distance, cracked in half. Her sister had gotten it for her on Ebay. . . .

Silly, she thought to herself, *you don't have a watch, and you don't have a sister.* That was strange. Why would she have thought otherwise?

Then, she had another weird thought: *Mr. Davis is going to stub his left toe and fall on his face.*

Suza was just picking up her bike from the pine-needle-choked lawn when Mr. Davis's left toe caught on a crack in the road and he toppled over.

Suza cocked her head. She'd known that was going to happen. . . . All the same, she needed to get going. Being early meant she had time to stop by the One Horse Diner. Her dad's friend AJ worked there and made the best breakfast sandwiches.

She coasted down to the end of the driveway and paused to button up her jacket—

And found Mr. Davis standing right in front of her. Another one of those weird predictions crossed her mind. *He's going to give me something.*

"Have to give you this," said Mr. Davis absently. He reached into his pocket and produced a small metal rectangle. It was the size of a stick of gum, with notches in its sides. The metal was bright silver, but it also seemed to glow with an oily rainbow pattern beneath its surface.

Suza stared at the object. For some reason, it looked familiar.

"Finally got it," Mr. Davis said, sounding relieved. Then, he leaned in close to her. "You have to take it to the diner," he whispered.

Suza took the object. It was cool in her hand. She saw a set of five symbols etched in a line across it, like those ancient Egyptian hieroglyphics or something:

Nervousness crept over her. This was familiar, but she wasn't sure how. "What do I do with this?" she asked.

"Not sure . . . You—you're supposed to take it to the diner so that we can—" Suddenly Mr. Davis froze. He looked around like there was a bug buzzing around his head and then slapped three times at the skin right behind his left ear.

MacDougals barked fretfully.

"What are you—" Suza began, but then a stern, deep voice spoke up in her head:

NEVER MIND THAT, SUZA. NOW, HURRY ALONG. IT'S TIME TO GET TO SCHOOL.

Suza reached up and absently slapped at the area behind her left ear, as if a bug were bothering her, too. She shook her head. . . . What had she been doing?

Oh yeah, going to school. She looked up at Mr. Davis. "Did you just say something?" she asked.

Mr. Davis looked down at Suza like he didn't even know her. "I— Did I?" He checked his watch. "Oh my. Come on, boy," he said to MacDougals. "Time to go!" He hurried off down the street. MacDougals looked back at Suza with big, pleading eyes.

Suza watched them go, then realized she had something in her hand. She gazed down at the metal object. What was this thing? She felt like she'd seen it before, like it was important—

THAT'S NONSENSE, SUZA. IT'S JUST A PIECE OF TRASH. The firm voice washed across her brain like gentle surf, erasing the footprints of her strange thoughts.

Suza immediately flicked the metal piece into the nearby storm drain, where it clattered harmlessly out of sight.

VERY GOOD. NOW, GET TO SCHOOL.

Right. Suza pushed back her sand brown hair, except for one curl that always sprang free and in front of her eyes. She strapped on her helmet, slipped on her purple-framed sunglasses, and lunged forward on her bike.

Cold, sweet air caressed her face. In the distance, a train horn echoed.

The road curved steeply along the side of a forested hill. Suza hurtled along, wind roaring in her ears. To her left, the town of Juliette lay in its perfect grid pattern, on a flat, high desert plateau surrounded by hills of amber grass. A pale sun had just risen over the distant horizon. The rays skipped across the flat brick building tops, bathing the hills and lighting the distant, snowcapped peak of Mount Randall. To her right, the white cylindrical tower of the Foster Observatory stood like a castle atop a rocky ridge. The dome of the observatory was just finishing its final rotation, its curved steel roof sliding closed like a weary eyelid.

The road flattened out and she entered waking neighborhoods, street after street of one-story ranch houses just like hers. Up ahead, a circle of orange plastic fencing had been erected in the middle of the road. A large sign beside it read: "**SLOW**." Inside the fencing, a manhole cover was open. As Suza swerved around the construction, a head popped up out of the manhole. It was a man wearing a yellow hard hat and an orange jumpsuit.

He'll stare at me when I go by, Suza thought.

The man stared at her as she sped past. She didn't get a clear look, but it seemed like he'd been wearing small, black sunglasses. Wasn't that an odd thing to wear down in the dark?

NOT AT ALL, the voice assured her. TURN HERE TO GET TO SCHOOL.

Suza almost did, but then she remembered her plan to go to the diner. She continued straight ahead, the houses giving way to short brick buildings, until she reached the traffic light at Main Street. Pickups and Jeeps grumbled by, their bumpers gleaming in sideways sun, tailpipes spinning clouds of exhaust.

Suza locked her bike to a parking meter and started walking down Main Street. As she did, more strange predictions arrived in her head.

It won't open for him, she thought as she passed a man dropping a quarter in the Juliette *Chronicle* box.

"Oh, come on!" the man shouted, tugging furiously at the handle.

I'll bump into a fat lady in a yellow dress, Suza thought as she pulled open the glass door to the One Horse Diner—and immediately collided with a large woman who was just stepping out. Suza bounced back and looked up.

The woman glared at her over a giant travel mug. "Why don't you—"

"I know. *'Watch where I'm going, half-pint,'*" Suza finished for her. She shook her head and stepped into the warm, bustling diner. She was greeted by the aroma of syrup, coffee, and bacon grease, and she felt a deep growl of hunger.

"Suze!" a voice called from behind the crowded counter. AJ was leaning through a narrow space between two customers. His white apron was already smudged with grease and ketchup and was currently dangling into an unsuspecting customer's eggs Benedict. "How you doing, little lady?"

"Um." Suza looked left and right. More predictions were coming. So many at once . . . An old man was going to sip his coffee then cough sharply. And he did. A young woman was going to erupt with a gaudy laugh and accidentally spit a hunk of pancake onto the lady across from her. And she did. Woman in a cowboy hat leaving the bathroom . . . Check.

"Earth to Suze," AJ called. "Not awake yet, are ya?"

Actually, it felt like exactly the opposite. Suza felt *too* awake. Too aware. She turned back to AJ, her face blank. *He'll ask me . . .*

"You here for the AJ Special? Bacon and peanut butter on whole wheat?"

Suza started to shake. It was like she knew *everything.*

"What's the matter?"

"You're going to be out of peanut butter."

"Nahh, we've got plenty of . . ." AJ reached down into the cabinet below him, then looked at her in surprise. "Well, I'll be darned . . . I—" AJ's eyes suddenly went wide. His voice lowered to a whisper. "Hey, where's the— the thing? Did you bring it?"

"The—" Suza suddenly remembered the piece of

metal. "Oh no . . . I threw it away!"

AJ glanced around worriedly. "You were supposed to bring it, weren't you?"

"I was?" But yes, of course she was. That was the *plan*. "I'll go get it," said Suza.

"Hurry," said AJ.

Suza left the diner, running back up the street toward her bike. Understanding flooded through her. *We need that piece of metal, because there's something wrong with this morning. But, not just this morning. Every morning. And that piece of metal is a key to—*

SUZA! the voice in her head thundered. YOU WILL COME TO SCHOOL NOW! CALMLY AND WITHOUT DELAY.

Suza stopped in her tracks. She slapped behind her ear. All of a sudden, she was calm again. Her breathing slowed. *Just get to school*, she thought. *Right*.

She grabbed her bike and rode slowly, arriving at school a few moments later. Buses were pulling up in a line, kids streaming off. Suza tossed her bike carelessly against the bike rack and walked straight through the double doors, down the hallway all decorated with pastel-colored murals of April flowers.

RIGHT THIS WAY, SUZA, the voice said approvingly.

She reached the office and walked inside, straight past the reception counter and directly into the principal's office.

"Suza," Principal Howard's deep voice soothed.

He sat reclined, filling the wide leather chair behind his dark wood desk, smiling kindly at her.

She started to think: *His smile is fake and I have to get out of*—

Stay right there, Suza, the voice in her head commanded.

Beside Principal Howard stood another short man in an orange jumpsuit and yellow hard hat. He wore black boots and small, oval sunglasses that actually looked more like swimming goggles, except that they were pure black. He stepped toward her. Suza wanted to move, but she didn't. She couldn't.

"It happens, dear, now and then," Principal Howard assured her. "But don't worry. . . ." The orange-suited man put his hand around her wrist. It felt neither cold nor warm. "We'll make everything just like it was."

Suza looked down, and as the first pulses of neon orange light began to spread from the man's palm, that feeling of knowing the future overwhelmed her. "No, you can't do it again!" she screamed. Principal Howard stopped smiling. "This is all happening over and over! You can't! I won't—"

But her voice faded as orange light washed over her.

A few minutes later, Suza walked out of the office. She headed straight to class, where she slid into her desk and sat at attention, eyes on Ms. Fells, her math teacher.

"Good morning, Suza," said Ms. Fells, smiling sweetly. "Nice of you to join us. Do you have a note for your tardy arrival?"

"Huh?" Suza wondered what she was talking about. She glanced at the clock and found that she was eight minutes late. How had that happened? Sure, she'd popped into the office for a minute, but . . . Why had she even gone there, in the first place?

"Suza?" Ms. Fells was now beside her. "It's all right, you're not in trouble." Suza watched Ms. Fells reach down and pluck a small, yellow pass out of her hand. "Now," Ms. Fells said, striding back to the front of the room, "let's get started."

Suza stared at her hand for another moment, then shrugged and began pulling her books out of her bag. What were they going to do in class today? She thought about it, but realized she had no idea.

After all, why would she?

part

ONE

JUST ANNOUNCED:

$25,000

AVAILABLE FOR
CREATIVE THINKERS!

THE
GAVIN KELLER FOUNDATION
PROUDLY ANNOUNCES
THE FIRST ANNUAL
FELLOWSHIP FOR ALIEN DETECTION

OVERVIEW

The Gavin Keller Foundation is pleased to offer this unique fellowship award and field research experience to creative-thinking teens nationwide.

AWARD

Winners will receive a fully funded, two-week research fellowship grant, publication of their field study report in *New Frontiers Mag-Zine**, and a $25,000 college scholarship annuity.

APPLICATION REQUIREMENTS

Applicants must submit a standard application and a detailed field study proposal, including:
  a) A well-researched hypothesis supporting the idea of extraterrestrial visitation
  b) A plan to research your theory in the field over a two-week period

BACKGROUND

Founded by Gavin Keller, a former NASA scientist and editor in chief of *New Frontiers Mag-Zine*, the Keller Foundation is dedicated to raising awareness of alternate narratives and credible scientific study in the fields of plausible phenomena and speculative forensics.

ACCREDITATION

The FAD is accredited by the NFUO (New Futures University Online) and endorsed by the CCN (Coalition for Crystology and Numerology), the NAP (National Academy of Phenomenonics), NHIP (Network of Highly Involved Parents), the RHSA (Rebel Home School Alliance), and over three other forward-thinking academic and parent associations.

APPLICATION
FINAL DEADLINE:
APRIL 1st

New Frontiers Mag-Zine is America's most popular online zine, devoted to illuminating our place in the cosmos as well as showcasing new culinary trends for the informed intergalactic palate.

chapter

Greenhaven, CT, June 30, 2:14 p.m.
Haley Richards gazed at the writing prompt on the board:

"My summer will be . . ."

"One more minute," Ms. DeNetto announced. "Please finish up the sentence you're on."

Haley glanced around. Most of her classmates had written a couple of paragraphs and were now sitting back in the stuffy air, waiting for these last few minutes of the school year to tick by. She looked down at her own page and saw nothing but light blue lines on a vacant landscape of white. Normally, she was one of the best writers in her eighth grade class, but today she hadn't written a thing. How could she? Haley had no idea what her summer would be. She knew what it was supposed to be; she'd had it all planned out in what everyone knew was very typical Haley fashion. But then, as everyone in class also knew, things hadn't quite worked out. And now, not only was Haley's summer a blank page, but it felt like her very future was unwritten.

"Okay, time's up." Ms. DeNetto walked to the front of the room. "And . . . " she said dramatically, "it looks like we will have time for a few last readers to end the year." A fluttering sound came from her hands. Ms. DeNetto was shuffling her Deck of Fates. Groans and sighs sounded from around the room.

Haley sat up, propelled by a rush of nervous energy in her gut. It was a feeling she knew all too well: a wriggling anxiety just below and behind her belly. She sometimes imagined that it was caused by a tiny creature, a parasite or maybe some kind of stomach gnome. The feeling had been with Haley her whole life, like an old friend, or maybe nemesis was more accurate, a little doubt demon riding shotgun inside her, questioning every move and pointing out every possible flaw.

She slapped her notebook closed. A playing card was taped to the front: eight of diamonds. Each kid had a card, and Ms. DeNetto had a matching deck. If she picked your card, you had to read aloud to the class. And while a blank page might get some of her classmates out of reading, Haley knew that if she got picked, Ms. DeNetto would just ask her to talk about her summer anyway.

If she had to, Haley could talk about it, but she didn't want to. Didn't want to deal with everyone's judgment about what she *wasn't* doing, and didn't want to bother trying to justify what she actually *was* doing.

She glanced at the clock. 2:15. Fifteen more minutes. That was about five readers. *Please don't pick me*, she begged the Fates. *Really, it's the least you could do.*

Ms. DeNetto drew the first card from the deck. "Five of spades."

Okay, one down. Little whispers of "Yes!" escaped around the room. Haley shared in that wave of relief, but only for a moment, because then she realized who had just been chosen. Madison Blake. *Well played*, Haley sneered to the smiling Fates. It looked like, as payment for not being called on, the Fates had decided to remind Haley of this summer's failings.

"My summer will be . . . a blooming garden of discovery," Maddy began theatrically. Haley reached back and pulled off her hairband, letting her brown bangs fall in front of her eyes so that she wouldn't be caught glaring. There were many things about Maddy that could inspire spite and jealousy: how she over-enunciated *t*'s at the end of words and treated *l*'s like they were made of ornately blown g-llll-ass, the big fuzzy boots that she wore when it was even a degree below fifty, the unspeakable way that she'd dumped their classmate Beckett, and how calm and poised she always seemed to be, in all situations: fluster-free.

But worst of all was her plan for the summer.

"First, I'll be planting fertile seeds of compassion at Habitat"—emphasis on *t*!—"for Humanity Camp. . . ."

That wasn't the part that bothered Haley, though it did sound fun.

"Then, I'll spend two weeks pruning and shaping my lll–ove for theater at Junior Shakespearean Society."

Not that part, either . . .

"And then . . ." Maddy added a dramatic pause and even seemed to spend an extra second on Haley as her gaze swept across the room. "The fruits of a long sunny summer will ripen at Thorny Mountain Music Camp."

That part. Haley glanced over at her best friend, Abby Warren. Abby gave her a sympathetic shrug. Abby was also going to Thorny Mountain, which was up north in the Berkshires of Massachusetts. She and

Maddy were the only two kids going from the whole school. Haley had applied, too, but she hadn't gotten in. It was frustrating. Thorny Mountain was fun, and Haley was good at the flute. It made no sense! She'd been twice in previous years.

But not only did Maddy get the thing that Haley wanted, she was also about to have the kind of summer that Haley was supposed to have, that you *needed* to have. Maddy was one of those kids who knew, like Haley did, that the summer after eighth grade was no time for goofing around, being a kid, and having fun. No matter what fuzzy old Mr. Kendrick, the school guidance counselor, said, you only had to do the math to know that you were on the clock: four summers— that was all that was left between now and when college applications were due. And college was the big time. You weren't just being compared to the little bubble of Greenhaven kids; it was going to be you against the whole wide world. You had to be prepared.

And grades weren't enough. You had to have *experiences*. That's why the Madison Blakes of the world had put together summers chock-full of high-protein college application goodness. And Haley had tried to do the same thing, only it hadn't worked out.

Maddy finished and Ms. DeNetto shuffled the cards again. "Jack of hearts."

Two down. The class was more vocal in their relief. Anders and Marco high-fived behind her.

But no, no! Haley couldn't believe it. As if Madison Blake wasn't bad enough, the next reader was Bradley Hong. Of all the people . . . Haley felt a tingle of fizzy adrenaline reaching her fingertips. Her head felt spacey, like it was bobbing in the water. She cast an evil eye up at the gleeful Fates. *This isn't subtle at all, you know.* Inside, the doubt demon squirmed with delight.

"My summer will probably be life changing," Bradley began in his quiet, painfully shy way. He stood in his eternal hunch, black hair a mess, gazing at the floor as he spoke. Haley liked Bradley. He was sweet, and definitely who you wanted to be paired with for a research project, and it wasn't his fault that what he was about to say might well make Haley barf.

"First I'll be at Camp Nucleus at MIT. . . ."

Not that.

"Then I'm, um, doing fencing camp."

Or that.

"And then I go to New York for the *Daily Times* Junior Correspondent Fellowship."

That. That was the one.

Above all else, it was Haley's dream to be a journalist, and JCF was the coolest, the *only* summer journalism program worth attending, anywhere, ever. This was the first year that they were old enough to apply, and if you won, you got to go to New York City for two whole weeks and work at the *Daily Times* as an intern for a real, actual, in-no-way-not-amazing journalist. And sure, you would spend a lot of time doing grunt research or fetching coffee (which in itself sounded somehow amazing), but also, *also*, your famous journalist mentor was required to read and edit no less than one original article by you, which would then be published in the *Times* online edition at the end of the program.

Haley had spent many moments during classes and meals, not to mention the hours orbiting the rim of sleep, imagining herself at the JCF. She could picture her first day: cresting the stairs at Fifty-third and Lexington in the hot July sun and staring up at the steel-lined, modern facade of the Daily Times Building. She would breathe in the air, and it would smell like hot dogs, and in her lungs and beneath the arches of her sweaty feet and in the beats of her heart she would feel the certainty of knowing that she was exactly where she was supposed to be, doing exactly what she was supposed to be doing.

Each day of the fellowship, Haley would be ready, ears alert for when the quiet pearls of journalistic wisdom were dropped in her vicinity. She'd be prepared, too, just in case there was ever a murmur in the offices of a Garrett Conrad-Wayne sighting—yes, *the* Garrett Conrad-Wayne, he of the grizzled beard and the velvet prose and the dispatches from East Africa that did that thing where they spun you dizzy with beauty and heartbreak at the same time.

Because what if, just *what* and in addition *if*, Haley could get Mr. Conrad-Wayne to notice her, maybe by mentioning that she followed him on Facebook and just so happened to have read all of his articles? And what if he was like, *cool*, and then, what if someday, years later . . .

A story would come through that he was too busy to take. . . .

And he would remember that plucky Junior Correspondent. . . .

And then it would be Haley, descending through turbulent tropical skies to a remote island village on the edge of the world, with sweat stains on linen shirt, weight of digital SLR on neck, stained-edge notebook on lap, sticking to knees.

Haley could picture it all, a big future in a big world, that started this summer . . .

Happening to Bradley Hong! This was so wrong! Writing wasn't even Bradley's favorite subject! Though he was annoyingly good at it. But his real passion was physics! *Physics!*

Meanwhile, Ms. DeNetto had chosen the next card. "Two of clubs."

Carl Powell sauntered up. At least he and Haley had no summer aspirations in common. While Carl read about basketball camp, working at the movie theater, and how there would be free popcorn for his boys, and a few lucky girls, if you knew what he meant (Haley never really knew what Carl meant), Haley just gazed out the window into the lazy June afternoon.

The air was faded tan, the fat green leaves of the maple trees swaying lazily in a hot, pollen-coated breeze. It was so June, so the-last-day-of-school, the world ripe with possibility, but . . . Haley wasn't going to New York this summer, or Thorny Mountain.

In fact, she'd be spending six of the eight weeks of vacation right here in Greenhaven with the Parks and Recreation Department, where she'd worked for the last three summers, and where life-changing opportunities included fishing trash and worse out of the filters at the town pool, planting flowers around town hall, and then pulling weeds and shoveling pet leavings and trying to keep those once-promising blossoms from wilting in the long, hot sun, day after day, running in place, time slipping by.

And yet . . .

All that said, the summer wasn't necessarily a total loss, because for those remaining two weeks of summer, there was something that Haley was doing. And when Haley could put aside her disappointment about the *Times* and Thorny Mountain, she was able to remember that this other thing was a *big* thing. Well, maybe. It might also be nothing. Haley didn't know yet, and that was the main reason for her blank page.

It was also the reason why she didn't want to get called on right now. It was one thing to go up in front of the class and talk about things like the JCF, or Thorny Mountain, or State Select Soccer or whatever because everybody knew what those things were, and they all sounded serious and legitimate. Haley's other thing might well be amazing. It was potentially bigger than anything anyone else was doing, but the problem was, it didn't sound like it from the description. In fact, it sounded kinda crazy. Haley knew this, and so she'd tried to keep it secret, but thanks to chatty parents and nosy teachers, there were no secrets in middle school.

She'd already heard the jokes, from kids like Kaz and Dawn and Carl. And she'd heard the rumblings from parents and from her relatives: What kind of summer opportunity focused on extraterrestrials? How could that at all be serious?

Yep, these were the joys of winning the Fellowship for Alien Detection. And yet, Haley knew that what she'd discovered, the theory that had led to her winning that fellowship, was actually very serious, mind-blowingly serious, at least, again . . . maybe. She wouldn't know until next week, when she got out on the road, and so, in the meantime, she just wanted to get out of this classroom without having to try to explain herself to a bunch of immature kids—

"Eight of diamonds."

Unbelievable.

"Haley," Ms. DeNetto said enthusiastically, probably thinking Haley would rescue the tone of the presentations after Carl's popcorn giggle fest.

Haley sighed to the Fates. *Fine.* She slid out of her desk and started toward the front of the room.

"Haley, aren't you forgetting your notebook?"

"No," said Haley.

Some annoying classmates had already started snickering to one another.

Haley reached the front of the room and felt a sudden surge of nerves. She felt her T-shirt sticking to her back, her jeans sticking to her shins, and her glasses sliding down the bridge of her nose. There was a hot sensation on the back of her neck. She should have left her hair up! She tried to take a deep breath, but her lungs seemed to hit a wall.

What if they're right? said the doubt demon. *It might all be silly. It might all turn out to be nothing.*

Quiet! she snapped. Then she took a deep breath.

You can do this, she told herself. *Forget about how the fellowship SOUNDS. Just tell them about the story.*

Yes. The thought calmed her. The story she'd uncovered, the story that had won her the fellowship . . .

Her classmates might be laughing now, but they wouldn't be after Haley told them about the mystery of Suza Raines.

chapter

2

Greenhaven, CT, June 30, 2:24 p.m.

Haley had uncovered the mystery of Suza Raines by accident.

But if you were to read *Hunting the Story*, the collected essays, musings, and cocktail recommendations of Pulitzer Prize–winning journalist Garrett Conrad-Wayne, or better yet, happened to own a dog-eared copy that you kept in your backpack at all times like Haley did, then you knew the truth was something different:

"Most people," Haley could quote at any moment, using a mildly pompous British accent, *"see the world as a presentation of events and moments, each of which*

is absolute. *In other words, they perceive each thing as it is now and accept it for what it is. The journalist, on the other hand, sees the now and immediately peers through it, asking how and why each thing came to be. Instead of seeing merely what is, the journalist seeks to know what was, to understand why, and to dream of what could be."*

Here Haley would often insert a burly chest cough, from years of good scotch whiskey and bad cigarettes, and also to crack a smile from Abby, before continuing: *"This awareness by the journalist is the Sixth Sense for Story. In most cases, the answers are quickly found by consulting our own learned knowledge or referencing the world around us for context, but in these other cases, when the questions cannot be immediately answered, the Sixth Sense tingles. And when it tingles, the journalist knows that somewhere behind the surface lies a story waiting to be uncovered, and the hunt is on."*

That was how it had begun for Haley, with a tingle in her mind, and this feeling just so happened to strike during some serious procrastination time on Facebook.

Thinking back on it now, it had been so random: Haley had been sitting around one evening, in the middle of January, enthusiastically avoiding a set of comprehension questions about *I Am the Cheese*. She'd been scrolling through the babble of status updates when she peeked down one of those random rabbit holes that can open up online.

First, an update had caught her eye from a mutual friend of hers and Abby's, named Mia. Three photos appeared in a row on Mia's wall. She was at a wedding. The first photo showed Mia with a microphone, her face beet red, hamming it up with two other girls doing karaoke. The second showed Mia standing in a group with the bride. And then in the third, she was by a sunny table of hors d'oeuvres, waving happily at the camera, with a big grin around a mouthful of food. Standing beside her at the table was a heavyset girl with a scowl and black-rimmed eyes and bright magenta hair.

And it was this inadvertently photographed girl that caught Haley's attention. Unlike Mia, who wore a flower-printed dress, this girl was in jeans and a maroon T-shirt. She had lots of jelly bracelets on her wrists, and her bangs were held back with thick black barrettes. *Kind of a weird look for a wedding,* Haley had thought.

She'd then noticed the writing on the T-shirt. It read, "We Are the Missing."

Haley maybe thought it was a band. So this was some typical emo chick whose parents were lazy and let her get away with too much, like going to a wedding without dressing up.

But . . . there was something more, and now, it was

hard to remember exactly what. Had it just been the T-shirt? Or had it also been the look in the girl's eyes, which seemed more tragic than just pouty. . . .

Maybe it had been that look. Haley ran her cursor over the girl, saw she'd been tagged, and clicked on her name: Stephanie Raines.

And that was just about the end of the line. Stephanie's profile was locked off for friends only, so you couldn't see anything.

However, there was one photo on her wall that had been made visible to everyone. It showed a smiling girl, leaning on her bike in a driveway. She wore oval glasses, and her face was covered with freckles. She looked maybe a little younger than Haley.

And the caption below it read: "Please help find my sister."

And then there was a link: www.wearethemissing.net

It wasn't a band name.

Haley slid over the photo. The girl leaning on the bike was tagged Suza Raines. Her profile was locked off, too. She was a happy-looking girl, someone who seemed down-to-earth and fun. She didn't look like a runaway, not that Haley really knew what that would look like. And she wondered: What had happened to this girl?

And even at that point, it may still have been mostly about procrastination, but as Haley had opened a new browser tab to search for "We Are the Missing," she'd felt the tingle growing. There was something here—she just knew it. And the feeling almost seemed dangerous. A voice in her head told her not to look any further, to go back to her schoolwork.

Maybe that voice knew how Haley could fixate on something that interested her, and that there was no time for this, not with homework and after-school newspaper club and flute lessons and, at the time, those unfortunate Irish-step-classes-that-shall-not-be-talked-about, and of course that essay Haley wanted to get a head start on for the JCF application. But Haley had not been able to fight her Sixth Sense.

The search results for We Are the Missing came up. It was a network of people claiming to have experienced alien visits. Their blogs and sites were full of wild claims, everything from having been taken aboard spaceships and turned briefly into animals, to accounts of being forced by near-maniacal extraterrestrials to go to drive-through windows and order hundreds of hamburgers, which they apparently had insatiable cravings for, and so on, but whatever these people claimed, the constant was that everyone reported experiencing missing time events—situations in which periods of time had passed that no one could account for—and some of them also claimed to have lost people: friends, family members, sisters . . . like Suza.

And from there, Haley was gone. Homework, flute lessons, even that JCF essay, none of it stood a chance. Night after night, all winter and into spring, Haley had spent endless hours reading accounts of missing time and missing people, and all that research had led her to discover a pattern. Then, the advertisements on various websites led her to the Fellowship for Alien Detection, and finally, the theory she described in her application, based on the pattern she'd found, won her that fellowship, and . . .

And . . . it had done more than that. Because if Haley were really honest with herself, she would have to admit that the story of Suza Raines had consumed her so much so that she had totally rushed her applications to the JCF and Thorny Mountain and had barely gotten them in at all.

It was this story, this mystery that her Sixth Sense had been powerless to ignore, that had not only led to her winning the FAD, but also to missing out on those other opportunities.

Of course Haley had wanted to win them all, but, when compared to her discoveries about Suza Raines, those other opportunities felt . . . safe. They were official, known, whereas the FAD was risky, wild. Its mysteries were uncharted, and it felt like it had the most potential for something Haley could only describe as "new map." Worlds unseen, horizons unexplored . . .

the FAD had the potential to change the topography of her whole life. Getting that story assignment from Garrett Conrad-Wayne when she was in college? How about getting a huge story next week? And then who knew what the future might hold after that, what undiscovered worlds Haley might be able to get to. New map. That was the thing. And even if her theory ended up being bunk, there was still the road trip and its promise of sights, sounds, and country that she'd never seen. Everything about the FAD was literally over the horizon from the life she knew. And that was what Haley wanted more than anything.

But the price had been losing out on those other opportunities . . . and having to stand in front of class and defend the FAD's oddities, now.

"You didn't write anything?" asked Ms. DeNetto, sounding perplexed.

"No."

"Well, can you tell us what you'll be doing anyway?"

Someone snickered. It was Kaz. She and Dawn and Carl were grinning at Haley now like hungry hyenas.

"Little green men," Haley heard Dawn mumble to Kaz.

"Little green boyfriend," Kaz replied. They both cracked up.

Haley wondered yet again at her classmates' ability to think they were so old, and yet act so completely juvenile at the same time.

The doubt demon seized control again. *They might be right,* it said. *How can there really be aliens out there? And if there are, how is some thirteen-year-old from Connecticut going to find them?*

This was a good point. One that had tripped up Haley more than once. Generations of scientists, not to mention crazy RV-driving, ham radio–operating, aluminum-foil-helmet–wearing freaks, had come up empty in the search for evidence of extraterrestrials and UFOs.

But no. . . . *No,* she told the doubt demon. None of them had what she had: an actual story. And so, no, she was not going to stand up here and be a joke. She was not going to give in to doubting herself, because she knew what she had. And in fact, she remembered now that she had her keys in her pocket, and on her key chain she had something that was better than a notebook essay. *Oh yeah,* she thought to herself, *that's what a real journalist would do.* And so after one last check-in with Abby's encouraging eyes, Haley went for it.

"Okay," she said brightly. "So, I won something called the Fellowship for Alien Detection, and while most of you might think that sounds silly, you won't after you hear my winning theory."

She dug into her pocket, pulled out her keys, and held her thumb drive out toward Ms. DeNetto. "May I?" she asked.

"Oh, um, sure," said Ms. DeNetto.

Haley slid the drive into a port on the computer at the front of the room. It was connected to the projector. She scrolled through and clicked on her files, stopping on a slide-show presentation called INTRODUCTION. She'd made it for when she was on her research trip, for introducing herself to interviewees, and on the off chance that she ended up being interviewed herself by any town officials or local media. This was actually the perfect opportunity to try it out and see if it worked.

On the white screen at the front of the room, a photo appeared. The mere presence of an image immediately quieted the class, and Haley felt a serious tone settle over the room. She wished she'd been able to squash the nerves and doubt demon earlier to think of this; it would have saved her so much anxious energy, but better late than never.

She paced in front of the photo. Her shadow was thrown at a high angle behind her.

"This is Suza Raines," said Haley, sweeping a hand toward the girl on her bike. "Originally from Amber, Pennsylvania. Reported missing six months ago. She remains missing to this day, and there have been no leads in the case." Haley let a beat pass. A paragraph change. She looked around. Even Kaz was suddenly staring forward.

"On the night of her disappearance," said Haley, "fourteen people in Amber reported experiencing the effects of Missing Time, meaning they believed they had skipped over a period of time that they could not at all remember. Their accounts varied wildly, and none could be confirmed, but what matters is that they all had one answer in common. When asked how long they'd been missing, they all said the same thing: sixteen minutes. Well, all except for Suza, because she didn't come back."

Haley clicked to the next slide.

This one showed a map of the United States. Red dots were drawn all over it.

"Now, people report alien abductions all the time. With the internet, there are thousands of reported cases, many of them by weirdos with stories that make no sense. But here and there, as the red dots indicate, large groups of people within a town have reported this phenomenon of having lost sixteen minutes of time."

Haley cued the next slide. Same map. Fewer dots.

"And in many of those same towns, at least one person has been reported missing at right around the same time, if not the same night, as the missing time event."

Haley stopped and faced her class. Even the gum chewing had ceased. "So you might ask, how did these people know about this missing time, and why don't they have any proof?" She clicked again, and the next slide showed a bulleted list that read:

- **Disorientation**
- **EMP Loss**
- **Network Reconnect**

"There are three reasons," said Haley. "First, the people didn't really understand what had happened at first. It took at least a minute or two for people to snap out of their trance and suspect what had happened. For some, they never even knew until they heard about it from someone else. Many people thought they'd just dozed off for a minute, as the event happened late at night, and so they just got on with their lives.

"Second, there is another interesting coincidence among these towns: They all experienced computer malfunctions and electric problems similar to an EMP burst—that's an electromagnetic pulse. The power went out briefly and many hard drives, appliances, anything with a microchip were either damaged or wiped clean. Internet service was down until power was restored, and servers were reset.

"Third, cell phones, if they weren't wiped out

completely by the EMP effect, would have reset, and when they connected to the network, the time would have immediately updated.

"As a result, the only people with any actual evidence of this sixteen-minute time loss were the ones who happened to have an analog watch, or clock, anything mechanical that was frozen for the same amount of time that the people themselves were. And some of those people just shook their heads and reset their watches before they knew any better. Add that to the disorientation, the data loss, and"—Haley finished—"there's very little proof that these things even happen. And, let's be honest, reports of alien abduction and missing time sound a little crazy."

"Then how do you know it's even true?" asked Madison, with her best skeptic's sneer.

Haley felt a little jolt. Time for the big reveal . . . "Well, one thought I had was to look at town webcams for the abduction nights, since lots of towns have cameras to keep track of live weather and traffic and stuff. I wanted to see if, you know, UFOs showed up or something. The thing was, the data for those nights had been messed up by the EMP effect. But then it was while I was looking at *this* photo that I noticed something."

Haley clicked to the next slide. It showed a photo of an old brick building with a tower in the center.

On the tower was a clock.

"Here's a webcam of the town hall in Gable, New Hampshire. Gable had wide reports of a missing time event back in March. This screenshot of the webcam is from two days after the reported incident, once they got things back up and running. But there's something wrong with this picture. Anybody see what it is?"

Her classmates squinted. Abby raised her hand with wild enthusiasm.

"Yes, Ms. Warren?" Haley asked with a grin.

"The time is wrong!" said Abby.

"Right." Haley stepped up to the photo and pointed. "The webcam is live. Here's the time next to the date. See it? Six-forty p.m. But the town hall clock says . . ."

"Six-twenty-four?" Carl asked as if telling time was new to him.

"Exactly," said Haley. "Sixteen minutes off. That clock has since been corrected, but it got me thinking. Lots of town clocks are antiques, big, old, analog. And someone has to manually fix the time when it's wrong. So I checked and found that Amber, the town where Suza went missing, had a webcam on its town green, too, and you could see the clock on the town hall. I called the town offices in Amber and asked to see their webcam footage. I said I was doing a story on the number of people using public spaces, and so

I was going to count the number of people on their town green by the hour each day."

"You lied?" asked Beckett, sounding shocked, or maybe amazed.

"Well," said Haley, "kind of . . . " She hadn't thought of it as lying, but more like how Garrett Conrad-Wayne had put it: *Stories are cunning and elusive, and often use people's own fears and insecurities as camouflage. The journalist must not be afraid to do what is necessary to see through this dense foliage, to, if necessary, camouflage themselves and their intentions in order to get the information they need.*

Haley liked that explanation better than *lying*, and like Wayne had said, it had been necessary.

"Anyway, so they sent me the files, and sure enough, right after the reported missing time and Suza Raines's disappearance, the town clock was off. . . ."

"Sixteen minutes?" said Beckett, on the edge of his seat.

Haley nodded with some theatrical flare of her own. "Sixteen minutes." She flipped through a few more webcam photos. "All this winter and spring, whenever new reports of towns with abductions and missing time appeared online, I would try to find a webcam with a clock tower, either in their downtown or at a mall or whatever."

"The clock over at the Waterbury mall is always

wrong," said Kaz, her tone now one part confused and one part trying to be helpful. "Is that aliens?"

"Mmm, I don't think so," said Haley. "I also got a couple other towns to send me files, like I did with Amber. And the sum of all this research is . . . "

Haley clicked again and a final map appeared, this one with just eleven dots.

"Over the past three years, these are the places where I have direct evidence of missing time events, in the form of these photos. There are over twenty others where the evidence is strong, but I don't have webcam images to back it up.

"And so for the next two weeks, I'm taking a road trip to visit these sites and interview the people there about anything they might—or might not—remember. Any questions?"

Silence.

A long, low beep sounded, announcing the end of the school year.

"Have a good summer," said Haley, and she walked to her desk, picked up her books, and started for the door.

Haley and Abby walked home through steamy afternoon air that smelled like hot tar and lilies. They briefly visited the ammonia cool of the SpeedyMart for diet grape sodas and cucumber-flavored soy chips, then stopped to eat them on a bench outside the town pool, awash in a chlorine-tinged breeze that was fluttery with laughter.

"That was an awesome display of nerd power," said Abby.

"Ha, thanks," said Haley.

"Are you still bummed about the *Times*?"

"A little," said Haley. "But mostly no." She'd moved fully to hoping that her award-winning FAD story could make it all the way to the tablet of Mr. Conrad-Wayne as he sipped chai in a Nairobi lounge. Likely? No. Possible? Yes.

They both drank and munched quietly. Haley wondered what was on Abby's mind, but she also thought she knew. Now that school was over and she was headed home, it was on her mind, too.

Finally, Abby said, "Did you tell your parents yet?"

Haley took a big bite of chips before responding. "Well . . ." she said around the mouthful.

"Haley . . ."

Haley swallowed and sighed. "Not really," she said, and by "not really" she meant "not at all."

"How's that going to work?" Abby asked, sounding worried.

It bothered Haley; she didn't like people worrying about her, but maybe she was more bothered right then because she knew her friend had a right to be.

"Well," said Haley, "I figure they don't really need to know. I mean, as far as they're concerned, we're just driving around for two weeks, with me interviewing people who think they were visited by aliens, seeing what they say. It never has to come up until I'm safe at home writing the article."

"Sure," said Abby, "but if any of it is true . . ."

And here was the problem that Haley and Abby had discussed before: If it turned out aliens weren't behind the events, then what happened to those missing people? And if, though probably very unlikely, there really were aliens out there, how were they going to feel about someone trying to uncover their story? Would that person end up missing, too?

That was maybe scary. And it was directly related to the one thing that Haley hadn't bothered to mention to her parents. . . . She hadn't told them about Suza Raines, or any of the other reports of abductions. Clock towers and missing time? Yes. Missing people? No. She'd left that part out of her application until *after* her mom had proofread it.

"They wouldn't have let me go," Haley said quietly.

"Maybe," said Abby.

Haley felt like it was a certainty. Missing persons cases were serious, after all, and bound to activate her parents' protective instincts. *Wouldn't they be right to feel that way?* the doubt demon pointed out. Sure, but

Haley would tell them if things started to feel dangerous. *Are you sure about that?* She was. Mostly. "And besides," said Haley, trying to ignore a rustle of nerves inside, "it's like Conrad-Wayne says, sometimes you have to camouflage yourself—"

"Yeah, but Haley, Garrett Conrad-Wayne is an adult. You're thirteen."

Haley didn't like talking about this. And she hated how the doubt demon was feasting on it. *What if she's right?*

Haley also hated having a secret from her parents, hated the cold, damp feeling she was getting down the insides of her arms from thinking about it. She stood up. "Yeah, well, they trust me. They told me this was my thing, and they would just be along for the ride . . . so, I'll just have to be careful."

She hoped it sounded like she meant being careful in terms of avoiding any aliens wrapping their long green fingers around her, but Haley maybe really meant about her parents finding out. Because she needed this. She had to get out there, to follow this story over the horizon.

Abby stood and looked at her seriously. "You better be careful. Don't do anything too crazy."

"I won't," said Haley, but she almost felt like she was lying again. Not like she was the type to do something crazy, but what if that's what it took? "When do you go to Thorny Mountain?" she asked, hoping to change the subject.

"Monday," said Abby. "Will you be in the Kingdom?" Abby was referring to *Macabre Kingdom*, the online world where they hung out to gossip and do battle with insidious demons.

"Whenever there's Wi-Fi," Haley replied. "Have fun in music land."

"You bet." Abby smiled. "My goal is a new boyfriend, preferably a cello player with a name like Nico or Alvin."

Haley smiled as big as she could. "Good luck."

"You, too. Be careful," Abby said seriously. She hugged Haley, and then gave her a mocking wink and a pretend boy-punch on the shoulder. "Have fun, bro." They shared a small laugh and parted ways at the next intersection.

Haley walked the last quarter mile home lost in thought. In two days, she was actually heading out to hunt a story. For real. And what would she find? What was possible? Were there really aliens out there? Maybe the missing people were just runaways or people looking for an excuse to get away. Maybe this was all a hoax. But maybe it was real.

A hot summer wind rushed over her, making her jeans stick to her shins, pushing her damp bangs into her eyes. Haley looked up at the sky, the blue washed to a pale haze. She smelled the sweet aroma of flowers bursting in yards, felt summer's whisper of possibility.

What would her summer be? Two days until the road. Two days till she would finally find out.

And only two more days during which she had to hide the truth from her parents.

Greenhaven, CT, July 2, 8:45 a.m.

Forty-two hours later, Haley was fuming over three more missing people.

She stood beside the open car door, gazing at her canary yellow house. Her parents and brother were in there, somewhere, doing . . . what? What could they possibly still be doing?

"Jill!" she shouted. "Allan! Liam!"

No reply.

Haley checked the time on her phone and cursed to herself. They were supposed to have been on the road at 8:00 a.m. For weeks, Haley had been picturing it. It was supposed to be: air still cool, shadows still long, that tangy smell of sprinkler water and wet grass. Sugary donuts at Dunkin' Donuts that you didn't have to feel bad about eating because it was too early to feel anything other than red eyed and too tired. They would glide through town, the businesses still closed, only the crowd of regulars at Paul's Restaurant, and then to the highway, a blazing start west to New York, through the mysteriously named Delaware Water Gap, and then beyond. No more New England, no more places you'd seen so many times. Moving, moving moving . . .

Only here she was, not moving at all. They were supposed to be in Amber by next morning, an all-day drive. Haley had made plans to meet up with Stephanie Raines at 11:00 a.m. Stop one of her field study. They had to make it.

And yet, standing there in the driveway, Haley was faced once again with the big, fat difference between getting out there in the world like she always imagined and being out on this field study, which was this: When you're thirteen, you do not get to go on a two-week road trip field study alone. You need someone to drive you around, not to mention get your hotel rooms and your food and everything else and, since Haley had no wacky jobless uncle looking for something to do, no older stepbrother home from college, nor a supercool cousin with a fresh driver's license and time on her hands, her companions in adventure had to be her mom, dad, and Liam, who didn't seem to understand that right now, they were on the clock. How could they not understand this? Each hour, each precious moment . . . There was no getting it back!

Haley marched up the flower-lined path, vaulted up the front steps, and went inside, the screen door banging behind her.

She found her father working furiously at the kitchen sink. He was wearing a baseball hat backward, a plaid short-sleeve shirt, and army green shorts. His skinny calves were pale, and he wore sport sandals, the kind that looked dorky but that Allan thought were cool because you could wear them to mow a lawn, hike a hill, and then jump in a lake, even though mostly he worked all day in an air-conditioned office in Glastonbury designing education curriculum.

"Dad," said Haley.

Allan turned. He was up to his wrists in foamy soap. Beside him was a pile of dishes. "Almost done," he said.

"Why are you cleaning the entire house if we're not even going to be in it?" said Haley.

"So it's clean when we get back."

Haley hated this logic, except she had done the very same thing with her room. Spotless, everything on her desk positioned at right angles. "But we need to *go*," she said.

"I know. So close!" Allan turned and continued scrubbing.

Haley headed upstairs. She saw a suitcase on her parents' bed, clothes splayed across its wide-open mouth. A pair of jeans fluttered through the air, landing on the pile.

"Mom," said Haley.

"Almost ready." Jill appeared, striding from the closet toward the bathroom. Her brown hair was tied back in a bandanna. She was in a tank top and shorts. "Just toiletries. That's it."

"We need to go," Haley repeated. She couldn't believe her mom wasn't ready. She'd gotten home late from the clinic where she worked, trying to get all her patient notes done, and as it was she was going to be doing more in the car. Again, hadn't Haley been up late perfecting her field study supplies and getting her notes all organized in her notebook? Yes, but still . . .

"Can you go make sure your brother is packed?" Jill called from the bathroom. There was a clinking of tumbling bottles. "I got him started but . . ."

Haley tromped down the hall. Why did she always have to help Liam? He hadn't been her idea, all those years ago. What would have been so wrong with a cat? A cat, which could have easily stayed behind for this trip.

Liam's door was shut. She popped it open, which

caused an immediate squeal and a series of thumps. Haley looked around the room, a wasteland of half-finished drawings, action figure appendages, balled-up clothes. Both windows were open, but it still smelled like burned toast and kid feet, which were like adult feet but with less cheese and more citrus.

Haley spied Liam's suitcase underneath his desk. The desk chair was overturned and leaning on an open dresser drawer. A squadron of figures held their position on the bottom of the chair against all invaders. The suitcase was the cleanest thing in the room. Empty.

"Liam," Haley groaned.

Soft footsteps. She whirled and caught Liam's arm as he attempted to smite her with a plastic pirate's sword.

"Yar!" said Liam, then, "Ow!" as Haley twisted his arm around his back.

"Pack," she whispered in his ear, adopting a pirate's snarl, "or you'll rue the day ye crossed yer elder sister."

"Fine," Liam sulked.

Haley moved to the dresser. She wondered if boys just got progressively less mature as they aged. Haley remembered her parents promising her, back when Liam was an irrational baby and constantly following her around and whining for every toy she had, that he would get less annoying. Now he was eight and Haley had seen little evidence.

"I would not have to be doing this if you were a cat," Haley muttered as she started tossing clothes into Liam's suitcase. She knew the four things that he always wore. "You do the underwear and socks," she ordered, and left the room.

"Hhhcchhh!" Haley turned to see Liam swiping claws at her and making a menacing cat face. She smiled. Maybe she loved him more than a cat.

"You're all packed?" Jill called as Haley headed back downstairs.

"Packed and ready to go two hours ago," she said.

"What about . . ." Haley turned to see Jill emerging from their room with a three-page, stapled list. The packing list. Jill's masterwork. But Haley was sure she'd thought of everything.

"Sunscreen?" Jill asked.

"Yes."

"The fifty and the thirty?"

"Yes."

"The face ninety? The sun is stronger down south."

Haley sighed and headed back upstairs. "And just in case we take a rocket to the sun," she muttered.

"Haley . . ."

"I'm getting it, but then we need to *leeeave*."

Haley returned to the bathroom then back outside to the car. She tossed the additional bottle of lotion in her bag and stood still, fists clenched, eyelids clamped, as a wave of anxious energy washed over her. Here it was, the first day of a two-week calendar, and it was slipping through her fingers.

"Let's GO!" Haley shouted toward the house. More slamming upstairs. More clanging downstairs.

In order to keep from losing her mind completely, Haley ducked back into the fleeting cool of the backseat and double-checked her supplies. Laid out neatly on the left backseat were the following items:

- Homemade fold-out tracking map with cardboard backing
- The pocket road atlas with the unbent spine
- Pocket-sized spiral-bound tracking notebook with green-tinted graph paper
- New pack of the best gel pens
- Pair of actual bona fide binoculars
- The family's tablet computer

The computer was the big score, because it had been deemed strictly for fellowship business for the duration of the trip, which meant it was *not* to be commandeered by Liam for whatever game he was currently playing that involved the grisly death of level after level of cutely animated creatures. That this would drive Liam insane with envy was maybe a small consolation for having him along in the first place.

Haley picked up the pad, flicked it on, and reread the email on the screen, which she'd gotten the night before:

Dear Haley,

Congratulations again on winning the Fellowship for Alien Detection! I'm thrilled to hear that you are heading out on your field study tomorrow morning. How exciting!

As was stated in your acceptance letter, you are required to email us the latest updates on your trip and research at least once a day. I have reviewed your itinerary and see that your first stop is Amber, PA, followed by Brownsville, KY. I can't wait to hear what you find out!

Also, please remember to use the debit card you received with your acceptance letter for all your family's purchases.

Again, I am so glad that you are going to have this exciting opportunity. Don't forget to keep your eyes wide-open, and go for it!

Fond regards,
Alex

ALEXANDRA KELLER
EXECUTIVE DIRECTOR
THE GAVIN KELLER FOUNDATION

The letter reinflated Haley's excitement for the whole experience. Alex sounded cool, pro. Haley couldn't wait to start sending reports. No: *dispatches*.

Now she heard a commotion behind her. Finally. She turned, only to find Allan rounding the corner of the garage with, not his bags and final items in his hand, but instead a shiny colander of lettuce from the garden.

"Perfectly good . . ." he stammered as Haley glared at him. "What? You can't just leave lettuce of this quality lying around to go bad . . . you . . ." His face cracked into a smile. "I'm so sorry," he said. "Five minutes, I swear. I wouldn't even be doing this if your mom was packed."

"Liar." Haley folded her arms.

"Just don't leave without us." He disappeared into the garage, and she heard him chuckle.

"This isn't funny."

"Nope," he called over his shoulder.

Haley huffed loud enough for him to hear.

Forty-five minutes later, they were finally on the road.

Altoona, PA, July 2, 9:15 p.m.

Twelve hours, three hundred and fifty miles, plus one stop to see a giant zucchini, three attempts to steal the computer pad by Liam, one fruitless search over three consecutive exits for what Dad called "a real coffee shop," one incident of Liam insisting that the sun through his window was burning him *to death* and he *had* to switch seats with Haley, and another time where Liam produced an inconceivably noxious gas and thought it was *hilarious*, they were finally out of the car and stuffed into a tiny cream-colored Relaxation Depot hotel room, just one exit away from Amber.

Haley sat on the bed, eating a trail mix bar and trying to get just the right angle with her computer pad to get the Wi-Fi to actually work, while feeling a mix of relief and frustration. Relief because they'd actually made it to where they needed to be, but also frustration, as her family continued what seemed to be their subtle daylong strategy of sabotage:

"I read that there's an entire mural made out of sunflowers just a few hours south of here," said Allan from the nearby sink, where he was using a small pair of scissors to snip the hairs in his ears. One time,

Haley had told him that was gross. Dad had shrugged and said, "Ear hair happens." He hadn't sounded happy about it.

"Dad," Haley groaned. "I don't know if we'll have time. We have a lot to do tomorrow. Besides, wasn't the zucchini enough?"

"Zucchini attack!" Liam shouted. He was bouncing up and down on the other bed, beside Mom, and now started deploying some of his orange belt karate moves to fend off imaginary produce. At least he knew better than to do that on Haley's bed.

"I also read about this sawmill that's from the seventeen hundreds and still works and everyone there is dressed in costume," Allan continued. "And they have a roller coaster!"

"Ooh," said Jill. She'd spent most of the car ride doing her notes, but now she was lounging on the bed, reading *Us Weekly*, also apparently under the impression that this trip was some big vacation.

"Guys," Haley pleaded.

"Haley." Mom smiled in that way that made Haley know something belittling was coming. "Dad's not trying to sabotage your fellowship, just squeeze in a little family time. It's not often we get to be together like this, nowadays."

"We were together for twelve *hours* today," Haley grumbled.

She pulled the wrapper down on her bar. Something moved in the corner of her eye: a little hand reaching carefully up over the side of the bed, fingers flapping until they hit the edge of the tablet computer.

"Ugh, Liam!" Haley snatched the tablet away.

"Come on, I want to play *MegaDuck*!" Liam jumped up and grabbed at it again.

"Get off!" Haley scooted away and shoved Liam off the bed.

"Ow, Mom, did you even *see* that?" Liam whined.

Haley yanked her headphones out of her sweatshirt pocket and slipped them on. She couldn't take much more of this. She was supposed to be on a serious mission, on the trail of a story, forging onto new map, her very future at stake! And yet instead she was fighting for breath, suffocated by family.

A pleasant ding announced that she was finally online, and she logged into *Macabre Kingdom*. On the screen, her little vampire avatar, Fang the Merciless, made her way through the Forest of Fugues. Haley was proud of her design, though Fang's spiky pink hair still needed some work. She stopped to help a trio of zombies do battle with an ancient ice demon, as Fang was lethal with a broadsword, then continued her search for Abby's avatar, Vane du Rose Noir.

Vane, u out ther? she typed.

Any aliens yet? Abby replied as Vane appeared,

spiraling around a waterfall of diamonds.

Only my parents, said Haley.

LOL.

They're trying to sabotage trip with roller coasters.

Fun! said Abby.

NO TIME 4 FUN! Haley felt a little bad typing it because roller coasters *did* sound kinda fun, but there was no time for intentionally going around in circles. Lines needed to be straight! Wish I was an orphan, she added.

A life of adventure! Abby replied. This was a running joke of theirs, about how when you were an orphan, or at the very least had your parents mysteriously lost or imprisoned, you'd end up living with some aunt or grandparent who didn't keep such a close eye on you, and adventure would practically crash through your door. But nothing ever happened with parents around.

That said, Haley knew she was lucky in the parent department. Were they perfect? No, but Mom and Dad were pretty cool considering they were in their forties, and they encouraged her without pushing, *most* of the time. That made her wonder once again: What if she just told them the truth about the missing persons stuff?

She'd heard them talking a couple nights after she'd gotten her winning letter, as she was heading down to the kitchen for a snack:

"You don't think it's too odd?" Jill had said to Allan as they both sat on the couch.

"Well," Allan had answered, "yeah, I think it's odd, but . . . I've scoped out this Gavin Keller Foundation. It's legitimate. Eccentric, sure, but if somebody wants to give money out to hardworking kids to research *aliens*, so what?" Haley could hear Allan getting fired up, as he often did when making a point. "I think it's great that this fellowship is so out there, so creative. It's a break from all the serious business that Haley has going on all the time."

Haley would have disagreed with that, but again, it was a fine conclusion based on the information they had.

"Look," Allan had continued. "She really wants to do this, and she didn't get those other opportunities. But that's not even the point, either, at least to me. If Haley had gotten the JCF and Thorny Mountain, she would have been gone half the summer. With this, we get an all-expense-paid two-week trip together! I wouldn't care if we were researching fairies and goblins. No summer camps, no late work nights, no distractions. Just us and a car, hanging out as a family."

"You've been practicing this speech, haven't you?" Jill had said.

"Every day driving home."

Then they had started kissing all gross the way adults do with the loud smacking sounds, and Haley had stopped listening.

In the end, she had parents who were willing to drive her around, and so maybe some silly daily attraction, like a sunflower mural, or a sawmill with a roller coaster, wasn't too high a price to pay.

How's Thorny Mountain? she typed to Abby.

Met a cute trumpet player.

Uh-oh, said Haley. A brass boy, eh? No sad cello?

Not yet. ☺

Ha. Good luck, time for bed. Big day tomorrow! Haley logged out. She turned off the tablet and got her spiral-bound tracking notebook from her shoulder bag. She flipped to a note she'd jotted down a few days before:

Blair County Fairgrounds, Livestock Barn 5, Stall #42.

This was the spot where she was supposed to meet up with Stephanie Raines, whom she'd found out when she talked to over Facebook, preferred to be called "Steph."

Haley felt a rush. Her first contact. No: her first *source*.

"Okay, bedtime!" she announced.

"Aye aye," said Mom.

"Yar!" shouted Liam. He came hopping up onto the bed they were sharing holding an open bag of

Cheesy Fingers, which he proceeded to spill all over the sheets. "Oops!" he said.

Haley looked at the orange flecks all over the spot where she was about to sleep. *Fine,* whatever. She lay down, back to Liam, and pulled the cheese-smelling covers up over her head. *You can endure it,* she told herself, and tried to return to the possibilities awaiting her the next morning.

Amber, PA, July 3, 10:12 a.m.

Actually, check that: She couldn't endure it, not a second more.

"But I want a snack and the pirate ship now!" Liam whined.

"Guys . . ." Haley had become a statue. Standing outside the gates to the Blair County Fairgrounds, the throngs of people around her were the only thing keeping her from screaming.

"Honey," Jill said to Liam. She had pushed up her sunglasses and had her hands on Liam's shoulders. "Just be patient; you can wait until after your sister—"

"Ooh, and cotton candy! Oh man, and look, they have a Scrambler! I want to ride the Scrambler!" Liam shouted, hopping up and down.

"Liam!" Haley snapped. "Stop acting like an idiot!" She couldn't help it, not after the snoring and kicking all night, and not after the incident back at breakfast with the syrup and the hair.

"Okay," said Dad, flashing a glance at Jill. "You take Haley? We'll hit the ship."

"Take me?" Haley felt a surge inside. She'd always imagined doing her research work by herself. "I can't go on my own?"

Jill sighed. "Haley, I know you can handle yourself, but I'd like to meet these people you're interviewing, you know, just so I know what's up." She shrugged. "Can't help it: mom's duty. I promise, I'll stay far out of your way for the interview."

Haley wanted to protest, but she knew how that usually went. So she just huffed, loudly enough for her parents to hear, and said, "Okay."

"See you guys in a bit!" Allan called over Liam's excited ranting as they headed for the fairgrounds.

"So," said Jill enthusiastically. "Where to?"

"I want to get a picture of the clock tower. Then we're meeting my source in the fair."

"Ooh, 'source.' I like it."

Haley frowned. "Mom."

"Sorry. Fly on the wall. I'm not even here."

Haley started up Main Street. Even with her mom in tow, she was starting to feel a sense of relief spreading through her. Finally, she was getting started. Out on the road, on the hunt. This was it.

They crossed a four-way intersection and reached a wide green lawn wrapped around Amber's historic town hall, a brick building with white trim, its clock tower rising into the hazy sky. The lawn was busy with people picnicking and throwing balls and Frisbees to one another and to their pets.

Haley pulled out her phone and aimed at the tower.

"The time is correct," said Jill.

"I know, Mom, it's been fixed for a while. I just want a photo for documentation."

Haley turned around and positioned herself for a self-portrait.

"Ooh, I can take that for you."

"Mom, I want it to be like this."

"Right." Jill took a couple steps back.

Haley snapped the photo and checked the results. The tower kinda looked like it was coming out of her head, but it was good enough. Now, to get on with the real story.

"Okay, now we go in," said Haley. She led the way back down Main Street to a line of white booths at the fairground entrance. She started to pull out her wallet. She had her own money from her allowance and had looked up what a ticket cost online, but then Jill stepped ahead of her. "I can get these," she said.

"Thanks," Haley said, and felt genuinely stuck between wanting to scream and being glad. This did leave her extra money for snacks, and yet it made her feel like such a *kid*.

They headed into the fair, joining a fluid stream of people. Haley could see the line of long red barns in the distance.

The crowd oozed down a central midway, the shadows from the Ferris wheel cars swooping over them like ghosts. As Haley crossed the fairgrounds, all of her senses felt heightened. She observed the details around her and imagined the first paragraph of her soon-to-be-award-winning report:

The Blair County Summerfest seems like exactly the kind of place where you would not *uncover an alien conspiracy. Kids with wide smiles ride on rickety rides, their proud parents snapping pictures. Fairgoers are lined up for roasted corn, ice cream, and elk burgers that smell like steak and oranges. A salesman hawks gleaming red tractors, while nearby, on the Kountry Karaoke stage, a white-hatted old cowboy croons to the passersby. . . .*

And there were even more details than that, so many it was overwhelming. Haley felt like she was just beginning to understand some kind of paradox, like the closer you looked at the world, the more there was to see. You'd never have time for it all! And yet something about that infinite possibility was electric, too. She'd write a hundred stories, if that's what it took!

Her excited thoughts quieted as they reached the barns. The first long building was full of cows. The next, pigs. Sheep in number Three, and gigantic-sized vegetables in Four.

Haley and Jill entered Barn Five and Haley found herself surrounded by wire cages stacked like apartments and housing chickens of all colors and feather styles. There were white ones, golden tan ones with black beaks, salt-and-pepper speckled, bright yellow, a pink chicken. Stacks of cages were numbered, starting at one.

On the walls there were posters made by the chicken owners, mostly girls, all with various colored ribbons. Some younger girls had drawings of their chickens. Older kids had inspirational quotes or song lyrics. Haley had never had a pet. Well, there had been gerbils, but they had been escape prone, and that had ended badly one winter's night.

Haley joined a tight row of shuffling bodies, inching down a narrow aisle. Feathers fluttered all around her. The light was dim and greenish, the air humid, thick like oatmeal, with the brown smell of sawdust, perspiration, and the countless tiny droppings that peppered the floor.

Forty-two was at the end of the aisle. There were five cages. A girl stood in front of them, bent over and looking carefully inside one.

"Excuse me," Haley began, "Steph?"

The girl stood up, a golden chicken with white streaks in her hands. She tucked it under her arm. "What?" said Stephanie Raines. She was shorter than Haley, but older, somewhere in high school. She wore skinny black jeans and an oversized black sweatshirt. Inside the open zipper, Haley saw the same maroon T-shirt from online: "We Are the Missing." One nostril was pierced, along with the other eyebrow. She wore a thick layer of eyeliner, her eyes so dark it almost looked like she'd been in a fight. It seemed possible. "Oh," said Steph. "It's you."

"Yeah," said Haley. She felt awkward suddenly, as she often did in moments like this. She always felt like she came across so average, at least compared to someone like Steph. Just a normal girl, no exceptional features, no attitude that immediately commanded attention. She knew she had cool ideas and talents, but those weren't first impression things. "Hi."

Steph just nodded. "I kinda wondered if you'd

actually show up."

"Yeah, well, here I am." Haley tried a smile.

Steph didn't return it.

"Hi, I'm Jill, Haley's mom." Jill reached around Haley and extended her hand. Steph gave her a blank look but then shook it. She glanced back at Haley.

Haley shrugged. "She wanted to meet you, and then she's taking off. Right, Mom?"

"Oh, yeah." Jill took a long look, like she was trying to absorb as many details as she could. Then she nodded as if she was satisfied. "Um, how about if I wait outside the barn? There were some craft tents across the way. How long will you need?"

"Like twenty minutes, I think," said Haley.

"Okay." Then Jill reached over and ruffled Haley's head. It had probably been an unconscious thing, but what a thing to do in front of this older girl! Haley couldn't help flinching away.

"Oh, right, sorry," said Jill. "Okay, see you in a bit." She merged back in with the passersby and continued around the loop of cages.

"Sorry about that," said Haley, rolling her eyes.

Steph's face stayed blank, dark. "Moms care. They can't help it."

A boy appeared beside Steph. He was slouched practically in half, in a similar black sweatshirt, with chicken-thin legs in tight jeans. He wore gold sneakers and a maroon fez atop his scattershot black and bleached-white hair. His long nose and narrow face made him almost resemble a giant relative of the fowl surrounding them.

"This is Gabe," said Steph.

"'Sup," said Gabe.

Steph ran her hand over the crest of sienna-colored feathers atop the head of the chicken she was holding. It clucked contentedly. "And this is Vonnegut," she said. "He's my big winner."

"Oh, cool." Haley now noticed that Vonnegut's open cage door had a blue ribbon on it. Three other cages had ribbons, too: two greens, a gold, and a red. Here was a story within the story: tough, intimidating Steph, the chicken champion.

"You read any?"

"What?" Haley asked.

"You're too young, probably," said Steph disappointedly. "Vonnegut's insanely good, but you can't just start in the middle with *Slaughterhouse*, like they make you do in school. You have to start with *Sirens of Titan*. It explains *everything*."

"Okay . . ." said Haley. Another silent moment passed. "So, I guess we should do the interview."

"What do you want to know?" Steph asked.

"Oh, here?" Haley looked around. She'd been imagining a coffee shop, well, a cool city café actually, even though that wasn't realistic, but at least a place to get out her notebook and stuff. Not a sour-smelling chicken barn.

Haley found Steph looking at her. It seemed like a disappointed look; then again, all of Steph's looks were like that, so it was hard to tell. "There are some chairs over here," she said.

Haley followed Steph across the aisle. A small area at the back corner of the barn was roped off. There were metal folding chairs around the border and a small table against the wood wall, holding plates of cookies and plastic pitchers of refreshments. There was one other person sitting there, an older woman who seemed to be mumbling to herself and staring off into space. Steph gave her a wary glance before taking a seat on the opposite side of the area.

Haley sat. Steph and Gabe looked at her. "Um, okay," Haley started, "so I thought first you could recount your experience the night of the missing time. And, you know, about Suza."

Steph stroked Vonnegut for a moment, then said, "We were hanging out, me and Gabe and a couple other kids, down by the river walk. It was a Tuesday night, really late, probably almost midnight. I should have been home. We were just messing around— there's not much to do in Amber, if you hadn't noticed—and . . . then we kinda blanked out for a second, and the next thing we knew, all the lights in town were out. We didn't know it had been sixteen minutes until later. We didn't really know anything at first, except that we all kinda felt weird, and Calla and Tony had been making out and they told us their lips were really sore."

"Sixteen-minute make-out," said Gabe.

"So we just thought it was a blackout," Steph went on. "Then we started hearing sirens and stuff, noticed people coming outside and kind of looking around. There were shouts. Everybody was disoriented. The power came back pretty quick. We figured it was nothing, but then I went home. . . . Mom was freaking out. . . ." Steph's voice quieted. "And she was gone. Right out of her room. Just . . . completely vanished." Tears gathered in Steph's eyes. She smacked at them with the back of her hand.

Haley had no idea what to say next. She'd thought about the idea of missing people, of a missing sister, but seeing it on Steph's face suddenly made it feel real, painful. She tried to imagine going into Liam's room and finding him gone, vanished. The thought made her queasy.

Gabe reached over and rubbed Steph's shoulder. "There's been no trace of her, and no evidence," Gabe added.

"Only a few of us in town really still believe we had

the missing time," said Steph, sniffling. "Most people have decided to believe it never happened, or have just gotten on with things."

"I'm sorry," said Haley, "about your sister."

"Yeah, well, it could be worse," said Steph.

"What do you mean?"

Steph didn't answer, but she stood up and crossed the little sitting space to the older woman. She wore a flannel shirt and faded jeans; her reddish hair, streaked with gray, was tied back except for one curly strand that hung loose in front of her face. Hair like Suza's. She maybe looked about Haley's mom's age, or younger, but the dark rings around her eyes, and the long lines around her mouth, made it hard to tell.

"Their dad died in Iraq," said Gabe quietly. "She was already in bad shape before that."

Haley got up and walked over. The woman was staring vacantly out into the sea of legs passing by and talking quietly to herself. Haley couldn't hear what she was saying until she was a foot away.

"Night sun descending," the woman said in a whispered monotone. "Night sun . . . night sun comes to earth, swallowed by the earth. . . . Night sun comes to earth . . . comes home. . . ."

Her arms were folded, her fingers twitching. Her pink sneakers tapped on the dirt floor.

"Hey, Mom," said Steph. She leaned down and rubbed her mother's shoulder. "That fellowship girl is here."

"Night sun descending and we are in the stars," said Steph's mom, her body rocking back and forth. "We are one with space and the sun comes home . . . um, huh?" Her eyes seemed to clear up, like she'd pushed through fog. "Suza?"

"No, Mom," said Steph, "this is that girl, Haley. The one who wanted to interview us."

Steph's mom looked at Haley. Just looked, and Haley felt a kind of hollow sadness open up inside her. She felt a pang of guilt, too, for acting so annoyed about her own mom, and her concern for Haley's safety.

Mom's hand shot out and she clutched Steph's arm. Still looking at Haley, she asked, "Does she know the sun's come home?" Her arm started to shake, then her whole body.

"Yes, Mom, she knows," said Steph, and she looked seriously at Haley. "Don't you?"

"I—" Steph's eyes seemed to say *play along*. "I do, yeah."

Steph's mom smiled. "The sun is home," she said, and the thought caused a sweet smile to break out, but at the same time, she started to cry.

"Daughter for sun. Suza . . ."

She clasped her hands, fingers twitching over one another, and stared back off into space. "Night sun descending to earth and we are in the stars, we are in the stars and the sun comes home, we give our daughters for sun, we . . ."

Haley just stared, her body feeling tight, trying to understand.

"It's a dream," said Steph.

Haley finally broke her gaze and turned to Steph. "What do you mean?"

"What she's describing: the sun falling to earth, all that stuff, it's from a dream she's had. I know, 'cause I've had it, too." Steph nodded to Gabe. "We all have, ever since the night of the missing time."

"You're all having the same dream," Haley repeated, trying to make sure she was understanding.

"More like a vision. A memory, we think," said Steph.

"A memory of what?"

Steph glanced up the aisles. "How much time do you have?"

"Um . . ." Haley checked her phone. It had been about ten minutes. "Some?"

Steph thrust her arms forward, tossing Vonnegut toward Gabe. "Watch them," she ordered, indicating

Mom with her chin. She turned to Haley. "I can show you, if you want. But we have to take a walk."

Steph was stepping backward. Haley saw a small door back beyond the refreshments.

"Where?" Haley asked.

Steph glanced around the barn again, almost like she was wary of eavesdropping ears. "I'll tell you on the way. You coming?"

Haley felt a flutter in her gut. Her thoughts started to spiral. Was this a good idea? Or was it crazy? She glanced back out over the sea of people. Could she be sure that Mom had really left the barn? Maybe she had taken up a post somewhere to keep an eye on her. But Haley didn't see her. Still, how late could she be before her mom came looking for her? And what would Jill think if she met Steph's mom, saw how damaged she was, and learned why? She would freak. It would be the end of the trip, Haley felt sure of it. And maybe she'd be right. This was serious stuff, maybe too serious, and it was also risky to just go off with Steph. Maybe she shouldn't—

Stop! she shouted at herself. No, she had not endured a day of car and hotel with Liam and her parents, watched others get the internships she wanted, and on and on, to *not* follow this story now. Garrett Conrad-Wayne wouldn't panic right now, he'd focus!

Look at this woman, at this girl, and now at this mystery of the shared dream. Haley was onto something here. Something big. And it was hers to figure out and solve.

Haley took a big breath. "I can't be long, but, okay," she said, and she followed Steph out the back door of the barn.

Amber, PA, July 3, 10:41 a.m.

"The dream started right after that night," said Steph
as they exited the barn into the brilliant hazy sunlight.
"Not everyone in town will admit it, but you can tell
by how everyone reacts when it comes up. Nobody
really knew we were all having the same dream at
first, but then, a few weeks later, this woman in town
painted a picture that she said was from a dream. It
showed this giant orange falling star in the night sky,
and when her husband saw it, he freaked out, and
then they posted it online and everybody remembered
it like we'd all seen it before."

Haley rushed to get alongside Steph. They were

walking across a vacant dirt space behind the barns. The sounds of the fair were quickly growing distant behind them and being replaced by the drone of summer bugs. "What do people think it was?"

"There are a lot of different theories. Mostly that it was a UFO coming down, but that's not how I remember it. I remember it more like my mom said: like a little glowing sun floating down from the sky. My view of it was from the river walk area. This neon orange kind of light appears and lowers over the hills to the south. Then it disappears."

They reached a chain-link fence and Steph started to haul herself over. Haley followed. The rusty links were hot to the touch. A leg of her capris snagged on the top, and there was a tearing sound as she dropped down into tall grass on the other side. Ahead was a thick grove of leafy trees, damp-looking shade beneath.

"This way," said Steph.

Haley considered the dark forest and wondered again if this was such a good idea, but she followed.

"There's more to the dream," said Steph. "After the falling star thing, everybody has this weird feeling of being in space, like, there are stars everywhere, above and below, except all the light is tinted orange like that sun star thing; it's like you're looking out from inside the star. But then it's weird because at the same time it's like there are rocks all around, rock walls and machinery and then space and people. It's confusing for everyone."

They were in the trees now, pushing through clutching undergrowth. Soon they joined up with a soft brown path. The air was like a damp cloth, blanketing Haley. Sweat beaded on her skin, soaked through her button-down shirt. Dirt was clumping in her sandals, and she made a stern note to herself that a real, ready-for-anything journalist would have at least worn sneakers. Bug spray, too, as mosquitoes were beginning to orbit her head and trying to land behind her ears.

Part of the dream sounded familiar to her. "I've read stuff on the Missing website where people say they've had visions of being aboard an alien spaceship, with all this light and stars. Your dream sounds like that."

"Yeah, people at other missing time sites have had the falling star dream. And everybody comes to that conclusion that it's because we were taken into space. But Gabe and I have a different theory."

"A theory about what?" Haley asked.

"That's what I'm gonna show you." The path climbed a short hill and then started down. They reached the edge of the trees. At the bottom of a short slope of sharp, flat rock slabs was a twisting dirt road. It ran from their left to right and ended at a fence. On the other side of the fence, the road continued briefly to a rock wall, and an old, partly caved mine tunnel that was crisscrossed with warped boards.

Haley followed Steph as they shuffled down the slope. She stopped at the fence. "Me and Gabe and our friends used to climb around in these mines. They've been closed for a bunch of years, but you can follow some of the tunnels. It's a good place to go if you don't want anyone to hassle you. Anyway, Gabe and I thought that the caves in the dream kinda looked like the mines. So a few weeks after the incident, we came down to take a look."

"What did you find?" Haley asked.

"First, we found this." Steph pointed to the gate. It was warped and half-rusted, with a clunky old chain wrapped around the bars, but that chain was fastened with a brand-new-looking padlock with a keypad and a flashing red light.

Haley saw that there was a small sign attached to the fence. It read:

DANGER! UNSAFE MINE
NO TRESPASSING
Private Property of
UCA
United Consolidated Amalgamations

She took a picture of it with her phone.

"The next thing is in there." Steph was starting to climb over this fence, too. Haley checked the time. Seventeen minutes since she'd told her mom twenty . . . She grabbed the fence and started up. Great, now she was trespassing, too. But at this point, there was no way she was turning back.

They dropped down to the other side.

"So, you think, what, that the orange light that fell from the sky is in here?"

Steph didn't respond. They reached the mine entrance and ducked between the diagonal boards.

Inside, the air was cool and moist. Within a few feet, the daylight had faded to near total darkness. "What about mine shafts and stuff?" Haley asked nervously. Flashlight, that had to go on the ready-for-anything list, too.

"Used to be an issue, but not anymore. Look." Steph had stopped just at the edge of the dim light.

Haley reached her. It took a moment for her eyes to get used to the dark, but then she saw it. A door. A solid, sleek steel door, housed in a similarly sleek steel frame that blocked off the entire tunnel. The metal was smooth and had a strange kind of shine, an oily rainbow pattern like Haley had seen on the inside of seashells.

The door had only two features: two round, black

disc shapes at about chest height. Haley stepped forward and ran her hand over the door, from the cool, dry-feeling steel down over one of the glassy black discs. Actually, she saw that they weren't quite round. They almost looked like they were meant to put your hands on. Haley tried it, pressing her palms against the smooth surfaces. They felt warm . . . but nothing happened.

She looked back at Steph. "I'm guessing you're going to tell me that this door didn't used to be here," said Haley.

"Nope. Not until after that night."

Haley stepped back to Steph's distance, surveying the sheer wall. "So, let me say this all out loud: There's a moment of missing time, and afterward everyone has this vision of a light falling from the sky. After that, there's this new secret door in an abandoned mine tunnel. And so you think that . . . someone put something down here?"

"Not someone," said Steph, "aliens."

Haley nodded, but maybe just for her own sanity, she had to voice another idea. "Well, what about the mining company that owns this place? Could they have—"

"What?" Steph snapped. "Stopped time? Lowered something from space? And taken my sister? What kind of mining company does that?"

"No, you're right, I just—"

"Besides, Gabe and I sussed them out online and it's just some giant corporation and there's like nothing about them out there other than profit reports and stuff."

Another thought struck Haley. "I haven't read about any mining stuff on the blogs. Have you told anyone about this door? Or your theory?"

Steph shook her head. "No. Feel free, but we're not."

"Why?"

"Because we're being watched. All of us. Probably you, too. And there are stories online that people who have new theories go missing. Rumors are that there are agents."

"Agents of . . ."

"*Them.* But by all means, if you want to report it in your little story, go ahead, but they already got my sister. They're not getting me, or anyone else I care about."

"What do these agents look like?"

"Nobody knows. If you see them, it's too late."

Haley considered this. Considered everything. That she was standing in a mine in Pennsylvania looking at a strange door. That she had been told a lot in the last—she checked her phone—oh man, twenty-four minutes, none of which she could verify. She knew Suza Raines was real, the missing time was real, this door was real, the sadness she'd seen on Steph's face before, the mother . . . But could the rest of it really be true?

Haley aimed her phone at the door and snapped the photo. The flash burst through the cavern, momentarily blinding her. As the light faded, she looked at the photo. It was good. She'd send it to Alex tonight.

But now she noticed something else. An orange light in her vision.

"Um," said Steph, her voice a bare whisper.

Haley looked up. At first she had to blink leftover flash out of her eyes, but then she saw that those two black discs in the door were no longer black. They'd begun to ignite in a magmalike orange.

Haley took a step back.

The lights grew brighter, glowing neon, bathing them, and now something began to appear, to materialize in front of them. A shape. A personlike shape.

"Crap!" Steph shouted.

Run. Had to run. Haley turned and started sprinting toward the mine entrance. It wasn't far, daylight already hitting her face—

She risked one look back, and in the blur of running vision she felt sure that she saw the orange light shaping itself, coalescing into a figure, and that figure starting to move after them. . . .

And then they were out, back into the sun, but instead of running to the fence, Steph was veering to the left.

"Wait! Why—" Haley began, but then she heard the roaring. Ahead she saw the small white truck that was speeding up the road, right toward them.

Haley slammed her feet into the dirt and sprinted after Steph, who was following the hill beside the mine back to where it met the rocky slope they'd first come down.

Haley made it to the slope and looked back. The truck burst through the fence and skidded to a stop. The doors popping open. Men getting out from both sides.

"Hey! Stop right there!" one of them yelled.

She churned up the rocky slope. Reaching the trees, one more look back . . . The mine entrance. Someone was standing there. A single figure, in a yellow hard hat and an orange jumpsuit. And black sunglasses. He, or she, seemed short.

The men from the truck were pounding toward her.

"Come on!" Steph hissed from the trees.

Haley ducked into the shade. They ran through the leafy, sun-dappled underbrush, back over the shallow hill. Steph veered sharply to the right. Here was the mine company fence again. They both scrambled up the side. Haley felt digging scrapes from frayed links. Her foot slipped out and she lurched and there was more stinging pain—a gash in her palm—then she was over and tumbling down to the other side, landing in the leaves, which stuck to her sweaty arms and shins as she jumped up again.

They kept running. Steph somehow found the forest path again and then they could see bright red barns through the leaves and then they were out in the tall grass, back to the fairground fence. Haley hit it full speed, bouncing against it with her hands outstretched. She turned, breathless, leaned against the hot metal, and looked back at the trees.

No one . . .

Still no one . . .

Steph, panting, tapped her shoulder. "Come on." She started climbing.

They got up, over, back down, and to the door of the barn. Steph ducked inside. Haley stepped into the doorway and took one last look back.

There, in the shadows of the trees, was a silhouette she couldn't quite make out with the glare of sun in her eyes, but she thought she saw the gleam of a yellow hard hat.

Haley lurched inside and slammed the door.

Back in the barn. Around her the mellow sound of shuffling fairgoers and clucking hens.

Steph had gotten Vonnegut back from Gabe and was looking at her, her face beet red, black makeup running down one cheek. "So," she said, between big breaths, "there's that."

Haley nodded. There was that, all right. Whatever that had been. Haley could barely wrap her brain around it, especially with the alarm going off in her brain. "I should go find my mom," she said.

Steph started rooting in her pocket. She held out her hand to Haley. "Here."

She was holding a watch. It was black and purple and featured an old cartoon character named Thundarr the Barbarian. He was standing there with a dinosaur, and behind him was a moon that was cracked like an egg.

"This was Suza's," said Steph. "Look at the time."

Haley did. It was behind. "Sixteen minutes?" she asked.

"Yeah. Take it. And if you find her, you can return it. Tell her it's from her sis."

Haley met Steph's eyes. "Okay."

Steph nodded. "Be careful."

"Yeah," said Haley. "I'll . . . um, I'll let you know what I find out."

Steph shrugged. "If you do find out anything, I'm not sure you'll be around to let me know."

"Well . . ." Haley didn't know what to say. Steph

might be right about that. "See ya."

She hurried up the aisle of cages, fixing her appearance as best she could. There would be no hiding the cut on her hand. She got a tissue out of her bag and dabbed at it. She could say it was from a chicken cage. That she'd knocked one over after Steph's chicken escaped from her arms.

She ran her fingers through her hair, tucked in her shirt. Checked her phone again. Thirty-one minutes. She was *so* late!

Outside, Haley scanned the crowd but didn't see Jill at the line of craft booths. *She went back in, didn't find me, and went to find security, she—*

"Haley."

Haley turned to find her mom sitting on a nearby bench. She was looking up from her phone. "Sorry," she said as Haley approached. "I got a chat from work, a patient whose prescriptions didn't go through. It was a whole big mess." Jill shook her head and stood up. "How was the interview?"

"Oh, fine," said Haley. "No big deal."

As they strolled back to the pirate ship, Haley told her mom the details of the shared dream, thinking that was safe to report.

"Sounds spooky," said Jill. "Any other good info for your report?"

"A few things," said Haley.

"And so what do you think?" Jill asked. "Are these people crazy, or just weird, or what? I mean, do you think there's anything to all this alien stuff?"

"You know," said Haley, "there might be something to it."

She braced for more questions, but then Jill flinched. There was a small horn sound, and Jill got out her phone. She'd gotten a text. "Oh, special request from Dad and Liam for fried dough. They say they can smell the stand from the pirate ship."

"Ha," said Haley.

They went to the fried dough stand and ordered four pieces with powdered sugar, then headed for the pirate ship ride. Haley wolfed down her dough and even took a ride on the ship with Liam. When the the rest of her family wanted to go on the Scrambler, Haley didn't join them. She felt scrambled enough inside.

Sitting on a bench, watching her family spin and lurch around, Liam between Mom and Dad, all of them with wide eyes and shouting, Haley wondered, *What have you gotten yourself into?*, and the thought caused a rush of fear in her gut. *You were in danger back there*, she thought, *real danger, weren't you?* Maybe, yes.

She thought back to the mine. The chase didn't even seem real anymore. Still, she'd have to be very careful from now on. And yet, at the same time, some of the fear was fading and being replaced by a kind of rush. What had been terrifying now felt more like an adventure, and it left Haley feeling something like thrilled. She had her story, and the hunt was on.

chapter

The next morning Haley sat with her forehead against
the hot window, staring at the miles of leafy trees
blurring by, feeling queasy. The car had taken on a
permanent odor, of food wrappers and sweat and sunscreen and cooked dashboard. Haley felt as if she was
coated in a thin film of grime that even the prickly,
jet-powered nozzles of another Relaxation Depot (this
one in Charleston, West Virginia; Dad was part of
the Frequent Relaxer program) shower couldn't completely remove. Her forehead had made a greasy oval
on the glass. She'd been in this position for a while,
just gazing out the window. She felt like her body was

humming at maximum, adrenaline coursing, nerves fried.

There were a number of contending reasons as to why she felt this way. It may have just been from the combination of plastic-packaged hotel breakfast burrito and bumpy highway. But it probably also had to do with all the looking over her shoulder that Haley had been doing at every stop since Amber. She never saw anyone who seemed to be following them or watching her, but she had no experience in these kinds of things and so she didn't know what to look for.

Plus, Steph had said that if you saw these agents, it was already too late.

Also in play was her lack of sleep: She'd sat up late into the night rereading the dream accounts on We Are the Missing and also researching the UCA corporation. What she had found out wasn't exactly your typical bedtime story. And when sleep had finally come, it had been uneven and plagued with dreams where Haley was trapped in tunnel labyrinths with glowing doors and small hard-hatted figures appearing and chasing her.

Then there were the aches and pains she had from the day before, which had been added to by Liam who, after insisting on an early morning swim with Dad, had gotten himself so overdosed on sugary cereal and hot chocolate at the hotel that, not an hour into the drive, he'd proceeded to have an insane meltdown when the battery on his Nintendo died because he'd forgotten to charge it overnight, which resulted in him accidentally kicking Haley in the leg. Now his sweaty head was slumped on Haley's elbow, a thin string of drool falling from his open mouth.

But the most likely reason for Haley's queasy feeling was the email she'd found when she got online at their last rest area stop.

Haley looked back at the computer. She'd already read it three times but started again anyway, hoping something might change this time:

Dear Haley,

Thank you for sending this update. I've had a chance to read it and to look at the pictures you uploaded. I also read your second email (from 1:30 a.m.! You night owl!) with the information about UCA's mine holdings. I've checked that myself and you are right. UCA and its subsidiaries own mines in far too many of your missing time towns to be a coincidence.

All this is fairly incredible, and, I have to say, a good bit more serious than I think my father anticipated when he launched this fellowship!

What I am trying to say is that while my father

and I thought that your field study theories were plausible and noteworthy, we did not necessarily expect them to lead to such concrete and, frankly, chilling results.

Obviously, you are onto something here. That said, I think we can agree that this is all too dangerous. I think what you've found out is already enough for a great fellowship report, not to mention something we can take to the authorities, and so I must request that you return home at this time.

I would imagine your parents are feeling the same way? Honestly, given what you've found, I'm surprised I haven't heard this from them directly. Perhaps you all still feel that you have to continue on in order to secure your award annuity, but please know that's not an issue! You've more than earned your scholarship!

I'm sure this is disappointing, given how motivated you are, but I imagine it's also a relief, after yesterday! Either way, it's for your safety. Please let me know your plans for returning home. I have notified the bank to deactivate your debit card in forty-eight hours, but that should give you ample time.

Best,

Alex

Nope, she hadn't misread a thing. Haley closed the email. A fresh wave of nauseous discomfort rippled through her.

She glanced up into the front seat, where her parents were having fun cycling through the radio stations and singing their own usually incorrect and always incomplete lyrics. *I would imagine your parents are feeling the same way?* Alex had said. *Yeah,* Haley thought, *or, my parents have noooo idea.*

Obviously she hadn't told them about the email from Alex. That would mean telling them about everything else. And that would mean the end of the trip. But this email was the end, anyway, wasn't it?

Because, after the rush of yesterday's discoveries had worn off, Haley had considered the potential danger she was in. Whether the missing time events and the missing persons were the work of actual aliens or people using aliens as a smokescreen, whoever was behind this was not going to want her finding out more about their plans.

Plus, Alex had just verified what Haley had learned last night: United Consolidated Amalgamations owned mines in many of the missing time towns she'd discovered. And now Haley had been at least spotted, if not identified, at the Amber mine. So, if she started showing up in other towns with mines, wouldn't the UCA people realize that she was onto them? And if they did, then what?

That answer was pretty obvious: She'd end up a missing person like Suza.

Haley dropped the tablet in her lap and sighed. It was over, and the cruelest irony was that her trip was ending early because she'd actually gotten her story.

And yet, she'd only glimpsed the surface! Where was Suza? Why were people being taken? What was happening in those towns during the missing time, and what did it have to do with the mines? What was that orange light that everyone remembered? Why was it being put underground? And how, *how* had a very similar orange light grown into a *person* right before her eyes?

Argh, there were still so many questions! And Alex was wrong. There wasn't nearly enough evidence to go to the police or whoever. Not yet. Nobody was going to be able to see that door in the mine without a warrant, and what judge was going to issue a warrant against a giant corporation based on claims of a shared dream about a glowing light from a bunch of UFO conspiracy weirdos? Sure, Haley had a camera photo, but she'd taken it while trespassing on private property! And she knew from TV that such evidence would probably be inadmissible.

Not only was what she'd learned not enough for the authorities, it wasn't going to be enough to publish, either. Sure, it might get her the scholarship, not to mention cause a frothing series of comments on the *New Frontiers Mag-Zine* site, but it was definitely *not* enough for a real newspaper like the *Times* to run it. She needed more.

So, no, Alex, this was not a relief. It was only failure. Only the glimpse of some huge truth, the shadow of a massive story, one she'd spend the rest of the summer, maybe the rest of her life puzzling over, wondering what might have been.

She couldn't give up on it. She just couldn't. Not yet. And so Haley had come up with a plan in three parts.

Part One was an email reply to Alex. Haley had thought about begging for more time, but she felt like Alex's decision was nonnegotiable, so her only choice was to try not to arouse her suspicions:

Hi Alex,

I understand about the danger and that we need to turn around. I'm relieved to know I can still have the scholarship and relieved to know that I'll be out of danger! We are turning around now, and I will update you every few hours about our progress home.

Thanks,

Haley

Part Two of the plan involved a route change: Haley checked her pocket road atlas again. "Dad?"

"Yeah?" Allan called over a shiny country anthem.

"How far to Brownsville?" This was the planned next interview stop on her field study plan. It was near Mammoth Caves National Park, which Haley hadn't thought much of until she'd made this connection to the towns and lights being put underground.

"Last sign I saw said one hundred fifty miles. So, a few more hours. Why, are we late?"

"No, but I got a message from my source there, and she needs to meet later," Haley lied. "So, we have a few hours to kill, and I just noticed, there's a park called Super Fun Wet! coming up in, like, fifty miles. It's got waterslides, bumper boats, and go-karts."

Liam jolted upright like a risen zombie. "GO-KARTS, YEEAHHHH!" he moaned.

"Oh, right!" said Allan. "Jill, didn't we go to one of those out in Kansas, back during our cross-country drive?" He was referring to the fabled journey he and Jill had taken back in their twenties to move Jill from Oregon to Connecticut, photographic evidence of which still hung in a collage frame in the guest bathroom.

"That's right!" said Jill. "I'm still mad at you about that stunt you pulled with the go-karts."

"Hello, people?" said Haley. "So, we're gonna do

that, then. Some family fun, okay? Also, they have Wi-Fi, and I really need to do more research."

This was the absolute only reason Haley was suggesting this stop. To buy time so that she could initiate Part Three of the plan, and that was . . .

She didn't know yet. Part Three was going to have to come from whatever she could find in this last-ditch search, some new clue that might get her closer to uncovering the real story. The way she figured it, she had forty-eight hours left before Alex would know that she hadn't turned around. At that point, not only did the debit card turn off, but Alex would no doubt start calling her parents. And then of course Haley would promptly be in huge, massive trouble, but . . . she didn't care anymore. If she could just crack this story open before time ran out, it would be worth any amount of punishment.

"Sounds great!" said Allan. He turned back to Jill. "It was not a 'stunt' I pulled. I'm just a superior driver."

While he and Jill went back and forth playfully, and while Liam pretended to drive a go-kart from his seat (complete with high-pitched screeching noises as he took sharp turns), Haley returned to staring out the window and simmering in her anxious juices. She watched the new road, the new parts of the map, sliding by, with every mile getting closer to a mystery, and yet with every minute getting closer to having to turn around. Unless she could find some way to keep going.

Two hours later, in the feathery shade cast by a plastic palm-frond umbrella, at a white table stained in brown-hued blotches of, at best, old ketchup and mustard, beneath the froth of squealing voices, water splashes, lifeguard whistles, frying burgers, and arcade game blips, while her family was tossed to and fro in the unnaturally blue water of a giant wave pool, Haley had her first experience with what Garrett Conrad-Wayne referred to as Scheduled Serendipity.

Most people, Garrett Conrad-Wayne said, *wait around for good luck to just randomly find them, as if luck is excrement from a bird that is just winging along going about its day, and it just so happens that, through a combination of wind and velocity, and due to no fault of your own, you are standing in the right place at the right moment for that smear of excrement to hit you on the head.*

The journalist knows, however, that luck is more like the excrement of a reclusive, flightless nocturnal ground bird, and it will only splat onto your head if you position yourself directly under the right branch of the right tree in the right part of the jungle at the right time of night.

Haley wasn't sure if bird poop was the best metaphor, but she got the point: You had to work to have good luck. And she'd been working, and working, and working, and then, there at the table at Super Fun Wet! she had encountered luck again, this time in the form of a typo.

Sitting there, at the only table in the outdoor area that was still in sight of her parents and had any decent Wi-Fi reception, a table that was also directly in the line of the blower from the snack bar grill, which had coated her already-sticky skin with a second layer of film that smelled like the charred edges of hamburgers, Haley had done search after search about United Consolidated Amalgamations. She'd found out that it was a multinational mining company that also owned a small genetic testing laboratory somewhere in Argentina. She'd found out that it was the largest producer of xenotillium, which was used in televisions and reportedly caused fish to grow extra heads in lab studies. She'd found out that it was the world's third-largest miner of coal and the fourth-largest miner of diamonds, not to mention, weirdly, the world's leading producer of frozen fish sticks. She'd found out that you could not find any information about its board of directors, or who its CEO was, or where its corporate offices were, because UCA was protected by some kind of vigilant internet security service.

Searches to do with things Haley had encountered

had come up essentially empty as well. A search for UCA Amber merely came up with information about the mine, which had gone out of service in the 1990s. Similar searches for other towns with mines came up with the same dry information. Most of the mines in missing time towns were closed, but even that wasn't a clue because then there were a few that were open. Haley did searches including the term "orange glow," but those either led back to the We Are the Missing site or similar blogs, or to some kind of pet cleaner called Dander-Off, which was apparently being sued for causing cats and dogs to briefly glow after application.

On and on the search results went, in all kinds of directions except the right one. After an hour and a half, Haley had followed so many links, tried to interpret so many search results and webpages, that she was feeling blurry. Her eyes hurt.

And it was then that she accidentally typed a search for "UCS Gable New Hampshire" and hit enter. Even as she watched the wheel spin and the page load, she saw that her finger had missed the *A* by one letter and typed an *S*. "Ugh," she muttered to herself.

Search results appeared. And as she was already retyping her search, her eye just happened to catch the second result:

UCS to Inspect Gable Mine on March 23.

For as tired as her brain was, some alert synapse

threw up a tiny red flag. Haley paused. Gable was one of the missing time towns where there was also a UCA mine. She looked at the date: March 23. She clicked on the link, and as she did so, she pulled out her tracking notebook and consulted her list of missing time towns.

The page loaded. It was an article from the *Gable Herald*, the town newspaper. In her notebook, she found Gable on her list. Their missing time event had been on March twenty-fourth. Haley read the article. A mine safety group, United Consolidated Safety, had come to Gable to inspect the structural integrity and environmental impact of the closed mine . . . the day before the missing time event.

Another search: United Consolidated Safety was a subsidiary of United Consolidated Solutions.

Search: United Consolidated Solutions was a subsidiary of United Consolidated Amalgamations.

Haley felt her fingers tingle.

She kept digging.

Search: UCS had run a mine safety inspection in Amber the day before the missing time event.

Search: same in Brownsville.

"Whoa," Haley breathed. This was it! She had the connection. Concrete. Solid. But . . . a minute spent thinking it through told her that this *still* wasn't enough. Because the actual missing time event was still completely unprovable, right? There was no hard evidence. Just people's accounts.

And then Haley found something. She clicked. A small article in the Local News page of a town website: *Mine Inspection Set for July 3*.

That was yesterday. The town was Fort Bluff, Arkansas. With shaking fingers, Haley flicked through her road atlas. There. She did some plotting. Fort Bluff was about four hundred miles away. A long haul for today . . . but they could make it by tonight, when, if all this evidence was right . . . There was going to be a missing time event.

Haley sat back. She stared at the computer, at the road atlas. If she could get to that town—well, not into it, but just near it—if she could *see* this missing time event happen, maybe see that light falling from the sky, and make a video of it, that would be the biggest piece of evidence, the last piece she would need to link the missing time, the shared dreams, and the mining company. . . . *But you're talking about going to where you think there's going to* be *a missing time event,* worried the doubt demon. Yes, she was. She was talking about hunting this story down to its lair.

Could she do this? What would it take? More lies . . . but only a couple more. And at this point, weren't they worth it? Then it would be over and she would have her story.

She already knew the next piece of information she would need. She opened a new browser window and ran a new search. Bingo. Now a couple more calculations. . . . And she had it. It was time to launch Part Three of the plan. First, another email to Alex Keller:

Dear Alex—
Our drive back is going great! We're going to stay the night in—

Haley flipped through her atlas . . .

State College, Pennsylvania. I'll check in again before bed.
—Haley

She sent and was clicking over to another window when there was a ding. *Macabre Kingdom* popped up. Vane was onscreen, standing beside Fang at the Lava Baths, where they'd agreed to meet. A chat from Abby appeared.

Hey! Just had dinner with brass boy! What's new with you?

LOL not much here, Haley replied. The sight of Abby made her nerves nearly fry. Abby, who'd been worried about her initial lies to her parents. Haley typed quickly: Can't talk right now. At a water park! Family fun!! More later. —H

She logged out of the Kingdom without waiting for a reply. Abby would never go for this. Better she didn't know.

"Hey, kiddo." Haley snapped up to find Dad walking over, drying off with a sunset-striped beach towel. "How goes?"

"Oh," said Haley, trying to sound breezy, "you know, fine." It was time for the next step in the plan. "Hey, Dad, I did some more research and I want to change the itinerary. Would that be cool?"

"Oh, um, sure, I guess. Why, what's up?"

"Well, I actually found a better source to interview. She has way more interesting stories than the girl I was going to meet in Brownsville."

"Better, like, weirder alien stuff?" Allan gave her a look somewhere between smile and worried.

"Basically. So, I'd like to go there instead." Haley flipped to the page on the atlas. "It's here," she said, pointing to Fort Bluff. "And check it out, there's a Relaxation Depot just up the road, at this exit. With your Frequent Relaxer privileges, it's not too late to switch the reservation, right?"

Allan checked his watch. "Nope. That will be fine. I love that program," he said with a smile.

"Okay, cool," said Haley. "The interview will be tomorrow morning, so we have to get there tonight."

"Sounds good," said Allan. "You're the boss."

Haley smiled. And now there was one final piece of the plan to initiate. The missing time events happened late in the evening, close to midnight, and so Haley's plan was to have them arrive near Fort Bluff nice and late. She wasn't exactly sure how she was then going to get within sight of the missing time event at that point, but she'd worry about that later.

Getting to Fort Bluff late at night meant that Haley needed something to occupy the family through the evening. And as if Garrett Conrad-Wayne was looking over her shoulder, there was something only an hour away from Fort Bluff that couldn't be more perfect.

"There's one more thing," said Haley, pointing to the map again. "Check out what's just over an hour east of Fort Bluff."

Allan followed her finger, and then his eyes lit up. Haley was pointing to Memphis, Tennessee, specifically: Graceland. "Oooh," he said.

"I thought you'd like that," said Haley. "And guess what? They're even having a karaoke-and-fireworks show there tonight. It's so close to Fort Bluff. I thought we could go to the show."

"No way," said Allan. He pretended to hold a microphone to his mouth and sang, "'*Ohhhhhh, since my baby left me, I found a new place to dwell . . .*'"

Haley smiled, trying her best not to look nervous. This was going well. "It's a bonus," she said, "since some people think that Elvis might have been abducted by aliens."

"That's right!" said Allan. "It might be valuable for your article." He shifted back into an Elvis voice, talking into the mic. *"I'd just like to take a moment . . . to thank my good friend, little green alien man . . . right over there . . . thank you, thank you very much."*

He looked down at Haley and smiled. "If we leave soon, we could probably make a tour, too."

Haley felt like it was taking all her energy to move the corners of her mouth into a carefree grin. "Yeah! Sounds good."

"Okay, cool! I'll go tell your mom." Allan bounced away, clearly happy about this new development.

Easy, Haley thought to herself. Lying was becoming all too easy. This was so much more than she'd ever done. But it was almost over. *Once I get through today,* Haley thought, making a deal with herself, *I'll tell them everything, get super grounded or whatever it will take, and never lie again.*

Haley did a little more research, reading about Fort Bluff. After that, she packed up and took a seat on a lounge chair by the pool. She watched the rest of her family emerge, laughing, from the waves, while inside, she tried to control her own waves of worry and guilt, but also anticipation. She hadn't thought it was possible, but that buzzing humming feeling inside had only increased, and it was showing no sign of calming down any time soon.

chapter

7

Memphis, TN, July 4, 9:18 p.m.

In the washed, khaki-colored hours of afternoon, as the car hummed west across Tennessee, Haley had looked over her notes about the missing time towns, studied the road atlas, and found another connection. Each town was pretty isolated from the other towns around it, and that included Fort Bluff.

She did some measurements. All of her missing time towns were at least five or more miles from any other town. This made her wonder if five miles was the limit of the missing time effect. Like, if you stopped your car just over five miles from a town, could you see the missing time event happen and not be caught in it?

This seemed like a random number, until she converted it to kilometers on a whim. Five miles was eight kilometers. And that got her brain working. First, eight and sixteen were related, in that they were both powers of two and even numbers and multiples of two and four. Also, if the missing time extended eight kilometers in any direction from the town, that might mean that eight was the radius of a circle extending around the town, and *that* could mean that the full circle around the town could be sixteen kilometers across. Could a missing time field be both sixteen minutes long and sixteen kilometers wide?

Haley couldn't be sure, but her current theory was that they could get about five miles from Fort Bluff and stop and watch what happened. She couldn't decide how crazy that theory sounded, but it was the best she had. And she still wasn't sure how she would get her parents to take her to the outskirts of town. A clever lie? And even more clever shading of the truth? *Just sneak out of the motel! Why not, at this point? You've already done all this lying, why not just go all the way?*

None of the options sounded good. Haley felt like she'd backed herself into a corner, and now she just had to hope that, as with her other discoveries today, the answer would come to her before it was too late.

"So what's the verdict?" Allan asked.

"On what?" Haley asked, her nerves singing.

They were sitting on the hood of their car in the large Graceland parking lot, near Elvis's personal jet, across the street from the mansion itself. They were among lines of cars with people sitting waiting for the fireworks show to begin at 9:30.

A crowd milled back and forth in front of them: parents, kids, grandparents, holding sodas, pretzels, cotton candy, some with stars painted on their cheeks, an Uncle Sam hat here and there. At the far end of the lot was a line of food booths. Besides that, an endless stream of Elvis impersonators paraded on and off a karaoke stage. Haley was beginning to wonder if karaoke was the true American pastime.

Allan was munching on a corn dog. They'd each gotten one, but Haley's hung absently in her hand, two bites taken. "The tour," said Allan. "Graceland. Did you like it?"

"Oh that," Haley said. "It was weird." How else did you explain a house with a jungle-themed living room, a basement room done all in blue and yellow with three televisions, or that whole room devoted to his jewel-studded costumes?

"Agreed," added Mom. "There's only so much cheese I can take."

"Cheese?" Dad made a choking sound. "But

couldn't you feel the sadness in there? The King's life had such a dark, lonely side. By the end, he was so isolated, so lost. And it killed him, too."

"How did he do it again?" Mom asked with more interest. Most of her favorite musicians tended to off themselves, like Elliott Smith or Jim Morrison.

"Painkillers," said Dad.

"Wait," said Liam. "So he wasn't abducted by aliens?"

"Well, some of *these* people might be alien abductees," Allan said, nodding to the crowd oozing past them just as two men in shimmery bikinis and Elvis pompadour wigs walked by.

"Ha," said Haley, but the sound died in her throat. She was wound too tight to laugh.

"How much longer?" Liam asked.

Allan checked his phone. "Ten more minutes."

"I should use the bathroom," said Jill. "Haley?"

"Er, yeah," said Haley. Part of her general buzzing condition all day was that she felt like she needed to go to the bathroom almost constantly. Other near-constant symptoms now were aches in her neck and her shoulders and ankles, in addition to feeling that her stomach was on edge. She also found herself constantly tearing at the skin around her fingernails, and having little mumbling conversations with herself.

Haley slid off the car. She slipped her shoulder

bag over her head. She liked having it with her, all her secret information close. She wished she had the computer tablet, too, but it was still in the car.

Haley followed Jill through the crowd, stepping carefully around and over blankets. The light blue of a long evening was finally deepening to purple. The last orange rays were lighting the tip of the jet's tail. The evening air was warm and thick.

The portable bathrooms were on the far side of the lot. They were halfway there when they entered a gap in the crowd. Before them was a giant clown. He had a white face and frizzy green hair. He seemed enormous, made of muscle, which seemed odd for a clown. Haley also noticed that, instead of wearing big clown shoes, he had on high-laced black combat boots. In fact, he had black pants on, too, and only seemed to be dressed as a clown from the waist up. It was not a very professional display.

He held a bundle of multicolored balloons and was just giving one each to a pair of little girls when he spied Haley and stood. The girl he'd been handing a balloon to hadn't quite grasped the string yet, and as the clown turned, the balloon leaped into the night, jerking up and away as if hooked by a fishing line from the sky.

"My balloon!" she wailed.

The clown glanced back at her with a blank but serious and not very clowny look. "Share," he said in a low voice.

The girls' eyes grew wide and they fled.

He looked back at Haley and held out a balloon for her.

"That wasn't very nice," she blurted out.

The clown continued holding the balloon toward her. It was lavender and bounced on the light breezes made by people walking to and fro.

"Take it," he said in that same unfriendly but authoritative monotone. "Please."

"How much?" Haley asked.

"Free."

"Ooh, a balloon." Jill had appeared beside her. "How much?"

"They're free," said Haley.

"How nice." Jill reached out, took the balloon, and passed it to Haley. "Come on, kiddo, we don't want to be stuck in a Porta Potti when those fireworks start."

"Right." Haley eyed the clown again. He looked back at her blankly.

"Bye," she said, thinking, *He's weird*.

"Bye," he replied.

She began to turn when she noticed that there was a small square of paper hanging from a loop at the base of the balloon. Haley turned it up. A hand-scrawled note read:

> If this balloon starts to change color,
> look at the moon.

Haley glanced up. A slim crescent of moon was midway up the evening sky, between the powder blue and the darker purple.

"What's that supposed to mean?" she asked.

"It's part of the show," said the clown, his voice flat like pavement.

"Um, sure. Okay . . ."

Haley turned and stalked off. She thought about just letting the balloon go, but Liam would like it, and a consequence of her high-strung day was that she'd snapped at him nearly every time he'd gotten within a foot of her. This would be a good peace offering.

They emerged at the long line of blue bathrooms. Only one had its handle turned to green. Haley handed Mom the balloon and went first.

When she came out, Mom gave her the balloon back. "Be right out."

Haley stood, holding the balloon, people jostling around her.

"Ladies and gentlemen," a female voice announced over a loudspeaker. "The fireworks will be starting in a few minutes."

Haley felt a vibrating in her pocket. Her phone was ringing. A flash of worry shot through her. Who would be calling her? She pulled it out and checked the caller.

Oh, no. It was Keller. Haley silenced the call and watched the name flashing until it stopped. There was a second of silence. Then a message that she had a new voice mail.

Haley just stared, frozen, at the phone. Then, it vibrated again. A text appeared, from Keller as well.

This is Alex. Debit card records indicate you are in Memphis! Please contact me. New developments and you are in great danger. I've sent someone to assist. Please contact ASAP!

Haley felt like she was shrinking in on herself. She'd been caught. But even more than that: What new developments? Danger? And . . . they were tracking her with the debit card? Someone was coming to assist her? With what? Haley could barely wrap her brain around all this—

And now she heard another sound. A familiar dinging, a sound like sonar. Her mom's phone. Coming from the toilet. . . . And she just knew. Keller was calling Mom. Had to be.

Ohhh, this was it. This was it and it was over! Crap! But not only that, they were in danger, too!

Haley heard the phone ringing. "Mom!" she shouted desperately at the stall. If she could just explain to Mom before she answered, maybe it would be better.

The ringing stopped. And now she heard Jill's muffled voice: "Hello?"

Oh, no, no. Haley was shaking all over, tears starting to leak from her eyes. This was horrible. What was she going to do? What was going to happen?

Silence from the stall. What was Keller telling her mom right now? What was Jill thinking? Oh, she was dead, so dead when her mom came out! Any second now.

But the danger! Haley's eyes darted around. Were there people coming for her? For all of them? She looked for more men like at the mine, but everyone just looked as normal and weird as a crowd dotted with Elvis impersonators would normally look. . . .

Then her sweeping eye noticed something strange. A glow. She looked up.

Her balloon was no longer lavender.

It had begun to glow, a weird neon orange, as if something inside it were lighting up. What did that mean? She tried to remember, but it was like her thoughts were moving slow. Oh, right, the clown. And it had to do with the show. . . . Her thoughts were so sluggish all of a sudden. . . . Right, the note. If the balloon changed color, she was supposed to look at the moon.

Haley turned, and it seemed to take forever. . . . It was like her muscles were taut rubber bands that didn't want to stretch. She looked up into the deepening evening, trying to turn far enough around to see the moon. Above, the balloon was positively radiating now, this brilliant orange, and it reminded her of the light from the mine door. . . .

There was something different about the sky, too. Wasn't there? It didn't look blue anymore, but more like gray . . . or, it was like it was getting gray, yes, that was it . . . right before her eyes—so hard to think, thoughts slowing— but yes, the sky was definitely losing its color. . . . And there was something else. A light. Growing. Above her. Neck straining to look up . . .

And that was when Haley saw the UFO.

Or at least something enormous and round—the belly of a helicopter?—hovering in the sky, pulsing with multicolored lights. Beautiful, strange lights, lowering toward her, and from its center, the brightest light of all, a searing white, flickering like a strobe.

Ppptht!

Haley felt a wicked sting in the back of her head, just below and behind her left ear. She winced and tried to grab at it but again the slow muscles and ow, it hurt so much, and now Haley was falling. She tumbled backward, landing so hard that it knocked the wind out of her. The back of her head thocked against the pavement.

The pain made her thoughts drift in the molasses. What was happening?

And there, floating above her in the air was her balloon. She'd let go of it when she'd fallen, but it hadn't floated away. It was just hovering there above her, the string dangling down, but it was still.

Everything still.

Where had the sound gone? Silence. The whole world was silent.

Now the balloon's color finally began to fade, the fiery orange draining, leaving a flat gray, just like the sky, just like everything, except for that brilliant white light overhead.

Haley couldn't tell what was happening, she didn't understand, she—

Yes . . . you . . . do. . . . she thought with a desperate, hollowing certainty. *They're . . . here. . . .*

There was a brilliant flash of white light, and Haley lost track of the world.

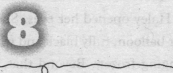
Memphis, TN, July 4, 9:26 p.m.

Sound returned first. Haley heard a voice.

"Well, that was easy." The speaker was male, his voice low and calm.

Now a second voice, female and bored-sounding, replied: "It always is."

"I know, but she's a sharp one. And this was risky. All these people."

"Still human, though," said the woman. "Once we leave and the lights start flashing, they won't know what happened. Besides, we couldn't wait any longer. She was headed to Insertion Point Beta Seven. And apparently Keller called in reinforcements."

"That's right," said the male. "I haven't seen anyone. You?"

"No."

Haley opened her eyes. She was still on her back. Her balloon, fully black and white, hovered above her, hanging frozen. Beyond that, a brilliant, pure white light flickered like a movie projector from beneath the silent craft. Those voices nearby were absolutely the *only* sound in the world other than Haley's breathing. It was as if everything had been frozen, except for Haley. She realized it would probably be a good idea to be as still as possible. She turned her head ever so slightly. . . .

In front of the now completely colorless bathrooms stood two people, a man and a woman. The man wore a yellow polo shirt tucked into his shorts. The woman had straight blond hair and wore a sky blue sundress with white polka dots. Other than the fact that they were both oddly pale, no color in their skin whatsoever, the only weird thing about them was that they seemed to be wearing identical tiny black oval sunglasses. And Haley felt fairly sure that these were the same gogglelike sunglasses she'd seen on the figure in the mine.

But from this close she could also see another feature of these two that she had not noticed on the mine figure: there was something strange about their faces. The skin was too clean— lineless and smooth, expressionless: *like a mask*. Their arms and legs looked that way, too, like they'd been taken from a mannequin.

"By the way, One, I hate these outfits."

"The Director says we need to blend in," the female named One replied.

"The Director. That's such a *human* title."

"For one with such concerns, Two," One sounded annoyed, "you've certainly embraced their moodiness."

"Please," the man named Two said. "Let's just get this over with. I'd like to get back for the temporal loop reset. I have some experiments that need updating."

The couple started toward Haley. "Poor girl," said One. "She should be at home writing some silly blog or doing her summer reading."

"Plenty of time for that," Two agreed, "once we get her back to Juliette and get rid of her troublesome thoughts."

It was all Haley could do to remain still, but they seemed to think she was frozen. If she waited for the right moment, she might be able to get away from them. *And go where?* There were no other sounds. It was like the world had ceased existing.

It has, Haley thought to herself, *in a way*. Because

she realized that this must be missing time. She was in it, right now. But . . . why wasn't it affecting her?

One spoke from right nearby. "Hmm . . ."

"What?"

"Is there some reason why she looks different?"

Haley heard a clicking sound, like buttons being pushed. "I'm reading the MT Field at full strength."

"Strange," said One. Haley heard the ruffle of her bending down—

And then she thrust herself into a roll across the gravel.

"What—"

Haley was up in a second, sprinting away. She glanced over her shoulder to see One jumping to her feet and Two racing after her.

Haley spun back around and finally began to take in the details of the world around her. There was no color left. Everything was black and white, and flickering in that strobe-like light from above. Every single person was frozen in place, some in midstride, others with mouths open in mid-conversation. A girl with a stream of water hanging between her water bottle and her lips; a small boy caught in the middle of a leap; a father with his finger raised, about to yell. All were still, silent, caught in missing time. All except for Haley, and she was being chased by . . . what? Steph's term flashed to mind: *agents*. What kind of agents?

But she probably knew that, too. *Alien agents*.

"Stop right there!" Two shouted at her.

Haley raced ahead, weaving through the statues. In the eerie silence, there was only the slapping of her sneakers on the flickering pavement, her quick breaths, and a light static hum like she was near large power lines.

"Now would be a good time for the sedative!" One shouted behind her.

"Working on it!" Two replied. He sounded close.

Haley hurdled a frozen dog. Something whizzed by her head. A dart with bright red feathers hit the black-and-white shoulder of a frozen man beside her.

"Rats!" Two called.

Haley dropped to her hands and knees, scurrying in between a thick crowd of bikers who were clustered around a motorcycle.

"I've lost visual!"

I was supposed to be frozen, too, Haley thought as she lurched back to her feet. So why wasn't she?

Ffftwwp!

Another dart just missed, striking a girl beside Haley right in the brim of her baseball cap.

"Almost!" Two shouted from somewhere way too close.

"Come on!" One shouted.

Haley risked a glance over her shoulder and saw

that One had jumped up onto the karaoke stage, her hair and dress an explosion of color among a frozen accordion band of Elvis impersonators. She spied Haley and pointed. "Over there!"

Haley raced on, her heart slamming against her ribs. Her lungs were starting to hurt. *At least,* she thought, *this pretty much proves my whole aliens theory.* . . . It would make a heck of a story, but if they caught her, it seemed certain that she'd never get to write it. *No,* she thought fiercely, *they are not taking my memories!*

Haley dropped down once more, sliding on her belly under a huge pickup truck. She jumped up and ran—

"Gotcha." Two appeared right in front of her. Haley crashed into him, and his cold hands gripped her shoulders. "You're quick," he said mildly, "but after this—" He grabbed Haley by the hair and held her at arm's length.

"Let go of me!" Haley shrieked.

"Relax, this is going to make you a happy camper," said Two. He raised his free hand, palm facing Haley. A disc of neon orange light began to glow around it.

"No!" Haley screamed. She thrashed against his grip, but it was no use.

"I almost wish you'd come to understand what you are onto, but this is much easier," Two said matter-offactly. "A few minutes from now, you won't remember a thing."

His smooth, pale face leaned closer to her, lit in orange. In the tiny oval reflections of his sunglasses, Haley saw her own eyes, her own tears. She realized that even this was something she would never remember again—

And then an even thicker, faster arm wrapped around Two's neck. The arm wore a fluffy, white shirt with purple polka dots, a white glove on its hand. Two gasped, his face turning purple. He let go of Haley, and the orange light ceased.

The face of the green-haired clown appeared over Two's shoulder. A smear of white makeup had been wiped off his face, revealing his olive-colored skin. Despite the considerable force he was putting into squeezing Two, he looked down at Haley calmly. "Just a moment," he said. Haley was surprised by his voice. He sounded more refined than Haley had expected from an enormous clown skilled at hand-to-hand combat.

The clown produced a stainless-steel syringe. He jabbed the long needle into Two's ear.

"Erk!" Two stopped struggling, his expression unchanged, and slumped over. The clown dropped him to the ground.

"Who are you?" Haley asked, her voice still shaking. "What's—"

The clown's hand shot out, covering her mouth. "Wait." He cocked his head. His hand dropped and clamped around her wrist. "My name is the Alto. The Keller Foundation hired me to get you out of here. You can trust me," he said, and dragged her into the crowd.

"Hey!" Haley struggled to keep her feet moving, following the giant man as he weaved deftly between the human statues. He reached the line of cars and leaped up onto a hood. Haley jumped, pulled off balance by his arm. Her shin slammed the headlight. She dragged herself up beside him. "What are you—" she began, but the clown was simply pointing ahead, and when Haley looked, her voice died in her throat.

Four cars down was her own. There was her dad, sitting frozen, midway through biting his corn dog. And . . . he was alone.

"Liam," Haley whispered.

"There." The Alto pointed into the crowd. "We have to hurry." He vaulted off the hood. Haley couldn't see anything other than frozen people, but she slid down and raced after him. Liam. Just like Suza . . .

She bumped into the Alto's back and spun around beside him. They had reached the karaoke stage. One stood onstage. She gazed at them, expressionless. Liam was sideways in her arms, frozen in a sitting position, flickering black and white, corn dog still in his hand.

A spear of orange light shot down from above, enveloping them.

"No!" Haley shouted. She started toward them.

The Alto threw an arm in her way. His other arm whipped forward, and something yellow flashed through the air.

"Gulp-tch!" A bright yellow ball slammed into One's throat. She contorted, stumbled backward, and crashed to the ground with Liam on top of her.

The Alto rocketed forward and lunged onto the stage. Haley hauled herself up after him. He grabbed Liam, yanking him out of the orange light. One shimmered and disappeared. The light winked out.

Something hummed deeply, making Haley's teeth vibrate. She looked up to see the UFO lifting into the sky, shrinking and darting off into the night. The parking lot was plunged into darkness.

The Alto flicked on a headlamp flashlight. He held Liam in his arms.

Haley just stared at her frozen brother.

"I'm sorry," said the Alto. "He'll be okay." The Alto pushed back his fluffy white sleeve to reveal an enormous wristwatch. It had two sets of hands on the same face. "Given my intervention," he continued, "they've cut the MT Field short, but it still takes eight minutes to cycle down. That should give us just enough time." He turned, still holding Liam, and hopped down off the stage.

"Wait, just wait!" Haley shouted. The Alto turned back to her, frowning. "What is going on? Who were those people?"

"You mean *what* were they," said the Alto. "And I think you know. This way. We have to put your brother back before the Missing Time Field wears off. That will minimize his disorientation. I can explain more later."

Haley followed the Alto back toward the cars. In the light of his headlamp, she saw that the people were flickering more slowly, traces of color returning to their faces.

"You did something to me, didn't you?" she asked.

The Alto nodded. "A field disruptor. Behind your left ear. The Missing Time Field can be circumvented by stimulating the balance centers of the inner ear. It's actually the same area that they incapacitate with their mind control."

"I probably don't know what you're talking about," said Haley, still catching her breath, "but I'm guessing that I was about to experience this mind control that you're talking about if they had grabbed me."

The Alto nodded. "After I gave you the balloon,

I positioned myself for the shot from the top of the airplane tail. That's why you had to look toward the moon."

In all the madness, Haley had forgotten that stinging sensation from right before the aliens had arrived. She instinctively reached toward the spot—

The Alto's hand shot out and caught hers. "*Not* now," he warned. "If you removed that, you'd freeze up."

They reached Haley's car. The Alto placed Liam back beside Dad. Their frozen faces both gazed up toward the sky expectantly, waiting for the show, having no idea what they'd just missed. Haley stared at them and started to cry. She thought of Liam jumping on the motel beds, his sweaty head asleep against her in the car, and felt horrible for ever being annoyed with him.

"It's okay, um . . . now," said the Alto. He shrugged and shifted on his feet. "You . . ." Her crying seemed to make him feel awkward.

Haley wiped at her eyes. "So, what are you, some kind of mercenary?"

"I make myself available for certain special operations," said the Alto. He slipped his thumb inside his clown shirt and produced a pair of silver dog tags. "I was in the military awhile back and . . ." He trailed off and glanced at the sky. It looked like he'd forgotten what he was going to say, or was maybe looking for something just out of sight above his eyebrows. "Other places since then . . ." he finished. "Anyway, the Kellers hired me earlier today. I had to wait for the money to be wired, and then I barely made it here in time."

"Okay, well, thanks," said Haley.

"I understand that they came after you because you found some connection . . ."

"Yeah." Haley shrugged. "A pattern of towns being put into missing time so that something can be placed in mines underground. There's this orange light, people have had this dream where it gets lowered from the sky . . ."

"Falling from the stars," said the Alto quietly.

"You know about that?" asked Haley.

"I—I'm familiar with it," said the Alto. "It was part of the Kellers' briefing. But they didn't seem to understand why you were here in Memphis. You apparently said you were on your way home."

"Yeah," said Haley. "Well, I actually figured out where the next missing time event is going to happen: Fort Bluff, Arkansas, tonight. I was on my way to go and see it, and stopped here to delay our arrival until later in the evening, so we'd have a chance of seeing it." Haley laughed darkly to herself. "I don't even know *how* I was going to pull that off. Maybe lie about an all-night ice-cream stand or something. I was working on it."

"Do you still want to go?" said the Alto.

Haley looked at him. His gaze was inscrutable, leveled right at her. "What do you mean?"

"Do you still want to go to this town you were trying to get to?" said the Alto. "Because I can take you there."

Haley considered this. She saw the Alto checking his watch again.

"We have to leave soon," he said. "My car has special modifications to avoid being tracked, but it's still best if we leave before the MT Field ends and take advantage of the confusion it will create."

Haley looked at her dad and brother. "Yeah but, what . . . are we all just going to pile in your car? How are we going to get them in there when they're frozen?"

The Alto shook his head. "Not them. Only you."

"Wait, what?"

"It will compromise the mission to take your family along. I can't keep that many people safe. Too many variables. Besides, the aliens are after you, not your family."

"They just tried to take Liam!" Haley shouted, feeling her motor ramping up again inside.

"That was only because they failed to get you.

Grabbing your brother was the next logical move, improvised, I'm sure, but still sensible. They could hold him as ransom to get you."

"Well, but won't they just try that again?"

The Alto shook his head. "We can leave your parents field disruptors, but also, this was a very risky operation for the aliens to attempt. They had the element of surprise. Next time, they won't, so they'll have to plan more carefully. And according to Ms. Keller, it sounds like you were probably keeping your parents in the dark about what was really going on anyway, which is why they hadn't turned the car around awhile ago."

"Pretty much," said Haley, feeling fresh guilt welling up with all the other feelings, like her mind was a crowded meeting hall.

"And that makes your parents less valuable, not worth the risk. Now, shall we?"

"I can't," said Haley, more tears slipping down her cheeks. "This is crazy. I was almost just abducted. I . . ." She looked up into the still night. "That's it. We have to turn around and go home. Those were the orders I got, anyway. I should have just listened. I got us all in danger."

The Alto reached over and patted her shoulder brusquely, a single time. "When you're on a mission, it is the hardest thing to turn back."

Haley nodded. She couldn't believe how she'd

acted, though. She'd ignored the dangers, so desperate to get her story. "Once this field fades," she said resolutely, "I'll tell them everything. And we'll head home."

Color was returning around them, clothes were brightening, lights warming. Haley found the Alto still staring at her. "What?"

"Well, unfortunately, going home will not be sufficient, at this point. As long as you know what you know, you're a threat to them. They'll come to finish the job."

"Well, then I'll forget everything!" Haley shouted. "I'll burn my notes, smash my computer!"

"That won't be enough," said the Alto. "I don't think you fully realize what you've gotten yourself into here. You uncovered their pattern, and they noticed. If you come with me, I can help you complete your mission—"

"It's not my *mission*!" Haley shouted. "It was a story, and . . . it's over now."

"No, it's not," said the Alto. "That's what I'm saying. Like it or not, there are only two ways that this ends: Either they find you, or you find them. I can help you. I can protect you, and we can find out what's really going on—"

"But my family!" Haley shouted. "I can't leave them!" And as she shouted it, Haley was thinking,

Wait, why was she even arguing about this? She wasn't really considering it, was she? That was crazy, and that instinct had nearly led to her getting abducted, her mind getting wiped. "I've been lying to them, I put us all in danger, I—"

The Alto checked his watch again and made a little sighing sound like he might be getting impatient, or bored. "Let me ask you something: How is your family going to feel if you're abducted and they never get to see you again? Because that is likely what's going to happen if you turn around. You're still a threat with what you know. That doesn't change just because you go home. You could still expose them."

"So I'm supposed to just run off with you? Isn't that basically the same thing for my parents?"

The Alto frowned. He reached into his pocket and produced two small rectangles. He held them out: phones. "Look," he said, stepping past her and slipping one into Allan's pocket. "Once we're safely out of sight, you can call them. These phones are shielded against the EMP effects that this Missing Time Field will cause. You can let them know you're safe, and we can give them instructions about how to meet up with us again."

The Alto held out the phone. Haley took it in her hand. She gazed down at it, then back at Dad and Liam. At their faces warming . . . at the lightening world around her . . .

You wanted adventure, said the doubt demon coldly. *You wanted to get out in that big world. Well, here we are. So now what?*

"This is the only way you're going to solve the mystery," said the Alto. "Hundreds of people are missing, many more than that are in danger, including you and your family now, and you have the keys to saving them."

"Ugh!" Haley threw up her hands. "How do I even know you're telling the truth?"

"You don't, except that I am. These were Keller's instructions: Rescue you, then bring you along and proceed to intercept the other fellowship winner."

Haley remembered the text Alex had sent her. Here was the assistance. . . . "Keller said there were new developments," said Haley. "What are they?"

The Alto raised his hands as if to indicate their current predicament. "You becoming a target."

"She wanted me to turn around and go home . . ." Haley repeated.

"Again, that was before you started attracting this kind of attention. Look," the Alto said, sounding almost flustered. "We can call Keller, if you want, but we're running out of time."

Haley tried to reconcile all this. "So now Keller wants you to take me with you to rescue the other winner." Haley had forgotten about the second winner. That had been part of the announcement: two winners chosen. The other was from Seattle, or somewhere. "Why? Is she in trouble, too?"

"He, actually. And affirmative. He also has information that we need. So . . . ready?"

No, Haley thought, she wasn't ready. Not at all. *You cannot do this,* she thought. As much as she hated to admit it, she was just a thirteen-year-old girl who still needed her parents. Look at how much trouble she'd caused trying to act on her own. Not to mention lying to them. To go on, to betray them further . . . how could she?

And yet, to continue the hunt . . . Haley felt that urge and hated it and yet there it was, that whirring inside. And really, was this insane, or was it yet another example of Scheduled Serendipity?

Because if the Alto was right, and by staying with her family she was leaving herself open to be attacked again, and taken. . . . Well, that result was even worse, wasn't it? She tried to imagine her family having to deal with that. They'd feel responsible. They'd never get over it. She thought of Steph and Suza's mom, rocking and mumbling. That woman would never be the same. . . .

Haley felt a hollow pit open up inside, an understanding, finally, far too late, of what she'd really done. Sure, leaving now was irresponsible, but was it any more so than lying to her parents again and again and putting them all in danger? She'd already hurt her parents without them even knowing it, deceiving them as she had, and while leaving them now was going to hurt them even more, it would hurt them less than if she was taken from them forever, without a reason or a phone call.

Haley glanced at the sky. Blues were returning. She saw a flicker of movement. Off in the distance, her lavender balloon was slowly rising into the night.

"Tick-tock," said the Alto.

8.5 kilometers west of Fort Bluff, AR, July 4, 11:18 p.m.

"Night sun descending . . ."

"The sun comes home . . ."

There was a tiny whoomp of air, a little push of warm breath through the cool darkness. That was all.

Moments later the light appeared, high in the sky, at first seeming to be just a bright planet. But it moved, floating serenely earthward like an ember.

Haley sat on the roof of a long, black sedan. It was parked half off a narrow country road, with shallow ditches and then endless fields of some kind of grain on either side. The air was cool, damp, swirls of light fog mingling just above the fields. The roof of the car was slick with condensation. There was a gentle drone of crickets, an overtone of frogs. Everything was blue-black, except for fireflies here and there in the grass, the stars brilliant and white above, and of course the giant falling light.

"Your calculations were right on," said the Alto. He sat beside her, arms around his bent legs. "See?" He held out his watch.

Haley saw that one dial was spinning normally, but the other had slowed to a near stop.

"Just over eight kilometers away from Fort Bluff, and we're right on the edge of it," the Alto said.

She'd told him about her missing time radius theory on the drive. That push of air had been the MT Field establishing itself.

The orange ember grew and lowered. Haley felt mesmerized by it. When she blinked, it left little green dots in her vision.

"Night sun descending," the Alto said again. Haley looked over to see him fiddling with something on his other wrist. It looked like a bracelet, a tarnished silver color, and it seemed to have a few objects hanging off it, like charms. It kind of looked like something a girl would wear.

"How do you know about the dreams?" Haley asked. "Were you . . . abducted or something?"

"I'm . . . not sure," said the Alto. He made his thinking face again, gazing up into his brow. "Something about my last assignment . . ." He trailed off.

"Okay . . ." said Haley. She licked at a coating of powdered sugar and barbecue on her lips. Somewhere back in the dark, they'd stopped at a convenience store. The combination of donuts, chips, and a soy shake had somewhat settled her nerves.

"What do you think it is?" she asked, gazing back at the falling light.

"I don't know," said the Alto, "but there is someone who does."

"Keller?" Haley asked.

The Alto chuckled. "No. The other fellowship winner."

"He knows what the aliens are doing?"

"I don't think so," said the Alto. "But he knows what that light is, and more importantly, he knows about Juliette."

"Juliette?" asked Haley. It rang a bell. "Those agents said her name. Do you know who she is?"

"It's not a who, it's a where. And . . ." The Alto made his searching face and sighed with frustration. "That's all I know about it."

"Why are you keeping things from me?" Haley asked.

"No—that's not what I'm doing. I literally don't

remember. Especially about my last assignment, but there are a lot of things in my head that are missing, large parts of my life that are a mystery to me. Things I can't quite piece together. But apparently the other winner's theory had to do with a place called Juliette. And I know that, for me, that's . . . familiar. But I don't know why."

Haley watched the Alto. She wondered if that could be true. Had he really lost parts of his memory? He'd returned to watching the star fall. And he was still fiddling with that bracelet. "Kerry . . ." he said softly to himself.

"What?" Haley asked.

"Nothing." The Alto pulled his sleeve down over the bracelet.

The orange ember had nearly reached the horizon. As Haley watched, it descended past the tops of the trees and gently vanished from sight. For another couple seconds, there was an orange corona above it. Then that winked out and the countryside settled into black.

Haley felt the Alto looking at her. "What?"

"You haven't called them yet." He looked down to where Haley was clutching the phone in her hands.

"Yeah, I'm getting to it." Haley felt a big nervous rush. She didn't want to think about her parents. Where were they? What were they thinking? How much were they freaking out? She had an urge to just wait until this was all over and rush back into their arms. But that was cowardice. She had to face what she'd done. Her parents were her responsibility now. If she didn't let them know she was okay, then the aliens might as well have gotten her. Of course, in a way, that would have been easier.

"They're not going to like it," said the Alto, "but not knowing is worse . . . in all things." He sighed. "Call your parents."

Haley held the phone up, gazing at it.

"You just press talk," said the Alto.

"Der," said Haley. She held her breath . . . then pressed. It rang twice.

"Hello?" Allan answered, breathless and confused.

"Dad, it's me," said Haley. She tried to make her voice sound normal, tried to keep the rising tremors that were wracking her body at bay. "I'm okay . . . A-are you?"

"Now that we hear your voice, yes, but Haley—"

"Dad, I'm sorry. . . . I had to go . . ." Haley choked up.

"Haley!! It's okay, just . . . where are you? Whose phone is this? Are you all right? What just happened?"

"Dad, listen . . . I . . ." Haley tried her best to speak calmly. "I'm with Keller's agent. His name is the Alto. He rescued me back there. It was a Missing Time Event . . . You won't remember it, but check the clocks once you're—"

"Haley, I know about the missing time!" Allan was practically shouting. "I checked my watch. We're still here. Your mom had just gotten a call from Alex Keller when the missing time happened, but now our phones are wiped out so we couldn't call her back. The police are here though, and we told them you're missing and now the FBI is on its way and they are issuing an Amber Alert and . . . Haley, we are looking everywhere for you!" He sounded desperate, frayed, and Haley could barely stand to hear it.

"That's good," said the Alto quietly. "Police, FBI. That will help keep them safe enough."

Haley heard Allan cup the phone for a second and then he returned. "Sorry, Haley, listen . . . just tell me where you are."

Haley wanted to, but she could see the Alto shaking his head out the corner of her eye. "Dad, I can't. But don't worry. I—I'm safe," she said, wondering if she really was. "And I'm—I'm going to be gone for a little while. This agent is taking me to find the other fellowship winner."

"Taking you?! What are you talking about, Haley?!"

"Tell them to drive west," said the Alto. "To head for Phoenix." Then he pointed toward the sky. "Before they trace the call."

"How do you know this agent is—"

"Dad!" Haley had to cut him off. Dad was asking a million questions and Haley could barely listen. She felt herself knotting up inside, tears leaking free, the tremors out of control. "Dad, listen, I have to go, this call could be monitored. Look, I'm so sorry. I lied to you guys about the danger we were in with the fellowship. The aliens tried to abduct me tonight, and if I don't go do this, they'll just come again. So I have to go. I have to make things right. The Alto says to head west, toward Phoenix. I'll meet you there."

"Haley, wait!"

"Tell him to find the vial of disrupters in the glove compartment," said the Alto. "But not to tell the FBI about those, because they'll just screw them up." The Alto clucked his tongue. "Amateurs."

"Who is that talking?" Allan shouted. "Haley, is that him? Is that the—"

"Dad, yes! Just, plee-ase . . ." Haley was crying now; she couldn't help it. Her whole body was shaking. "Just get the vial out of the glove compartment. Wear those disruptors behind your left ears and head west."

"What vial? Disruptors, what are you talking about?"

The Alto's watch started to beep. "Time's up," he said.

Haley swallowed hard. "Dad, listen, I gotta go. It's okay, really, and I love you guys and I don't want you to worry. . . ."

"Haley, no! Are they making you say this?"

"No, not really, I mean, just trust me that I'm okay."

"Okay, okay," Allan's voice got low, a desperate whisper: "Haley, th–this man you're with . . . If he's kidnapped you or hurt you, just say something . . . say 'How's Liam?'"

Haley glanced at the Alto. "I'm sure I'm fine," she said, hoping it was true. "I gotta go, Dad," Haley caught a sob, holding her breath until it passed. "I love you."

She held the phone out in front of her.

"Haley, wait!" Allan shouted from the receiver. "No, don't hang up!"

She couldn't. No, she couldn't hang up, she couldn't go through with this any longer—

The Alto pulled the phone away. He hit End, flipped the phone over, popped off the back, and yanked its guts out. He flung the mess out into the field. "Sorry." He turned and opened the car door. "We should get going."

Haley swiped at her eyes. Took a deep breath.

"See?" said the Alto. "Better."

"No," Haley whispered. It wasn't better. It was maybe worse.

Haley felt her bag moving. She looked down to see that the Alto had removed her phone.

"What are you doing?" she snapped.

"Any calls or messages you send can be traced." He had already flipped open the back.

"Don't—" Haley began.

The Alto pulled a chip free in the back and tossed it into the night. He held out the phone. "Camera will still work."

"Great," said Haley. And then she realized she hadn't thought to take a picture of the falling light. *Some journalist you are,* the doubt demon scolded. *Yeah, well, I've had a lot on my mind.*

The Alto hopped off the roof. "Let's roll," he said.

Haley slid off the car and got in. She slumped in the cold vinyl seat. The Alto gunned the engine, wheeled the car around, and shot off down the black road. Haley noticed a plastic hula girl bobbing on the dashboard, smiling at her.

She stared out the window, crushed, squeezed dry and wondering if this could really possibly be the right thing to do. Sure, she'd just seen the falling light, connecting the dreams to the mines. It was all real, everything she'd uncovered, the whole giant story. . . .

But now it felt different. Her anxious yearning to find new map, to get out over the horizon, to not be held back . . . Well, here she was and instead of the pure kind of wind-in-your-face exhilaration that she thought it would be, this was something new: She felt alone, small, an insignificant speck in an enormous universe.

Haley shivered, wrapped her arms tightly around herself. She had no idea what came next, and all she could see were the cones of headlights on pavement, the black of unknown countryside, and the flicker of a billion stars, worlds away.

Juliette, AZ, April 25, 6:45 a.m.

Suza Raines was getting suspicious. As her alarm clock blared, she lay in bed, eyes still closed, thinking: *It's too early. The clock is wrong.* She wiggled her shoulders, nudging the covers up over her head. Just a few more minutes of sleep . . .

But now she noticed the strange music coming from the clock. This wasn't KJPR. Trumpets squealed and strings warbled. It sounded kind of like that Billie Holiday music her dad liked to listen to, except this gobbling voice was male, and definitely not singing English:

Chaque jour je me réveille et c'est pareil,

Je ne peut pas se comprendre de ce que j'ai perdu

The clock looked weird, too. Not just because it was a boxy old digital with red numbers and fake wood sides—her dad thought the big numbers would be good for her to see when she woke up, before she could put on her glasses—but also because the numbers were wrong, somehow.

This is it, she thought, *I'm finally going blind.* Suza sat up and shook her head. *No, stupid. I'm just tired.* That was probably it. She'd taken advantage of Dad and Angie being out late last night and stayed up watching TV and guzzling diet root beers and munching barbecue chips. Late-night TV watching was the absolute only good thing about having Angie around: Otherwise, Suza didn't like her one bit.

She felt the same way about morning. Wanted nothing to do with it. How annoying was morning, anyway? Night was way better. It always felt just a little wild, like if you stayed awake long enough, you could almost make the next morning never come. Hang on to the same day forever.

The day that happens over and over, she thought randomly.

Suza grabbed her glasses from her bedside table, slipped them on, and looked back at the clock. Well, she wasn't going blind. Not today, anyway. The numbers on the clock were definitely messed up, like some of the digital bars were on the fritz. It looked like nonsense:

So, at least one of those odd thoughts that kept popping into her head was wrong. Although, her fear of going blind had felt different than those other two thoughts, about the time being wrong and the day happening over and over. Those had seemed more . . . *certain*.

She sat up and turned off her alarm. It was definitely time to get a new one. Maybe she could go to Base Surplus and Consignment after school, or tomorrow—

There won't be a tomorrow!

The thought shot through her head like a searing laser. Suza winced and shook her head. Without knowing it, she reached back and slapped behind her left ear.

The feeling passed as quickly as it had come. What had that been? Suza had no idea.

She got dressed and shuffled into the kitchen. It was nice to find it quiet. Usually, Angie was up by now, wrapped in her so ugly, baby blue robe with the fuzzy collar, her mane of blond hair everywhere. What Dad saw in her, Suza didn't know. . . . Why did her mom have to leave?

Another weird thought popped into her mind: *She didn't leave; I did.*

Suza unknowingly slapped behind her ear again. Of course her mom left, a while ago now. Still, Suza could remember her, always wearing those silly pink sneakers. . . .

Suza sighed. Her dad had tried hard to explain to her why things hadn't worked out. Something about people being *incompatible*. They didn't fit each other. But then what about Suza, who fit with them both? Shouldn't they have been like three Lego blocks, with Suza in the middle? How come it didn't just work?

A voice drifted through the kitchen window. "Darn it all, MacDougals!"

Suza looked out and saw her neighbor, Mr. Davis, sprawled in the road.

He tripped, Suza thought to herself. *Well, duh, that's obvious*. She turned away.

It occurred to her now that if Angie wasn't up, Suza would have plenty of time to go see AJ down at the One Horse.

She needed to say bye to Dad, though. Suza headed down the hall and peered into the still-dark room.

Two lumps lay buried in the covers, Angie making a light, yucky snore.

"Dad," Suza half-whispered. "I'm leaving for school."

Matt rolled onto his side. "All right. Did you eat something?"

"Yeah."

"Okay, love ya, kiddo."

Suza felt a little double beat in her heart. "Love you, too," she said quietly.

Outside, Mr. Davis and MacDougals were gone. Suza walked over to her bike. She bent to pick it up when she noticed something shiny perched on the edge of the seat. Someone had carefully placed it there for her: a shimmery silver rectangle of metal, about three inches long, notches in its sides and symbols etched in a line across it. *Right,* she thought. She picked it up—it seemed to weigh almost nothing— and slipped it into her pocket.

As she got on her bike, another thought arrived: *Show it to AJ.* Why AJ? Well, AJ was a grad student in astrophysics, and he spent most nights up at the observatory. He was also always talking with Matt about his theories on how there were aliens visiting Earth. How they were already here and practicing mind control. That always made Dad laugh.

Another thought suddenly arrived. *Hurry, before they notice.*

Suza hopped onto her bike and raced down into town. She passed that fenced-off construction area again, causing a man in a yellow hard hat to stare at her. Wasn't there something weird about him? *Don't worry about that. Keep going.*

Reaching Main Street, Suza locked her bike and headed for the diner. On her way, she heard a voice that seemed familiar:

"Come on! Excuse me, who do I talk to? This thing took my quarter!"

As she neared the glass door to the One Horse Diner, a large woman in a yellow dress walked out.

The words "half-pint" floated across her mind as she ducked into the diner.

"Suze!" AJ was standing at the end of the counter, filling coffee mugs. His white apron was already smudged with grease, ketchup, and Hollandaise. "How's it going, little lady?"

"Hi," Suza said. She was feeling odd. Like—things were wrong somehow. She looked down the long row of booths. An old man was coughing on his coffee. A young woman was looking at her friend with red-faced embarrassment as the friend wiped at her shirt.

"Earth to Suze," AJ called. He came around from

behind the counter, filling a few mugs at the tables along the front windows. "Hey, I know why you're here."

"You do?" Suza asked, feeling a flash of worry.

"Yeah, but, bad news. We're fresh out of peanut butter."

"Oh, right. I know, or, I *knew*, but . . ."

"What's the matter?" AJ asked, stopping beside her.

I have to show him, quick, she thought, *before . . .* Before what? She couldn't remember. But there was something. Some time pressure. Suza reached into her pocket.

AJ's face suddenly grew serious, and his voice dropped to a whisper. "Do you have it?"

"You mean this?" She held up the metal piece. It seemed to gather all the light in the room and reflect it back out, making a glittering diamond pattern on everything, like a disco ball.

"Whoa," said AJ.

"I . . . I was supposed to bring it here, right?" Suza asked.

"You . . ." AJ's face twitched as if he was working through a complicated thought. "The—the um, the plan. That's the key to the plan. . . ."

Now Suza noticed that the diner had become silent. She looked around to find the entire restaurant gazing at her. People were twisted around, half-standing to get a good view; passersby outside were even pressed up against the glass, looking in from Main Street, their faces wide in wonder. All staring at the metal piece, making twitching, problem-solving faces, like AJ.

"But . . . this doesn't work," AJ murmured. "We've already tried it. We . . . we have to take it straight to the observatory, instead."

Hearing these words, a great flood of relief and certainty rushed through Suza. *Yes!* she thought. *This is what's supposed to happen. AJ is supposed to take this to the observatory.* "Okay, here." She held the piece out toward AJ.

But he stepped back, shaking his head. "No, that's what I'm saying . . . it doesn't work. If I take it, they'll just . . . They always stop me. Every time I try, I—"

He started slapping behind his left ear. Suza watched him do it without surprise. Now she heard a similar sound around her. Other people were slapping, too, and in moments the entire restaurant was doing it, some lightly, some harder. It sounded like rain on a roof.

There's something wrong with us, Suza thought. *With all of us. We're being controlled—*

Suddenly her head was flooded with a commanding, monotone voice:

SUZA! YOU WILL COME TO SCHOOL NOW! CALMLY
AND WITHOUT DELAY!

The volume made her wince. Suza turned back to
AJ. "You have to take it!" she said. "You're *supposed* to
take it!" She felt certain of this. That was the only way
to stop this— whatever was wrong with them, he—

NOW, SUZA! RIGHT NOW!

Suza shook her head. *No!* she shouted back at the
voice. *I won't do what you say!*

"Suze." AJ stumbled into the counter. The coffee-
pot slipped from his hand, shattering on the floor. "It
doesn't work if I take it," he said breathlessly. "We've
tried this already. I don't even know what I mean by
that, but . . ."

The slapping in the room grew louder, like the
rain had become a downpour.

"Please!" Suza shouted desperately. "AJ, please!
We—"

The door to the One Horse slammed open. By
the time Suza whirled toward it, the four orange-
suited construction workers in yellow hard hats were
already inside. People screamed. Two of the short
men grabbed AJ by the arms.

"No!" he shouted as they dragged him behind the
counter.

The other two grabbed Suza by the arms. She
tried to lunge away, but one man spun her around. He

had torn the metal piece out of her hand in an instant.

"No, give it back!" she screamed.

The construction workers were barely taller than her. Their faces looked oddly blank and smooth, like their skin was made of plastic. Their eyes were hidden by black oval goggles.

There was a crash behind the counter. Suza tried to look, but she couldn't.

Stay calm, Suza! the voice commanded. All this will be over in a moment.

Suza heard AJ shouting from the floor behind the counter. "Not again! Suze! You have to take it! Next time you take it!"

The workers dragged her out of the diner and down the street. Suza tried to break their grip, but it was no use.

Calm down, Suza. Down. Down.

And she was calming down, despite her panic. This was the only way, wasn't it? She didn't need to worry. No more bad thoughts.

As Suza was led away, everyone on the street stood perfectly still, watching her pass. As soon as she was by, each person would slap at the area behind their left ear and then suddenly resume what they were doing. It happened in a wave down Main Street.

"Well now, this is a continuing problem for you, isn't it?" said Principal Howard, a pitying smile on his face. "But don't worry. We'll get the bugs out of Suza Raines eventually. . . ."

The worker took her by the wrist, but this time, Suza didn't yell. Instead, she hid as far inside her head as she could get, clinging to a single thought, trying to burn it into her brain. And as the orange light washed over her, she kept repeating it, over and over— *Next time I take it— Next time I take it— Next time I take it— Next time I take it—*

Until all of her thoughts were gone.

part
TWO

Port Salmon, WA, July 3, 8:52 a.m.

The day before Haley and the Alto disappeared into the dark countryside, and just under three thousand miles away, Francis "Dodger" Lane sat alone in the corner of an unfinished kitchen, head in his hands. He looked like he was crying, sitting there, head slumped over between his knees, but he wasn't. He had the first three fingers of each hand pressed against his temples, and he was listening as carefully as he could.

He heard a persistent plinking; a leak had formed in the plywood roof over a year ago and now a small cascade collected in a permanent shallow pool on the brown tiles. The floor was sagging there. He also heard a tiny scraping, probably squirrels, or maybe the rats that always tormented Dodger's mom's tomatoes. Distantly, cars droned by on I-5. However, none of these sounds were what Dodger was listening for.

"Francis!"

Neither was that. But Dodger looked up, all the way to the mold-splotched ceiling, and sighed. "Coming," he replied, though not loud enough to be heard. It was time to go; he knew his father, Harry, was itching to get on the road before the Seattle traffic got bad, to get gas at that one service station south of Bellevue that had "The Only Reasonable Price in Town," and then get down to Eugene and check in to the Relaxation Depot before the pool closed because, as Harry Lane had espoused for as long as Dodger could remember, you had to use the pool and exercise facilities. Otherwise "What These Places Charge Is the Royal Rip-off."

And Dodger could just see how it would go wrong, like it always seemed to: how there would be freak traffic in Seattle, how that service station would be out of 87 octane (and if you were going to fill the tank with that premium stuff you "Might As Well Shove Your Wallet in There, Too"), how the hotel pool would be closed because a kid went to the bathroom in it and the exercise bike wouldn't be out of order but the calorie counter would be off and then, "What's the Point?"

What's the point of this trip? Dodger thought to himself. Then again, staying here didn't hold much promise. June had been miserable in Seattle, it always was, as if the Pacific Northwest took pleasure in mocking the calendar's proclamation of summer with a purgatory-like dirge of fog and rain. Through the clouds, you could practically hear the rest of the Northern Hemisphere getting on with the fun of the season, and all you could do was wonder why, why would anyone live here? Of course, July was usually so stunningly sunny that you forgot about all that, but of course, in typical fashion, they were leaving just before that sunshine was due to arrive.

But Dodger didn't have anything to do in the nice weather anyway. At least when it was dreary, nobody criticized him for hanging out in his room playing *Civilizer 4.2*, a computer game where you planned and constructed perfect homes, cities, and towns for this endearing little race of creatures called Darwees. Or, even better, for hanging out over here at Number Two Orca View with his maps.

They were scattered around him now, some of the jewels of his extensive collection of paper maps, which he kept carefully stored in the stainless-steel oven on the wall above him. It was the only appliance in the kitchen of Number Two. There were just holes where refrigerators and dishwashers were supposed to go. There weren't even countertops. Only one of the walls was finished. Everything else was just raw board, most of which had greened and warped, sagging in the moisture. Other than the oven, the only finished item in the kitchen was the "Sedona Dream" floor tile, which was serving as a sturdy lake bed.

Such had been Harry Lane's attempt to capitalize on the big real estate bubble a few years ago. Orca View Estates was supposed to be twenty-six luxury homes descending a gentle slope of sustainably harvested forest in a soothing S and ending at a private beach with a clubhouse and a heated pool. There would even be real sand volleyball courts. Each house would be modern and spacious and filled with a bright young family seeking community and solitude. Meticulous landscaping, magical lights at the holidays . . .

It was supposed to be.

But Harry's timing had been six months off, and the market had collapsed. Only one house had been completed, Number One Orca View. Dodger lived there. Number Two had been started and abandoned. The street only extended twenty feet beyond its lot, and at the end was a heaped pile of sand, now green with blackberry, that had once been the perfect fine white for beach volleyball.

Lane Real Estate was gone, too, and now Harry worked at *Viva Value!* It had taken a lot of wrangling for him to get these two weeks off in prime summertime, and so Dodger knew that meant they had to "Make the Most of It" and that they were "On the Clock," and yet here he was, hiding out next door when his dad was ready to go.

Dodger actually did want to go on the trip. In fact, he really wanted to go, to do his field study, to research the theory that had won him the Fellowship for Alien Detection. The fact that he was actually associating the words *want* and *research*, an academic word, had been enough to win his mom's support for the idea, and one of Harry's famous looking-to-the-left shrugs. And yet that was the problem: Going on the trip meant being in the car for two weeks with his dad. Mom couldn't go. Her firm had just started a big trial.

What would they talk about? When did they ever sustain more than a two-minute conversation? And those were only ever about current events in space science, the one place where Dodger's and Harry's interests actually converged, albeit only somewhat, like two ships passing in a fog, briefly visible to each another as ghostly lights.

Those conversations went something like:

Harry (*innocently*): Hey, did you hear about that new Mars probe?

Dodger (*tentative*): Yeah, it . . . sounds cool.

Harry (*possibly interested*): It's apparently got tools for trying to find microbes up there.

Dodger (*optimistic*): Yeah, they think with the sub-surface ice, there could be actual life.

Harry (*like Harry*): Well, it's not exactly little green men, but hey, it's not my money.

Dodger (*shrugging*): Yeah.

And that would be that. How would they possibly manage two weeks—three hundred and thirty-six hours—together?

And yet, not going was no longer an option. Not just because Dodger had actually managed to win this fellowship ("I know," Harry would say, "who'd'a thunk, right?"), and not just because all that annuity money was on the line ("A big chunk of student loans," Harry would say, "if somebody ever decides to get his act together for college,"), and not even because of the aforementioned two weeks of *prime* vacation time ("Say good-bye to Maui *this* year." They'd never been to Maui), or even just the general notion that Dodger could win something. (Harry had a lot of sayings for this, like back in the unfortunate soccer era: "My boy's not exactly what you'd call clutch," or, after the incident with the football tryout: "He's just never been very aware of himself in space.")

In all of those past moments, Dodger felt like he could have saved Harry the disappointment by telling him beforehand that things weren't going to go well. But Harry always seemed to think that if they just found the right outlet, the right fix, then Dodger might stop being a sullen, lonely kid who slouched around like a marionette, and become a real boy. Dodger didn't buy it. He felt like he couldn't have done all those things well even if he'd wanted to. It was like something inside him didn't work right, or like he was stuck inside the wrong life, one that was a size too big and fit him all wrong. And that was the biggest reason why he knew he *had* to go on this trip, a quiet painful certainty that he felt deep inside: *because I don't know if I can survive staying here.*

It was a feeling that seemed to be getting worse this last year. Maybe it was the idea of high school coming up. Dodger didn't know who he wanted to be, couldn't picture a future with him in it. And this fellowship might be his only hope for fixing that.

But before he was going to strap himself into the car beside his dad, he needed some inspiration, or maybe *assurance* was the right word. That was why he was over here in Number Two hiding out.

He'd already tried looking at his maps. Usually

some time spent with his favorites did the trick. There was French Polynesia and the Cook Islands, a polar view of the Arctic Circle, satellite map of Mars, schematic of ancient Rome. . . . These maps always took him away, not just out of this house or Port Salmon, but out of his life completely. He could imagine himself as someone else entirely, perhaps with a name like Stefanos or John Carlton Wescott, perhaps with a fair dame he'd rescued from savages along the way or even just a cool, quick-witted dog. No matter the specifics, he would always be off exploring, seeking out new worlds, hidden archipelagos, lost caverns, solitary nooks in ancient temples. In short, places to call his own.

The maps weren't working today, though, not even the one he was using for his upcoming field study, which showed the greater American West. Sure, it held the promise of the mystery that he'd discovered, the theory that had won him the fellowship, but right now he needed to be sure that mystery was real, and not just something he'd made up.

And so he dropped his head and started pressing against his temples again. He closed his eyes and searched in the dark, trying to get away from the outside world, the leaking of the unfinished house, the humming of cars and scurrying of rats, searching. . . .

And then he felt a strange, tight sensation, like he

was being yanked out of his own head and traveling through a hollow black space. Suddenly there was an earsplitting voice—

"Good morning, ladies and gentlemen! This is DJ Alpine at KJPR and it's a beautiful spring day here in Juliette! The forecast calls for partly cloudy skies with a forty percent chance of UFO sightings, hey-o!"

The voice lit up his mind, syrupy and electric. Dodger felt himself sinking into it. A peaceful feeling washing over him as the DJ continued. A DJ on a radio station he could hear in his head, from a town called Juliette.

A town that, as far as Dodger could tell, didn't exist.

chapter

11

Port Salmon, WA, July 3, 3:47 p.m.

"You just heard three in a row by Pluto's Fancy, and coming up we've got a brand-new smash by those visitors from another planet, the Orbiters!"

There was a swell of static and the voice retreated, like a wave rushing away from him. Dodger pressed harder on his temples, squeezed his eyes tighter, trying to look into the black behind his mind and find the radio station again.

It had started a little over a year ago, or maybe longer than that. Dodger couldn't be sure because it used to be something that only happened during dreams. Dodger would wake up with memories of this exact voice, this DJ Alpine and his radio broadcast, from somewhere called Juliette. He'd thought it curious even when he'd assumed it was just something his subconscious had created. Usually the radio voice would be part of some larger dream where Dodger would be in these familiar and yet unknown places: a weird murky collage with vacant black borders, the way dreams usually were. Dodger figured the radio was another symbol of this ideal, unknown place he was hoping to find for himself.

Still, some things had been consistent in most all of the dreams with the radio voice, things like the sunny spring weather and the distant mountain covered in snow. There were other images, too, like dark corridors that were maybe caves, and a weird orange light. It made Dodger wonder if his brain was trying to tell him something.

He'd even started drawing his own map of this dream place called Juliette. It had been fun, re-creating that world, an even more satisfying escape than the South Pacific or Patagonia. This place was all his, a world of his own creation.

But that had all changed last fall, when the radio station suddenly started, or more accurately, tuned in, while Dodger was wide awake. The first time it happened, he'd been sitting in the middle of class, decorating one of his book covers. He used duplicate maps to cover his books, and he'd been drawing a serpent curving in and out of the South China Sea, when *Bzzt!* KJPR had started broadcasting in his mind.

Dodger had looked up in a panic, but around him class had been proceeding as usual, with all the other heads hunched over a social studies text and Mr. Laramee droning on. Dodger could see his classroom, but the sounds of the world were gone, replaced by DJ Alpine. Actually, class hadn't continued as usual for very long, because heads slowly started turning in Dodger's direction. He didn't understand why until he caught his neighbor Sadie glancing underneath his desk. When he looked down, he saw that his legs were twitching and his feet were tapping rapidly against the tile floor. It took all of his concentration to get that under control.

There had also been tears coming out of his eyes, and apparently his hair had been kind of floating like someone had rubbed a balloon against his head. This caused a few smirks and whispers among neighbors.

"What?" Dodger had tried to say, and the radio voice had suddenly cut out, leaving Dodger empty, spent, and lonely feeling. And then class had proceeded.

Since then, the station had arrived in his head in one of two ways: either randomly, and in these cases Dodger had learned to recognize the signs that it was coming—teeth chattering, tingly fingers, the urge to pee—and either get to a solitary place or at least brace for it. Or he could tune it in as he was doing now, by concentrating and searching. He couldn't always find it; sometimes weeks went by with no signal, and Dodger would feel certain that it had left him forever. This thought made a hollow pit form inside him, but the radio always returned.

"First let's check in with Dan Spirit for a look at the weekend weather. . . . Okay, looks like we'll have a little cold front blowing through later this evening, and maybe even one last April snow squall. Oh, and one more thing, when you're out and about today, be sure to watch out for all those construction sites in the roadways. Rumor has it, all the cable lines in town are being upgraded."

Dodger knew that hearing a radio station in his head was in no way normal, and yet, when it was broadcasting, it didn't *feel* weird. If anything, it felt familiar, even comforting, like he somehow knew this voice or this place.

But that was where it got really weird. Once Dodger started hearing the station while he was awake, he'd also started trying to figure out where it was coming from. He'd pored over his extensive collection of United States maps, looking for a town called Juliette. And he found one almost immediately. The problem was, the Juliette he'd found was in Georgia, and besides the fact that the radio in his head was always mentioning canyons and mountains, Dodger also knew that radio station call signs east of the Mississippi began with a *W*. The *K* in KJPR meant that this Juliette was somewhere out west. . . . But there wasn't one. Anywhere. As far as Dodger could tell, the town of Juliette that he heard in his head did not exist in the real world.

Another strange fact about the radio station was that the broadcast Dodger heard was always from the same day: April twenty-fifth, over and over, like the station was on a loop. But not a full-day loop: Sometimes Dodger heard the Juliette morning show late at night, and vice versa.

All of these oddities had led to a disturbing possibility: What if this radio really was all in his mind? Like he was going crazy, his brain malfunctioning?

The one thing that had saved Dodger from diagnosing himself as insane had been winning the FAD. He'd run into the application while reading accounts of alien abductions on a website called We Are the Missing. He'd found that website when he was searching for Juliette online. It had been the source of the only two references that seemed promising.

The first was on a message board of posts under the heading: *"Anybody else hearing voices?"* Far down that very odd thread, there had been a woman in her eighties who lived in a nursing home in Tulsa and claimed that a voice in her head named B. J. Carmine sang her to sleep each night. He was from the Big War, and he called her Julianne. . . . B. J. Carmine and Julianne . . . not too different from DJ Alpine and Juliette.

But it was the second message board that was more promising. This comment thread was titled *"Anybody hearing aliens on their radio?"* and here were a number of posts about people tuning in weird voices from the stars. Buried in this thread was a comment and a series of replies that looked like this:

Thanksforthefish42:
    Anyone else tried the PhoneHome radio that EyesOnTheStars sells on EBay? Am getting some kind of strange radio signal from some place called Juliette. DJ is corny LOL but I can't figure out what it is. Maybe hoax or what???

Reply posted by PiperMaruKrycek:
    We have one and yes, weird broadcast! Hadn't tuned it in well enough to make out specifics. R U going to Heavenly Frequencies gathering? It is July 4 weekend at PhoenixTail Ranch and Spa in Oregon, near Bend. Great frequencies at those high altitudes, boosted by sacred sites and

ancient wisdom! Largest gathering of amateur radio enthusiasts in the U.S. My wife and I will be there!

Reply posted by Thanksforthefish42:
  You bet! I'll look for u!

Here was at least some evidence that Dodger wasn't making up Juliette. Maybe it was really out there, somewhere, this place he'd sketched, a place from his dreams, a place that felt like . . .

Home.

Dodger knew that was a weird thing to feel, and yet, he couldn't help it. He felt like, maybe, if he could find it, and see those streets and mountains that he'd dreamed of, and drawn, maybe it would feel like he belonged there.

But how to find it? He'd need to get on the road, and get to this gathering in Oregon. Applying for the Fellowship for Alien Detection had seemed like a good way to do that.

His parents had been shocked when he'd asked to apply. And they'd become silent, in that way that Dodger always assumed was a kind of unspeakable dismay, when they'd heard his fellowship theory, entitled: *Broadcasts from Missing Town as Proof of Alien Abductions*. And they were even more silent, nearly catatonic when he actually won. Dodger did not usually win things.

"Thanks, Dan. Okay, now back to the hits here on KJPR with—"

"Francis?"

The radio voice cut out and a splitting pain stabbed across Dodger's brain. That had been a pretty long connection, and the longer he listened to the voice, the more his head always hurt afterward.

Dodger looked up, eyes watering, to find Harry peering in though the vacant window frame at the far side of the kitchen. He was looking at Dodger with a slightly squinting expression, as if Dodger was a sign written in another language.

"What are you doing?" he asked.

"Nothing," Dodger muttered, letting his head fall back against the metal oven door.

"Nothing?" Harry repeated. "We . . ." He looked away, into the space by the counter. "We were supposed to leave, like, ten minutes ago."

"I was just checking my maps," said Dodger.

Now Harry's eyes tracked around the unfinished room. "You know I don't like you over here."

"Sorry."

Harry sighed. He breathed in like he was going to say something, then didn't. He checked his watch. "I thought this fellowship was important to you."

Dodger frowned. "It *is*. I just . . ." Dodger had a sudden urge, one that came over him from time to time. What if he just told Harry? *I'm over here because, you know that radio signal that I wrote my fellowship report about? You know how I said you could hear it on special radios? Well, my head is one of them.*

But Dodger could imagine Harry's reaction to that. He'd freak out and start calling psychiatrists and neurosurgeons, anyone who could explain such a crazy statement. And it *did* sound crazy, but at least if he were to say it, then Harry might understand that Dodger wasn't *trying* to disappoint him all the time.

And yet he hadn't before and he didn't now. "Sorry. I'll be out in a sec."

"Are you packed?" Harry asked.

"Yeah." He wasn't. "I just have to grab my bag."

Harry's mouth shrunk. He shrugged. "Come on, Dodge, I don't want to hit that Seattle traffic."

"Okay, I'll be right there." Dodger started to fold up his maps.

"Hey."

Dodger looked up.

Harry was peering at him. "What's that on your face?"

"Huh?" Dodger saw that Harry was indicating his own upper lip, beneath his nose. Dodger checked himself and felt something moist. He pulled his finger away and found a red smear on it.

"Is that blood?" Harry asked.

"Um, I . . . I guess."

"What happened?"

"Nothing. I was just sitting here. Maybe it's the dry air," Dodger said, despite the persistent sound of rain on the roof.

Harry gazed at him strangely, then blinked and looked away. "I'll meet you at the car." He turned and left the window, hiking back out through the tangles of blackberry. Dodger heard a ripping from thorns and his dad cursing to himself.

Dodger wiped at his nose, making a streak of blood on his hand. Had the radio caused this? That couldn't be good. He gathered the maps around him, folding each with extra care to avoid getting any blood on them. He tucked the favorites inside his sweatshirt, closed the others back in the oven, then headed out of Number Two Orca View.

Over the years, his travels in and out of the house had carved a narrow track from the front door through the blackberry jungle to his yard. Dodger shivered in the gray drizzle and hunched over to further protect his maps. His head was beginning to clear, the pain from the radio headache subsiding.

He had reached the front steps of his house when he heard voices from around the side. His parents. They were over by the car, but only the huge rear end of the Lanes' Dodge Maximus was visible.

Dodger couldn't make out the words, just a frustrated tone from Harry and a soothing tone from Sophie. Dodger edged a few feet across the small front yard and listened.

"It'll be a dead end, Sophie, just like every other time!" Harry was saying in a livid whisper.

"You don't know that," Sophie replied. "You may get out there and figure something out."

Dodger peered around the corner. Sophie was standing by the open car door, clutching a shawl around her small frame. Harry was sitting in the driver's seat, his arms stiff and his hands clenching the steering wheel.

"Like what?" he said. "What's left to figure out? We should just—"

"Franny." Sophie had spotted him. "Hey, are you ready to go yet?"

"Just gotta get my bag," he said, and he caught Harry's glowering look as he turned and headed inside.

So his dad thought this trip was pointless. Great, but not at all surprising.

Dodger headed upstairs to his room. His suitcase was open on the bed, empty. His floor was covered in a sea of maps. Dodger quickly grabbed a few that he knew he'd need, folding them and placing them in his suitcase along with the ones from his sweatshirt. Then he threw in an extra pair of jeans, a couple T-shirts, socks and underwear, and his black hat with the green embroidered alien face on it. He slapped the suitcase shut and headed out.

Only he stopped at the door. A strange feeling had welled up inside him, a kind of shivery question mark that made him turn back and survey his room carefully. The bed with the navy and green plaid comforter, his computer, the maps all over his walls and the floor, mostly covering the solar system rug that he'd had since he was very young.

Take it all in, he thought to himself. Just in case. Just in case what? Just in case he found what he was looking for: aliens, Juliette, whatever it was.

And never came back.

The thought made Dodger shudder, and he didn't know if it was something he hoped for or something he feared, but whatever it was, it was exciting. He turned and headed back out of the house. On the stairs, he tapped his pocket. The map of Juliette was there. The place he was setting out to find.

The place that he hoped, somehow, would feel like home.

12

Near Bend, OR, July 4, 4:08 p.m.

"You listen to these people, and you have to think to yourself, what kind of a person would act like that? Tell you what, if I had my way, they'd all be sent back to where they came from!"

"That's right," Harry agreed.

Dodger sat slumped in the passenger seat. Harry had been listening to the *Surge McFarlain Show* for the three hours since they'd pulled out of the Relaxation Depot in Eugene, which had turned out much like Dodger had expected. The pool had been open but only lukewarm, and there had been no exercise bike but instead an elliptical machine, which Harry couldn't use because of his hip. Plus they'd ended up in a room with a king bed instead of two queens because apparently the other rooms had been prioritized for "Frequent Relaxer" customers, and Harry did not believe in reward programs. So, they'd fought for control of the covers all night. All of this had led Harry to deliver his verdict as they left: "Well, that was the Royal Rip-off! If we didn't have this fellowship debit card, I'd have asked to see the manager."

They'd also listened to Surge for a good chunk of the six-hour drive from home to Eugene, especially during the stretch around Tacoma where the traffic had been miserable.

"Can we listen to some music?" Dodger had asked at one point.

"This calms me down," Harry had said through gritted teeth, glaring out at the traffic and riding as tight to the bumper in front of him as possible. Dodger couldn't see how Surge McFarlain could calm down anyone, but then again it was better to have Harry talking back in agreement to Surge than railing against the drivers around them.

Dodger spent the first couple hours after Eugene trying to get the mobile version of *Civilizer* to work on his meBox, which Harry had gotten him on a promotional special at *Viva Value!* The meBox was neon green with a big red button on the side. It was made by *Viva Value!* and Harry claimed it was "Just Like One of Those Apple Products but Without the Markup." Yet, as far as Dodger could tell, the only thing the meBox did well was freeze during games. Oh, and take pictures. In fact, there seemed to be no way to stop the meBox from snapping photos, since the big red button on the outside of the device was a direct link to the camera, and it would take a picture anytime you touched it by mistake or slid the meBox in or out of a pocket or bag. There was no way to disable this, at least that Dodger could find. As a result, Dodger had inadvertently taken hundreds of blurry or dark pictures.

The meBox was also unable to do the one thing that Dodger actually needed it to do, which was get on Wi-Fi so he could send email. As a result, Dodger had yet to send any updates to Alex Keller. He supposed he could have found another computer, but he felt like he had nothing to report yet anyway. After a few more unsuccessful tries at *Civilizer*, he slid the stupid meBox into his backpack.

Finally, as they crossed over the pass east of Eugene and entered the high desert of Oregon, Surge's signal got so static-filled that Harry turned it off. "I pay good money for that satellite radio," Harry grumbled. "It is *not* supposed to have reception problems. That's the whole point of having it!"

They sat in silence. Around them was a dry world of orange-barked pine trees drenched in sun. The Maximus hummed over the highway. Dodger watched a snowcapped peak float by in the distance.

"So," said Harry after a couple miles. "We're going to this radio convention thing to try to find out more about this missing town."

"Yeah," said Dodger. He felt himself tensing up. Other than a quick conversation about what to eat for dinner last night and a check-in about the sorry state of the Mariners, this was the first time they'd really talked.

"Juliette," said Harry.

"Right," said Dodger. He looked down at the map of the West, where he'd highlighted their route. It ended at Bend, which was up ahead, because Dodger didn't actually know where they were going to go after that. In his fellowship application, he'd said they were continuing from here to Devil's Tower, Area 51, and Roswell, but he'd only said that because you were supposed to have some sort of plan, and those were all classic spots in alien visitation lore.

His map showed the West from the coast to Colorado. It was one of his favorite maps, with the big green national parks, the giant splotches of national forest, the mountain ranges and deserts and volcanic formations. Still, he had little to go on regarding Juliette's location. He'd heard a few details in the radio broadcast: about the canyons, a ski area nearby, references to the high country, but that was most of the Rocky Mountain West.

"Any idea how a town can be missing?" Harry asked.

Dodger did not want to have this conversation. "Not really." He sighed. "But people hear it, on radios."

"And how do you know it's not a hoax?" Harry asked.

Dodger shrugged. Without revealing his own head-radio situation, what was he going to say? He felt like he could almost hear Harry holding himself back from just completely belittling this whole crazy idea. Really, Dodger was amazed they were even out here at all, except then Harry reminded him of the primary motivation.

"Well, even if this is all a scam, you'll still get that cash. Unless the whole fellowship is a scam. Now that would be a new level of Rip-off."

The Imperial Rip-off? Dodger wondered, thinking of what would be even more serious than "royal," but all he said was "I guess."

They passed through Bend, where the price of gas was "Outrageous!," and then drove south and west in the glaring sun, back into the pine forests. They turned off onto a dirt road with a brown sign indicating the Green Springs Ruins, which Dodger had read were ancient Native American sites. There was also a brightly painted sign for the Phoenix Tail Ranch and Spa and the Heavenly Frequencies gathering.

"This is going to be one of those places where clothing's optional and people enjoy their natural body aroma, isn't it?" Harry looked over like he meant that as a joke.

"Probably," said Dodger, just to humor him.

Harry, driving fast, came up behind a turquoise Volkswagen camper van. He slowed down dramatically. "Yeah, exactly," he muttered. "Come on." Harry then proceeded to tailgate, even though so much dust was being kicked up by the camper that he had to use the wipers.

Finally, they reached a dirt parking lot. To the right, a wide-open pasture stretched beyond a fence made of split logs. There were three horses munching on the yellow grass.

"More cars than I would have thought," said Harry as he pulled into a spot. There were maybe fifty cars, Dodger guessed.

They got out. The sun was hot, direct. Dodger felt a lightness in his head. They were at altitude here, nearly six thousand feet above sea level, and it almost seemed like they were closer to the sun.

Their footsteps scattered the bone white dust. Dodger adjusted his hat backward on his head and squinted through the bright. Ahead was a small sea of tents of various colors.

"Hello, curious minds." An older woman sat in a folding chair beneath an umbrella. She had a roll of tickets. On a folding table beside her was a box with a hand-written sign that read *Suggested Donation $15 Per Person*.

"Thank you for lending us your ears," she said. She had long gray straggly hair and wore a shapeless lavender dress with embroidered flowers and leather sandals. A baseball cap was perched on her head, made of red mesh and a white front displaying the phrase "I'm Listening" in purple letters.

"Hello." Harry handed her a twenty-dollar bill and then held his hand out for tickets. The woman looked at it for a second before frowning, stuffing it in the box, and ripping off two tickets. She waved them on.

Dodger tried to give the woman a look as he passed that said, *Sorry about him*.

"Can't use that fellowship debit card here, and it's not like we're actually going to participate," Harry said, as if justifying what he'd paid.

"Mmm," said Dodger.

The tents were arranged in loose lines. Some were the classic kind you'd see at fairs and markets: white with one open side, either with information on a table or wares inside. Others were simply people's tents, with chairs and tables outside them.

Dodger saw people selling homemade radio kits, knitted hats with copper antennae coming out the top in various shapes, polished stones and crystals of every possible color, wooden sticks with prisms attached to the end with leather straps, dream catchers, and books and pamphlets with titles like *Alternate Truths*, *The Aliens in Washington DC*, *The Alien-Mining Syndicate*, all of which looked like they'd been printed on copy machines. There was a booth selling alien figurines, and another selling only tiny glass jars of what was advertised as ET Oil: "Rub It on Your Head! Enhance Your Frequencial Powers!" The head of the bald man in the booth glistened.

As they walked, Harry was silent except for an occasional "Huh," which meant that he sensed the presence of the Royal Rip-off.

At the end of the aisles was a square area denoted by yellow rope. A sign read "Listening Zone." Dodger noticed strips of copper and little black rings that he thought were magnets hanging at regular intervals on the rope.

Inside, people were clustered around tables with all manner of radios, from complex contraptions of silver and black to one group with phones that had cords snaking up to big antennae that were duct taped to the top of stepladders. The space smelled like electricity and burned metal. Dodger saw smoke from people soldering connections on circuit boards.

There was a whine and Dodger saw a man speaking through a megaphone. "Remember, folks, let's everybody hold off on actually using your radios until tonight's group tune in at eight p.m., so that we can all be present in the moment of connection. We don't want to subvert that positive energy."

"Sheesh," said Harry. "So, do you want to talk to these people or what?"

Dodger wasn't sure. He wasn't great at making conversation. Plus, this all looked a little crazy. "Maybe we should just go set up and come back in a few hours for this group tune in."

"Suits me," said Harry.

They'd decided to camp some nights on the trip, and this was one of them. The ranch had an adjoining campground. They returned to the car and drove up the road to the campsite entrance. A sign on the self-serve station read: FULL. They had made a reservation, and Dodger was grateful to see their name on the white board; otherwise he couldn't imagine how Harry would have reacted.

Harry grabbed an envelope. "Twenty-five dollars?" he exclaimed. And then when they drove in and saw that the campground's pool was half-filled with greenish water and pine needles and that their site was right by the noxious smelling bathrooms, he could only sigh. "Can't anything ever be like it's supposed to?"

Harry started unpacking the tent. Dodger unloaded the cooking supplies. As he set up the propane stove, he heard Harry cursing to himself. He turned to see Harry standing in the tan grass, wrapped in a tangle of green fabric and blue metal poles. His shirt had come untucked, exposing the sagging rim of his belly. "It's like you need a degree in astrophysics to put this thing up!"

Dodger wondered if he should help, but as he watched Harry lay out the metal poles on the fabric, then swear to himself and rearrange them, he felt certain that trying to help would only make things worse.

"I think I'm gonna take a walk," Dodger said.

"Hmm?" Harry looked up from the mess.

"A walk, for a bit. Is that okay?"

For just a moment, that look returned to Harry's face: like Dodger was another complicated gadget that Harry couldn't quite comprehend. But then Harry sighed and said, "Sure. If I ever get our five-star hotel here put together, I'll get the fire going and do the dogs."

Dodger shuffled up the campground road, his

black T-shirt untucked, his jeans hanging loosely, his sneakers mostly untied. The campground smelled sweet with burning charcoal. He passed the other sites with RVs and tents, some with families at play with their little kids. Everyone seemed to be having fun. It bothered Dodger to see.

He was just going to take a loop around the campground, maybe see if there were any maps of the area on the check-in board, but then he passed a sign that read "Green Springs Ruins Trail."

A path led off into the shade. Dodger decided to check it out. The large trunks of the ponderosa pines were close on either side. Dodger could see blobs of sap congealed on their thick slabs of orange bark.

His footfalls were nearly silent on a soft layer of yellow needles. The air smelled faintly sweet, like syrup. Though Dodger didn't spend a lot of time outdoors, he'd always liked woods and trails. He felt his shoulders loosening, his entire body unwinding.

He reached a little rise where the trail broke out into a small meadow that spread over the top of a hill. Dodger could see back down to the campground and to the little gathering of tents at Heavenly Frequencies. It looked like an encampment, like some traveling army of yore. Off to the east was a hazy blur of Bend, and to the west were the enormous volcanic Mount Bachelor and the Three Sisters.

Dodger sat on a little island of rock. He had a small notebook in his back pocket—he always carried one—with a pen. He opened it to a new page and started sketching a little map of his walk so far, with the campground in one corner. He sketched the tents, then the trail to this clearing, spinning the notepad in his lap to get his compass directions oriented.

Doing this excited him. His hand flew across the page as he imagined himself as the intrepid explorer, making a log of his journey. When he'd completed the map of this area, he breathed deep. This was good. Being out here, he felt a kind of ease and possibility that he hadn't anticipated.

Dodger continued on. The path fell back into the trees and farther into a shallow gully. There was a dry streambed. The trees began to change, lots of black char on their trunks, and then Dodger entered a stand that had been entirely burned. The trees were jagged sticks, the ground speckled with cinder chunks. The soil had changed, too. It was dark, with black chunks of bubbly-looking rock. Remnants of a lava field. That made sense. He'd read that this was a very active volcanic area, geologically speaking.

The trail weaved to avoid crumbly piles of the volcanic pumice. With the black stones and dead trees and the grass now sparse, the place felt alien and sort of ominous, like he was on another planet, a lone visitor far from home.

There was a rock wall on one side of the trail now, and Dodger spied a set of sienna-colored petroglyphs there. Wispy figures running after animals and circular symbols. Communication, thousands of years old.

And then Dodger saw the circle.

The trail ended in a round, open space where the chunks of lava had been cleared and piled into a circular wall. The black trees around the edges felt like tribal elders. The floor was made of dirt. In the center was a small square structure, only a foot high. A few of the top blocks were broken, as if this had once been something more substantial.

Dodger walked into the center of the ruin. As he approached the little square structure, he felt a strange sense of light-headedness. At first he wondered if it was the sun and the altitude. He probably should have brought water with him. He wasn't sweating, but the air was so dry, it was likely evaporating right off him.

But then, things started to open up in his mind, and Dodger realized that he was feeling the symptoms of the Juliette radio about to arrive. He stopped over the little structure. Maybe it had been a chimney. He looked inside and saw a pile of crushed beer cans.

The radio feeling grew, a warm wave of energy in

Dodger's mind. He put his fingers to his temples.

But then he heard voices.

They were coming up the path. Dodger didn't know who he might run into out here in the woods, and almost out of instinct, he looked around for another way out of the ruins, but the path he'd followed was the only way in or out, unless he tried to climb over the rock piles.

Two boys appeared. One was a good foot taller than Dodger, lean, with shaggy blond hair and extra-long limbs that were dotted with freckles. He wore a T-shirt and jeans tattered with holes. He had a cable looped over his shoulder and was carrying a thick, black square under the other arm.

The second boy was shorter and just as lean. He was carrying a lunch box flat in both hands. The lunch box had two antennae coming out of the top, each with a clump of aluminum foil at the end. It was adorned in artwork for what Dodger guessed had once been a TV show called *Battle of the Planets*.

The older boy saw Dodger first. "'Sup?" he said.

Dodger wondered what he should say, and he hated how even these basic little moments with other kids always tripped him up. "Hey," he ended up saying.

The two boys stopped in front of him.

"You here for the gathering?" the tall boy asked.

"Oh, well . . . I guess."

"You guess?"

"Yeah," Dodger said, and then he noticed the green lettering on the tall boy's yellow T-shirt. It read *Where Is Juliette?*

"You heard of it?" the boy asked.

"The town that isn't there," Dodger mumbled blankly.

"Yeah," said the boy. "So you know about these." He pointed to the lunch box.

"Um . . ."

"PhoneHome radio," said the younger boy. "No?"

"Oh, I have heard of those."

"Cool." The tall boy pointed to his shirt. "This came free with the radio. My name's Sid." He stuck out his hand.

"Dodger." He hesitated at the thought of the handshake, feeling an all-too-familiar worry, like he wanted them to like him, wanted things to go well, but also like there was no way they possibly could. Handshakes were a particular problem. What grip were you supposed to use? How long did you shake for? But Sid grabbed his hand and it went fine.

"We came out here to try the radio before the big listening event," said Sid. "People say these sacred spots have extra power for tuning it in."

"It?"

"Juliette." Sid dropped to his knees and placed the big black box on the ground. Dodger saw that it was a car battery. And the cord was a set of jumper cables. Sid connected the clamps to the battery and uncoiled the rest. "Come on, dude," he said, and smacked the shorter boy on the back.

"Ah, come on," the boy moaned.

Sid looked back at Dodger. "That's my little brother. His name's Randall, but I call him R2. Different moms, that's why he's a lard butt."

"Shut up," R2 muttered. He knelt and placed the lunch box on the ground beside the battery. He affixed the two clamps at the other end of the cables to the bottom corners of the box. "Okay . . ." he said. The side of the lunch box where the handle would have been located now had two black dials and an orange switch. R2 flicked this. There was a snap, a spark flying free, and then the switch lit up.

"Watch it!" Sid snapped. He dropped to his knees beside R2 and shoved him out of the way. "Let me try."

"Come on!" R2 whined.

Dodger could hear soft static emitting from the lunch box now. "Do you guys mind if I listen, too?" he asked.

"Sure. If we do tune it in, the more witnesses the better."

Dodger cautiously knelt beside the radio. His hands felt clammy, his fingers tingling. If he could hear Juliette through this radio, that would prove it was real, or at least that he wasn't going crazy.

"Ah." Sid pushed the radio back to R2. "You do it." He turned to Dodger. "So how do you know about Juliette?"

"Well . . ." Dodger wondered what to say. "Just the rumors online." He considered sharing his story with these two. He was hesitant, but maybe these kids seemed fine. "I'm actually researching it for a fellowsh—"

"Hold up," said R2. He twisted furiously at the knobs. "I might have something."

"Dude." Sid shoved him out of the way again. "Let me see, you malfunctioning droid."

R2 frowned but didn't protest.

"Have you ever heard it before?" Dodger asked.

"No, just read about it. Our dad is really into radio stuff. But he's more into pulling in radio frequencies from outer space. He thinks the Juliette thing is ridiculous."

The hissing sound grew into a static. There was a warble of radio music, but it sounded like some kind of old-timey jazz, maybe another language, too, not what Dodger usually heard on KJPR. The static crescendoed but then faded down.

"Ah," said Sid disappointedly.

Dodger felt certain they had just missed it. Back during that little crescendo, he'd felt a glimpse of that warm, syrupy sensation. "Mind if I try?" he asked.

Sid seemed to size him up for second, then pushed the radio toward him. "Be my guest, but it's my radio, so if you find it, we still get the credit."

"Oh, sure," said Dodger. Such a thought hadn't even crossed his mind.

He moved his fingers toward the knobs. He'd try tracking back toward that little swell in the frequencies. . . .

But the moment Dodger's fingers touched the knobs a surge of energy flooded through him, and all at once his brain ignited and the radio voice returned.

"Now, friends, I've got an important message for all you folks out there who just aren't getting enough get-up out of your old car. Our good friend Hank White, owner of High Country Auto, wants to invite you all down to his showroom to see his Spring Melt Specials, including a huge sale on all 1993 model-year clearance items. Hank's got the guaranteed lowest prices on the pickups with the pickup you need. You'll be glad you visited High Country Auto, out on Juniper Canyon Road in North Juliette. Now, back to the hits!"

Music cut in, a country shuffle that ripped at

Dodger's ears. The radio was so much louder than normal, seeming to echo around inside his skull. His vision blurred static white.

It felt like his entire body was humming, his molecules unsticking. Tears slid from his squinted eyes.

He looked up to see Sid and R2 staring at him, mouths open. Dodger wondered why, but then he noticed that the station sounded different. This time, he seemed to be hearing it through his ears, not just in his head, like it was outside, blaring into the sunny evening, but not from the radio. Dodger felt a strange humming around his jaw and eyes, and understood even more.

Oh no.

The radio was broadcasting out of *him*, out of his entire body, as if he were a speaker.

Near Bend, OR, July 4, 6:45 p.m.

Dodger couldn't close his mouth. His teeth were vibrating like his mouth had been invaded by an army of tiny dentist drills. He tore his hands from the radio.

The broadcast ceased. Dodger toppled back on the dirt, banging his head on the stone square. He gasped for breath, his eyes watering.

"Dude . . ." Without turning his head, Sid reached out and punched R2 in the shoulder.

"Ow! What?"

"What do you *think*, you Spice Mine reject?" Sid pointed at Dodger. "He's one of *them*."

"O-one of who?" R2 stammered.

"What do you think? He's an . . . he's an alien. Or a hybrid, or something."

Dodger fought to get to his elbows. "Sorry, I—" he stammered because he couldn't think of anything else to say.

Sid was peering at him. R2 looked like he might run away screaming. "What are you?" Sid asked.

Dodger just stared back at him. "I'm not anything. I just . . ." Dodger thought he might as well admit it. "I get this radio station in my head sometimes."

Sid glanced at the lunch box radio. When he looked back at Dodger, his eyes had narrowed and he was almost grinning. "Do it again. Can you do it again?"

"I—no," Dodger said. He started to back away on his elbows. His head was throbbing from banging it, but also inside. It felt like everything had been rattled, like he could barely figure out which way was up and which way was down.

R2 rubbed at his chin. "It was when he touched the radio. Like he connected with it."

"Yeah . . ." Sid's eyes lit up. He stood and started toward Dodger. "You gotta do it again, kid." He lunged and grabbed Dodger by the arm. R2 scrambled over and grabbed the other.

"Let go!" Dodger tried to writhe away. He was able to flip onto his stomach. His face hit the earth, dirt filling his mouth. He gagged.

"Oh man, we'll show the whole gathering!" said Sid. He grabbed Dodger's leg and yanked him backward. "You'll show us where Juliette is, and we'll be the ones who found it!"

Dodger thrashed his legs, but Sid's grip held firm. He yanked Dodger back to the radio and slapped his hand onto it.

The broadcast burst back to life out of Dodger's mouth. **"And don't forget those winter storm warnings for tonight."**

"Nice!" Sid shouted over the noise.

"Dan Spirit says the squalls could be rolling in by ten o'clock, so best to be home and off the roads by then—"

Dodger felt like he was going to explode inside. He couldn't breathe, his heart pounding, overcome by the sound. He felt like his head was leaking out of his eyes and ears, pressure everywhere.

But there was light, too. Through the rigid vibrations, Dodger was able to glance down and he saw that the entire lunch box radio was glowing an electric neon orange, from every seam.

It grew brighter the longer his hands stayed connected to it, and now Dodger had a strange sensation. He felt a warmness building inside him, like he had connected to this light, like the light and the radio voice and his body were all weaving themselves together in a kind of warm unity. The feelings of pain became distant, unimportant, and Dodger had a strange sense of being inside his head, but so deep inside, like he'd become detached from the outside world and was now floating in space.

What could he do with this energy? He felt it coursing through him, rushing to and fro, and nearly beating at his toes and fingers to escape. It would move for him, if he wanted, he felt sure of this.

In this calm, he found that he could lift a hand away from the lunch box. And as his hand rose, the glow of light stayed with it, a corona around his fingers and palm. The energy was right there, right at the edge, and if he wanted, he could use it.

He pointed his hand at Sid.

Sid looked up and saw this. His eyes went wide.

Dodger flicked his hand, like he was shaking liquid from it.

A burst of the orange light leaped free and slammed into Sid's chest.

"Gah!" It flashed like a water balloon of light bursting, but then there was smoke and searing and a round black burn appeared in Sid's shirt. Sid lurched backward, his body convulsing, his eyes rolling back in his head.

"Oh my God!" R2 shouted over the blare of the

radio. He stumbled to his feet, tripped, landed on his backside, then turned and started scrambling across the dirt.

Dodger got to his feet. He let go of the lunch box, and the radio ceased. His hand, however, still glowed.

"Stop," he said to R2.

R2 stopped and flipped back around and stared at Dodger, panting. Sid groaned and his eyes fluttered open.

Dodger held his hand out toward them. He pushed just a little of the energy flow out, making it glow in a corona around his fingertips. He could feel that this wouldn't last long, that without being connected to that radio it would run out, but they didn't know that.

"I'm keeping the radio," Dodger said. His head was calm. There were just thoughts, easy, no doubts attached to them. "And if you tell anyone you ran into me up here . . ." He pushed a little more light out, the glow increasing. "I'll come for you."

Sid started to nod. R2 was crying.

Dodger couldn't believe he'd actually just said those things, it was so unlike him, and yet, not unlike *this* him. *Who is this me?* he wondered, and then he thought: *the alien me.* That didn't make sense, and yet . . . in a way it felt right, didn't it?

"Okay, okay . . . we're going, we . . ." Sid and R2 got up and took off out of the clearing.

Dodger watched them go. He listened until their footsteps faded. Then he turned and knelt beside the radio again. He placed his hands on it, and the box began to glow in its neon orange and the bubbly DJ voice began to blare out of him, and yet he knew now that he could control that. He had to apply pressure to the power inside him . . . find his own muscles and be in control of them. Mouth shut. Hands . . .

He moved his fingers and flicked open the latch on the lunch box. He pulled up the lid and the light increased.

Inside he saw three things. Against one wall was a small green circuit board, blotchy with soldering. Next to that was a small round speaker. And in the center of the box was a rock. It was a shard of crystal, about six inches long and glowing an incredible orange from its core, as if someone had chipped off a piece of a star. Two wires connected the crystal to the circuit board. Dodger took his hands from the radio. The crystal went dark, becoming a glassy black.

Dodger tore the wires free, then placed his hands over the crystal and lifted it. It exploded in brilliance again, and it was hot to the touch, so hot that Dodger wondered if it would burn his skin, but instead he felt like the skin of his hands had become irrelevant, as if the crystal was part of him.

Dodger sat. He pulled the rock close, pressing it against his chest, the glow warming his torso and spreading through him.

He lay back with the crystal like this and stared at the sky, the rim of his vision glowing in warm orange, and watched the afternoon blue deepen and darken. A flock of birds. No, darker. Bats.

Dodger lay there in the footprint of the ancient ruin, the crystal clutched close against him, until the first stars began to wake in the sky. All the while, the radio voice of KJPR burbled at a low, syrupy boil in the back of his head.

"Checking scoreboards, the Suns beat the Spurs last night, 99–97. They close out the season today in Denver against the Nuggets, and then they'll move on to face the Lakers in the playoffs on Friday."

And whereas, in the past, the radio had overwhelmed his brain, here it was just another pleasant sound along with the wind in the pine needles, the shrieks of birds and later the sonic whines of bats, the thrumming of Dodger's heart, and the static of the vast universe, above, around, and within him.

"Time for another three in a row!"

Time unspooled in light and space. Dodger saw the stars from among the stars, he saw the Earth from beneath the Earth, and he saw the caverns, rooms, and streets of the place he'd only before known from dreams. Juliette. He was there. He was everywhere. He was something more than himself.

Near Bend, OR, July 4, 8:55 p.m.

"Francis!"

Dodger's eyes opened. There were more stars, only a faint blue on the rim of the sky. He felt deeply relaxed, refreshed.

A flashlight beam fell on his face. Dodger threw a hand over his eyes.

"Francis . . ." Harry's giant face appeared. "Where the heck have you been?!"

Dodger sat up on his elbows. "Fell asleep," he mumbled.

"Well, get up!" Harry yanked Dodger to his feet. Dodger wobbled, his balance unsteady. "I've been looking for you for hours! I searched that whole freak show back there! If they hadn't mentioned this trail . . . Come on, Francis!"

"Sorry," said Dodger.

"You—" Harry began, but his brow furrowed into a knot and he stopped.

Dodger suddenly flinched. Where was—

The shard of crystal was by his feet. Harry didn't seem to have noticed it. But he was looking at the lunch box.

"What is that?" he asked.

"It's a radio," said Dodger. "I got it from some kids."

"Kids?" Harry asked. "You were hanging out with some kids? Who?"

"Nobody," said Dodger, "just people from the radio gathering. Anyway, it doesn't work."

Dodger placed his foot gently over the crystal. "Dad, I'm sorry. I was just out here, and I swear I only meant to relax for a second."

Harry kept looking at the radio. Then he looked back at Dodger, and then off into space near Dodger. "I was just worried," he said. That word surprised Dodger a little. Worried? Maybe Harry had meant it like *disappointed*, but the way he'd said it was different. Could this be actual worry?

"The gathering down there is almost over," Harry continued. "I was in there for a bit, looking for you. . . ." He breathed slowly, like he was trying to calm down. "They, those people down there, are saying they hear all kinds of stuff: aliens, spy transmissions, Elvis. . . ."

"We don't need to go there," said Dodger. "It's kinda weird."

Harry made a slight chuckle. "I'll say. But what about your research . . ."

"I got all the information I needed from these two kids I met," Dodger lied. Though, in a way, he had.

"Um, okay." Harry seemed to be weighing this. Then he shrugged. "I still can't believe you fell asleep out here."

"Sorry."

"You must be hungry. I can reheat the dogs and beans." Harry turned and started out of the ruins.

"I'm starving," said Dodger. He knelt and scooped up the crystal. It immediately began to glow, but he pressed back against it, keeping its energy at bay as he stuffed it in the back of his jeans.

He followed Harry back to the campsite, his head still fuzzy and spacey feeling.

As he walked, he thought about the broadcast he'd heard. A new detail had stood out: the bit about the 1993 model-year clearance sale . . . which meant that in Juliette, it was 1994.

How was that possible? And what did it mean? Was he hearing a broadcast from back in time? In that case, maybe he couldn't find the town because it no longer existed, like it had been abandoned sometime in the last twenty years. But then how would its radio station still be broadcasting, and why would it be broadcasting its signal from that day? Also, nobody on the station was talking about the town shutting down or closing or anything like that.

So maybe instead it meant that Juliette was still out there, but stuck in 1994. Like, repeating the same April day over and over again? Did that mean it was in some kind of time loop? And if so, did that mean that it was put *in* the time loop on that April day in 1994?

Whatever the explanation, Dodger realized that this meant something: Even though Juliette wasn't on any maps now, it might be on an older map, something from before 1994. Dodger knew that none of his maps were that old. The oldest map he had was probably from sometime in the 2000s. It would take a lot of searching online, if there was something there at all, because all the maps on Google or the other usual map sites were completely up-to-date.

A library might have something. Dodger could find one to go to tomorrow. He also knew what direction they'd head in the morning from another clue in the broadcast. The sports reporter had given a Suns score, and even though Dodger barely cared about professional sports, he at least knew that the Suns were an NBA team from Phoenix. A possible clue that Juliette was in Arizona, too, or New Mexico. They didn't have a professional basketball team either, and so might follow Phoenix. Dodger knew that, for example, people as far from Seattle as Idaho still followed the Mariners. Regardless, he at least had a general direction: southeast. And a new goal: Find an old map.

And on the way, he could continue to work on the biggest question of all: *What am I?*

It was a mystery that he couldn't wait to explore.

chapter

14

Burns, OR, July 5, 11:14 a.m.

The next morning Dodger stood beside the librarian
of the Harney County Library. He had managed to
get from her a look similar to what he often inspired
in Harry.

"Wait, explain that again?" the librarian asked,
standing up from the shelves along the interior wall of
the small, brick building. She pulled her glasses down
from her black-and-gray-streaked hair and peered at
Dodger like he was something written in very small
print.

"I need a road atlas, or state maps, or a guidebook, of the Southwest, but I need it to be old. These

are all too new."

"You mean like historical maps? We have a few of those books of gold rush era maps, but I'm afraid they're only of local areas, the kind that people around here would be interested in."

"They don't need to be that historical," said Dodger, "just kinda. Like from around 1993."

"1993. But wouldn't a new map be more up-to-date?"

"No," said Dodger. "I mean, yes, but that's not what I'm looking for."

The librarian squinted, like this was hurting her head. "You know, we spend a significant amount of our budget each year trying to keep our reference books current. Why would someone come to the library for a guidebook or an atlas if it was outdated? But then here you are asking for exactly that."

"Sorry," said Dodger. "It's for a project."

"And it has to be from the early nineties?" she asked, as if that decade could not have been less cartographically important.

"Yeah. Or a little older, I guess. I mean, really old could be good, but that might be too old."

The librarian gazed at her stacks again. She kept staring, and Dodger wondered if she was hoping he and his weird request would just disappear if she gave it enough time. Finally she shook her head. "I'm afraid you're going to have to try a used bookstore, though I don't know what value they'd find in keeping a not-new but also not-old atlas. Otherwise you should probably try to find yourself a map collector." She sighed. "But even then, the nineties . . . I don't know."

"Okay," said Dodger, "thanks. I'll check those historical maps before I go."

So, after futilely trying to get his meBox to connect to the Wi-Fi, Dodger spent some time online via the library computer. A half hour of searches taught him that finding a map that was not new but also not historical was nearly impossible.

He did, however, find three map collectors that were roughly along their route toward the Southwest. Of the three, a place in the town of Lucky Springs, Nevada, seemed the most promising. Not only because of its reportedly giant collection, but also because it turned out that Lucky Springs was also a town that was mentioned on the We Are the Missing website. A handful of people there had claimed to have experienced missing time and alien abduction. A fortunate coincidence. If his map search came up empty, maybe Dodger could talk to these people or something.

It didn't occur to him to email Alex Keller with an update until he was back in the car. Oh well. He didn't know how that would help, anyway. Plus, he liked this feeling of being off exploring, his whereabouts unknown.

Lucky Springs, NV, July 5, 2:25 p.m.

"So, why are we going here again?" asked Harry as another hour of the *Surge McFarlain Show* came to a frothing close.

They'd been humming across Nevada for two hours and were now winding down a rocky canyon road.

"I told you," Dodger mumbled, gazing out the window at the canyon walls made of gray rock that was crinkled like tinfoil. "There's a museum here that's supposed to have good maps."

"And you need an old map," said Harry.

"Yeah. A few of them."

"And that's because this town that you're looking for doesn't show up on the GPS or in a normal old atlas or anything. . . ."

"Yeah."

"And so, why is that again?" Harry had that perplexed tone again.

"Because the town is too old," said Dodger, thinking that wasn't technically a lie.

"So, it's like a ghost town."

"Yeah." Dodger wondered how he would answer the obvious next question, a question so obvious in fact that Dodger was kind of amazed it hadn't come up before. Surely now would be the time for Harry to ask, *What are you expecting to find in Juliette?*

But instead, Harry leaned forward and started smacking at the display behind the steering wheel. "You know," he said, "I think that gas station back there may have gypped us. This tank is going down too fast." He peered at the gas gauge. "Typical," he muttered. "Small town gas station looking to stick it to the tourists." His large hands flexed on the steering wheel. "Probably think just because we drive a nice car that we're made of money."

Dodger shifted his body to stare more fully out his window. Not that he at all enjoyed Harry's paranoid theories, but he was glad to have avoided that question. Because what *did* Dodger expect to find in Juliette? He wasn't sure. A town stuck repeating the same day, he thought, but also a town that he was connected to by the black crystal, and the abilities he'd gotten from it.

He'd spent the drive with the shard of crystal tucked in the back of his belt, so that as mile after mile of Nevada passed by, it pressed against the lower half of his spine and made a warm humming sensation like a massage chair. He felt the power coursing through him like he was a toy with a new battery clipped into its socket. Every once in a while he felt a rush, and the faintest tinge of an orange glow would start to build at his fingertips. But he could push it back in, keep it hidden.

What was in Juliette? Dodger thought there must be more of this crystal. Otherwise, why would he hear the radio station through it? Actually, he thought there might be a lot more, perhaps even the *source*, whatever this crystal had come from.

As to why he was connected to the crystal, all he could come up with was what Sid had said the day before: because he was an alien. That couldn't make any sense, could it? Sure, he'd always felt different, and it had always seemed like life didn't fit him right, but still, he'd gotten enough scrapes and cuts in life to know that he didn't have green blood or anything like that. And hearing a radio station in his head was one thing, but he wasn't seeing spaceships or little green men.

But he had seen Juliette, or something that seemed like it, in dreams, so much so that he'd drawn a map of it, and then he'd seen it again last night in the ruins. And he didn't know what the reason might be, but he felt a strange certainty that Juliette was somehow . . . home. There was no logic to it, but it seemed right.

Could he really be from this other place? But

how? After all, he looked like his parents. It wasn't like he could be some sort of alien baby that had been switched at birth or whatever. And yet, first the radio in his head, then the crystal, then his ability to control its energy. Dodger couldn't help thinking of these developments as stages . . . of what? *Of me changing, or . . . reverting.* He didn't quite know, but he wondered: What would be next? Reading minds? Flying a spaceship? Would this continue the closer he got to Juliette? He had no idea, but he found that the thought excited him.

But until he could find the town, he was pretty sure he had to keep just about *all* of this from Harry. He glanced over at the man silently gripping the steering wheel, while every now and then stealing glances over at Dodger as if he were suspicious of him. Thirteen years of Harry Lane had made Dodger pretty sure of what would happen if he found out about Dodger's radio stations and glowing crystals and fingertip lights.

It would be hurtling-back-to-Seattle time, Harry on the phone with lawyers to go after the Keller Foundation, and doctors and psych wards to deal with Dodger. It was one thing for Harry to have to put up with a kid who was a constant disappointment. It was another for Harry to have to contend with having an actual paranormal freak for a son. He did not see Harry dealing well with that at all.

Luckily, despite last night's events and the strange glances now, Harry still seemed to be on board with this trip, if for nothing more than the big payout. He reinforced this with his reaction as they crossed a small steel bridge and wound up the other side of the canyon to the town of Lucky Springs.

"Would you look at that . . ." he said, sounding as close to awestruck as Dodger had ever heard.

Lucky Springs was nestled snugly into a narrow valley just above a frothy river that cascaded through rocky chutes. Gray peaks towered high overhead like the bows of upended ships, their flanks quaking with aspen groves. The town was quaint and looked like it had been unchanged since the eighteen hundreds.

That was, except for the giant parking lot full of buses that had been built just below town.

And now they could hear why through their open windows: the dinging of slot machines. Though it still appeared to be an antiquated pioneer town on the outside, every building on the short, S-shaped strip of Main Street had been gutted and turned into a single giant casino. A banner over the street read "Lucky Springs: Where the Gold Rush Lives On!"

They parked among the buses and walked up the hill into town. Dodger still had the shard with him. He'd thought about getting it into his backpack, but didn't want Harry to notice.

Crowds of pastel-outfitted people milled in the street. The metallic plinking sound was everywhere. At each door they passed, they were met by a cloud of sour-smelling cigarette smoke.

They passed the High Stakes Saloon, a wooden building ringed with porches, swinging bar doors, and a sign that read "Bar fight every hour, featuring the Rough & Tumblers." Dodger glanced inside and saw the neon blur of slot machines around an antique bar. Next was the First National Bank Buffet and Black Jack's General Store, a room full of card tables.

Harry peered inside. "I don't suppose that fellowship debit card will work on those."

Dodger saw a half-smile on his dad's face and knew he was making an attempt at a joke. "Probably not."

"One lucky spin in there and say good-bye to *Viva Value!*," Harry mused. "We could double our money this trip."

"Why don't you head in there?" Dodger suggested, thinking this might be the perfect excuse to get rid of Harry and his suspicious glances. "This map place will be boring."

They stopped. Harry seemed to be considering it, but he also flashed a strange look at Dodger. "You'll be okay, on your own?"

"Yeah," said Dodger. Wasn't he always on his own?

"Well . . ." Harry glanced into the card room again. Dodger thought he could see Harry fighting between some notion of his responsibility as "a good dad" and what he really wanted to do, which was fulfill his dream to "Double Down and Hit It Big," like he did sitting on the couch with the little hand-held casino game he'd gotten a few Christmases ago. Against that feeling, the dad instinct didn't seem to stand a chance. "All right, let's meet out here in . . . how long?"

Dodger checked his meBox. "Maybe half an hour?"

"Okay, sounds good."

Dodger turned and started up the street.

"Don't fall asleep in any forests."

Dodger glanced back. "I won't," he muttered. He saw Harry staring at him with a look that seemed . . . concerned? Dodger felt a little rush of nerves and almost asked *What?* but then Harry shrugged and lumbered into the card room.

Dodger continued up the street. The museum was another block up, just after the road turned back to rocky dirt from the fresh pavement in the casino section. That change was enough to draw an imaginary border, and the street in front of the museum was nearly deserted.

It was a crooked wooden building set into the base of a perilous rock wall. Gold letters painted on its wide, dusty window read "Aunt Violet's Gold Mine Museum."

Dodger climbed a rickety porch, pushed through a creaking screen door, and entered a dark, dusty shop crammed with trinkets. The warped floorboards creaked, but otherwise, the shop was silent. The tingling chorus of hundreds of slot machines echoed discordantly behind him.

Above one aisle, a sign with an arrow read "Maps." Another aisle had a sign that read "Mine Tours." Dodger started down the map aisle. He passed shelves of fool's gold, cowboy hats, and turquoise beadwork. All the souvenirs were coated in a thin film of dust. He squeezed between two racks of fringed leather jackets and reached a narrow, dimly lit doorway. There was a heavy wooden door with a worn wooden handle. The door had no latch, and with a hard push, it slowly creaked inward.

Dodger entered a large room. He'd expected something like a library. Shelving with narrow drawers, maps laid flat inside. High windows, large flat tables with lamps, lots of dust, a brown smell, but this room was nothing like that. It was hexagonal, the walls made of loosely fitted vertical boards. Every few feet, a huge railroad spike stuck out of the wall. There were maybe twenty in all. Tied to each was a thick frayed rope. These ropes ascended diagonally to the center of the high, wooden ceiling. Here, each rope wound over a pulley, then dropped straight down into a wide, dark hole in the center of the room. The wood plank floor made a hexagon around this chasm. A mine shaft, Dodger guessed. He stepped to the edge and peered gingerly over. Cool air met his face. The ropes groaned, twisting in the slight breeze from the depths. Whatever they led to was hidden in darkness.

Dodger wondered about them, but his more pressing thought was one of disappointment. There were only six maps in the room, one per wall, each set in a shabby frame with cloudy glass. That was it? Some museum. Even he had to admit this was starting to look like a classic Royal Rip-off.

Dodger shuffled over to the nearest map. It was drawn in black ink, its edges tattered and brown with a parchment-like quality and a coffee stain in the right corner. Among rounded sketches of mountain chains, towns were drawn as clusters of miniature buildings. The script writing was difficult to read, but Dodger saw Lucky Springs tucked in the left corner, and the larger grid of Boulder to the northeast. Rivers were drawn in squiggly lines, and small symbols—two pickaxes crossed like an X— dotted the map, indicating mines. A legend in the corner dated the map at

1868. There was no Juliette on this map, but Dodger found himself transfixed by it anyway. Modern maps were always so complete, every area accounted for and organized, but this map was unbound, the land unfinished and wide-open with possibility. Dodger tried to imagine living somewhere in that map, back in the time of tiny towns connected by rail and wagon track, traveling with your wooden trunk containing all your worldly possessions, over wide, blank swaths of country yet-to-be-drawn. Out there, you could draw your own town, find your own place.

Lost in the brown wrinkles of the map as he was, Dodger barely heard a rusty squealing sound. Suddenly a voice spoke: "That one's not for sale."

Dodger spun around to find a hunched little woman standing in a waist-high box, dangling at the rim of the mine shaft. Ropes at each corner of the box connected to a large double-pulley system, just above the woman's head. She held a rope in her hand for controlling the makeshift elevator. It swung back and forth lightly.

The woman wore faded overalls with a ragged wool sweater underneath. Her gray hair was tied in two braids that fell down over her shoulders. She peered at Dodger, her eyes squinted deep within tan folds. "D'you hear me, boy?" she said. "You took a wrong turn. This isn't part of the shop."

"I—" Dodger stammered.

The woman huffed and reached down by her side. "Come on now, kid. You got something to say for yourself, then say it. Can't stand a body that doesn't know what to say for itself." She pulled a long wooden cane out of the elevator. Reaching out with the hooked end, she snared one of the angled ropes and pulled the elevator over to the edge of the shaft.

"I'm . . ." Dodger felt a familiar hesitation. Like he couldn't say who or what he was. "I'm Dodger, and—"

"So? You got a name. So does everybody." The woman swung a stocky leg over the side of the box and planted a scuffed cowboy boot on the edge of the floor.

"I came here to look at maps," Dodger finally said. "Is this it?" he asked, indicating the walls.

"It?" The woman finished exiting the elevator, letting it swing free over the shaft, then brushed off her overalls with a heavy sigh. When she looked up at Dodger, she squinted even harder. Her weathered face seemed like it might fold over on itself. "This isn't enough for you?"

"No, well . . ." Dodger glanced meekly at the maps on the walls. "It's just—"

"What, did you think it was going to look like a department store?"

"I—"

The woman waved a hand at him. "Relax, kid, I'm giving you a hard time. Now, you say you came to look at maps?"

"Yeah?"

"Is that a question?"

"No? I mean, no."

"How old are you, Dodger?" the woman asked skeptically.

"Thirteen."

"Lord!" She took a step forward and raised her cane at him. "What's the matter with you, anyway? Why aren't you playing video games or asking out girls?"

"I—"

"Man alive." The woman shook her head.

"I like maps," Dodger mumbled. "But I'm looking for something. On a map."

"Hmm . . ." The woman peered at him. "By the look of ya, I thought you were another one of those moron kids that youth is wasted on."

"Um," said Dodger.

The woman stuck out her wrinkled hand. "Name's Violet. Call me Vee. So, what are you looking for?"

Dodger shook her hand. It was very dry, coarse. "I need maps of the Southwest, but not new ones. More like from—"

Vee shook her head violently. "No no, not what

maps. What *thing* are you looking for?"

"Oh, like, a town."

"A town? And you need old maps because it's . . . what? Ghost town or something?"

"Sort of. I don't know that it's abandoned. It's more like a missing town."

Dodger expected Vee to think this was a weird thing to say, and yet she nodded her head. Her eyes seemed to widen with interest. "Missing how long?"

"I don't really know," said Dodger. "At least nineteen years, but maybe more."

Vee chuckled. "That's not that old. Well, maybe to you it is."

"Do you have any maps from back then?"

Vee turned and leaned dangerously far out over the mine shaft, snaring the elevator rope with the end of her cane. "Of course I do. Come on."

She swung back into the little elevator box. The ropes whined. Dodger was amazed by how she could move.

"Where are we going?" Dodger asked.

"You want to see the maps. Well, they're down here." She looked back at him crossly. "Come on, boy, quit your rubber-legging and let's go."

Dodger stepped up to the edge of the mine shaft, then took a queasy look down into the blackness. He was not a big fan of dark bottomless holes, or being this close to one, or the idea of going down *into* one in a rickety wooden box.

But Vee grabbed his sleeve and he stumbled out into space, grabbing the rope and sliding into the box.

Vee pulled in her cane and they swung out to the center of the shaft with an unnerving whine from the ropes. The pulleys squealed as she let out the rope, and they began to descend into darkness.

The air was cool. Dodger could barely see his hand in front of his face. Above, the entrance to the shaft was slowly shrinking. Below, there was only more black.

"Hang on, boy," Vee advised through gritted teeth. The pulleys shrieked and they lurched to a halt. The elevator swung lightly. "Welcome to the permanent collection."

Dodger couldn't see a thing. A match ripped to life. Vee held up a greasy, red metal oil lamp and lit the wick. Warm light bloomed out through the lamp's soot-stained glass belly.

Now Dodger could see what Vee meant. He also understood what those ropes hanging down into the mine shaft were for. All around them, at various heights, beginning just above and stretching down out of the reach of their meager light, hung tall, skinny wooden boxes, like crates stood on end. Each box was open at the top, with the ends of rolled maps sticking out.

"Cool and dark," Vee was saying, holding the lamp out and peering at the boxes. "Up at the surface, too many temperature changes. Go down any lower, and the moisture becomes an issue. This depth is perfect for keeping maps fresh."

Dodger wasn't really listening. He was busy gazing around and below them, wanting to unroll each old map. Even if it took days, years. He'd move here. Sleep in a tent. Pay rent cleaning the slot machines. Whatever. And yet, the shiver of anticipation returned. Juliette was here; he knew it.

Dodger peered over the edge of the elevator, into the darkness below. "What's down there?" he asked.

"This is an old shaft from the gold mine. There's a whole tunnel system down there, but those wretched UCA people blocked off most of it."

"The who?" Dodger asked.

"UCA is the company that owns the mine. They walled off sections for safety a couple years ago. My mine tour business has never been the same. If I still owed payments on this building, I'd have lost it. Bastards."

As Dodger looked down, he noticed the crystal getting warmer against his back. Almost as if the crystal was responding to the idea of this mine shaft. Dodger had this weird sense from the crystal, almost as if it wanted to go down there. Maybe he was imagining it.

Dodger looked back around at the hanging map boxes. "How many do you have?" he asked.

"I don't keep count," Vee was saying, "Keep count, and you might start to think you have enough. Numbers are outlaws—bandits. They make rules in your mind." Each box had a label marked with jagged handwriting in charcoal pencil. Violet leaned from one to the next. "My rule is: You can never have too many maps. I collect every old one I can get my hands on. Ahh, here we go."

She leaned far out of the elevator, her feet momentarily leaving the floor. Dodger watched her and thougth that, though he normally explored maps on his own, it was fun to have someone to share the wonder of new discoveries with. Actually, it was maybe even better.

Vee shuffled through a crate. "Something in here should work. . . ." She returned with a long roll of paper. "This is from 1990. I collect them on the decade. Most people think a map like this is worthless, but that's exactly what they thought two hundred years ago, and why there are so few of those maps left. People need to have the long view on the world."

Dodger reached out carefully, afraid to damage it, but Vee thrust it right into his hands. "Go ahead," she said. Dodger was surprised by how she treated them. Not like they were precious, but like they were tools.

He was reminded of how he left his maps scattered on his floor and tossed them around in the car. A map that was wrinkled and hard to fold back up had been used for important things.

Dodger unrolled the map. Vee raised the lamp over his shoulder.

He found the compass rose, oriented himself to north, then found the major cities: Denver, Santa Fe, Reno, Flagstaff. . . . He first traced the bright blue veins of the highways, the red arteries of U.S. routes. He looked for the gray bones of railroad lines, curving along beneath and behind.

Up, down, across he looked. Wyoming, Colorado, Utah. New Mexico . . . skirting the wide swaths of forests, the emerald national parks, following the squiggles of rivers, slowly back and forth across the map—

And suddenly there it was.

Juliette.

Dodger felt a deep squeeze of adrenaline. His heartbeat kicked up a notch.

"Found it?" Vee was leaning around his shoulder, nodding.

"Yeah," Dodger said, suddenly short of breath. It was in the northern highlands of Arizona, west of Flagstaff, southwest of the Grand Canyon. It was just there, like any other town off the highway, in medium bold black font which indicated a town of around twenty-five thousand. The town where the radio came from. Occupying a tiny gap where on his maps there was nothing.

It all really did exist. Dodger had believed it before, but this put any doubt to rest for certain. "Yeah," he said again.

"Get the coordinates and landmarks," said Vee. "I'm afraid I can't let you take the map."

"Thanks." Dodger slipped out his little notebook. His fingers were slippery, clammy, making it hard to flip to a fresh page. He had already figured out the latitude and longitude: $35° 23'$ N, $113° 49'$ W. It was habit. Memorizing strings of numbers was easy for him, a skill that none of his teachers had ever suspected. Writing them down, though, that would be good, just in case. He scribbled quickly, then drew a sketch of the surrounding area.

"Exciting, isn't it?" Vee murmured. "I remember the first time a map did that for me." She leaned over his shoulder.

Dodger clutched the coordinates close to his chest.

Vee chuckled. "Don't get your bloomers in a bunch, boy. I've no interest in your mystery town. Your interest in it is enough for me."

"Sorry," said Dodger. He still couldn't believe he'd found it. He started rolling up the map. "And thanks for helping me."

"You're more than welcome. It's—" Vee stopped. Dodger saw her brow furrow. She looked up.

Dodger followed her gaze, and as he did, he noticed a strange humming noise.

It took a second for his eyes to adjust to the comparatively bright circle of light up at the surface.

Once it did, he saw movement. Two forms, silhouettes. People. People with lights on their heads, rappelling down the mine shaft on ropes.

"That can't be good," said Vee. She looked at Dodger. "Friends of yours?"

"No," said Dodger. "I don't have any friends."

As the two figures zipped toward them, Dodger noticed a strange white light beginning to flicker around them, bouncing off the walls, a black-and-white light like a strobe.

"That can't be good, either," said Vee.

chapter

15

Lucky Springs, NV, July 5, 2:46 p.m.

The flickering light increased. It seemed to be at once lighting the walls and draining the color from them. "Nope, not good," Vee repeated.

"We have to get out of here!" Dodger said. He looked around wildly. Would it be paranoid to think people were showing up because he'd just found the Juliette coordinates? Or would it be naïve to think otherwise? Either way, there was something completely unnatural about that flickering light.

"Nowhere to go," Vee muttered. "That's the only way out."

Dodger looked up helplessly. The figures were

closing. The flashing light was starting to hit the pulley above his head.

Dodger looked over the side. "What about down?"

"Just a dead end down there," said Vee.

But as Dodger had said it, he'd almost felt like the crystal had heated up, like it was agreeing with him. Plus, the strobe light had started to flicker around them, and Dodger had a peculiar sensation of slowing down, like the air was becoming oatmeal. Moving was getting harder—

"Just do it!" Dodger shouted. "Down!"

"Well, all right, I suppose it's worth a try." Vee fiddled with the rope. Above, the figures were no more than twenty feet away.

Dodger's arms felt heavy, his thoughts getting stuck in his mind . . .

Suddenly the elevator dropped downward with a screaming chorus of ropes and pulleys. The rushing blackness extinguished the lamplight. Dodger heard shouts of surprise from the figures above, but they were quickly erased by rushing wind.

Dodger gripped the sides of the elevator. He felt sure they would smash to a rocky death any second.

"Okay, hang on," Vee called over the wind. Sparks began to rain down from the pulley and the elevator slowed, then slammed hard against the mine shaft floor.

"Out," Vee ordered.

Dodger scrambled over the side. He fell out and landed on damp clay ground.

The world was utterly black around him, the air thick and sweet smelling.

He heard the sound of boots hitting the ground. "Dodger, where are you?"

Dodger turned. "Where are you?"

"Over here," Vee called. She sounded close, but Dodger couldn't see a thing, and he couldn't place Vee in the darkness. "We should go this way."

Then he heard the zipping of lines from above. He looked up to see the two headlamps getting closer. The ropes were buzzing like furious bees.

"Dodger!" Vee's voice had gotten farther away.

That flickering light was now shining on the elevator. Dodger scanned the dark, looking for some sign of Vee. All he saw was the rough outline of round tunnel walls. Close. Miles of rock in all directions. Dodger felt like it was crushing him.

"Vee!" he hissed.

No reply.

He got to his feet and backed away from the elevator, running his fingers against the wet wall. The lights were getting close. He wondered if he should try to run around the elevator, toward where he thought Vee was. Or turn and go behind him. She'd said this was a dead end, so what was the point? Maybe he should just sit down and let whoever was coming get him.

And then they arrived.

Dodger took a few more steps back as three lights dropped into the tunnel, like little stars. Two were pale and constant. The third made the point of a triangle beneath them. It was a more brilliant white but flickering, the source of that strobe light. Only now it went dark.

"Rats," said a male voice.

The two lights bobbed, and Dodger thought of those deep-sea creatures, with the bioluminescent lure and the giant translucent teeth.

There were two clicks, and then the lights dropped another couple feet. Boots crunched on the ground. One headlamp swung around and lit a figure.

"What's the problem?" a low, female voice whispered impatiently.

"It's a proximity effect," a male voice answered. "All the parameters are set now. It just needs to recalibrate." He sounded only mildly frustrated.

"I told you we should have just activated the field the moment he arrived in town."

"And I told you that the Director was very clear that we not repeat the mess in Memphis. The FBI is still all over that scene, and we have no idea where that agent and the girl are. The best move was to wait until the boy was isolated and we were sure he'd tracked down the coordinates."

"It was the best move until your field generator stopped working," said the woman.

"One . . ." said the man like he was exhausted.

Dodger thought their bickering sounded a lot like his parents.

"Don't get annoyed with me, Two," the female named One said. "Just make it work. No more mistakes or the Director will flip out."

"'Flip out,' nice *human* phrase," Two huffed. His headlamp shone down on the shiny metal box in his hands. It was still flickering faintly.

"Oh, and what's that," the female countered. "Do I hear you trying to employ their sarcasm?"

Two just sighed. "It's almost there. I just needed to correct for our proximity to the amplification node."

One turned away, her headlamp sweeping around the room. Dodger backed up carefully, sliding his sneaker soles over the soft earth. "He can't have gone far."

Dodger tried desperately to keep still, and also to keep up with what he was hearing. One and Two were here to get him because he'd found the coordinates. They'd tried something in Memphis that hadn't worked and now there was a secret agent on the loose . . . and they were using a field thingy to catch him—that must have been the glowing—but it wasn't working because they were close to some kind of node?

Oh, and there was Two's comment about a human phrase, which meant that these two . . .

Weren't.

"Okay . . ." said Two, "here we go."

A brilliant white light began pulsing from the shiny box in Two's hands. Dodger could see that he was short and square, wearing khaki shorts and a Hawaiian shirt like many of the casino revelers up in town. The outfit looked out of place with climbing harnesses and headlamps. The light increased, and Dodger could see One. Her climbing gear was buckled over smooth khaki capris and a flower-printed, sleeveless shirt. They both had skin that almost seemed to reflect the light, like plastic. And why were they wearing black goggles in the dark?

The light spread from the box, flickering like a strobe, becoming so bright that Dodger had to squint and turn away. A humming sound accompanied it, like being near power lines, growing louder.

Dodger backed up. Whatever this field was, it did something to reality, or time. He'd felt that strange slowing down when it had touched him before.

"Wait . . ." he heard One say. "Two, over there . . . do you see . . ."

Both lights swung right toward him.

And then Dodger realized that he was slightly glowing. *No!* he thought. *Not now!* He tried to press the glow back inside himself, but his heart was racing, his nerves sizzling, and he couldn't gain control, especially because it felt somehow *stronger* now. There was suddenly far more energy at his back. The crystal felt like it was positively burning.

Their footsteps started toward him.

"How is he doing that?" One asked.

"Don't know, but let's get him."

Dodger turned and ran. He'd only taken three steps when he tripped on an unseen rock and fell over. A tearing at his knee and a bright stinging pain and that coolness running down his leg definitely meant blood. He needed light! He jumped up, extended his hand in front of himself, and pushed out, creating a warm glow around it, but not enough.

Around him, the walls were beginning to flicker with that black-and-white strobe effect.

Dodger kept running. He could hear their footsteps behind him. He reached around and pulled out the black crystal. He held it straight in front of him and pushed himself into it, connecting with its energy as hard as he knew how.

The crystal burst with light, illuminating the entire tunnel around him.

And the radio broadcast began pouring from Dodger's body again.

"Howdy, folks, the time is seven forty-five here at KJPR and that means it's time for another four in a row of continuous hits!"

"What is going on?" he heard Two shout.

"Freeze him already!" shouted One.

Dodger could see the tunnel now, the rocks on the floor, and though he was lit up like a neon sign and blasting radio, and though his knee was killing him, he ran like he never had, hurtling rocks and darting back and forth.

"Now, folks, before we get to the music, I actually want to read you a special bulletin from the Weather Service. . . ."

"I have the field set to maximum!" Two shouted.

The flickering increased around Dodger, the strobe light reaching ahead of him down the tunnel wall.

"Heavy winds are expected later tonight along with those snow squalls."

Dodger began to feel that slowing sensation again. Whatever this field was, it was causing his body to grind to a halt. *No!* Dodger thought desperately. Had to keep moving!

"So please be sure to be in your homes before they start, which should be around ten p.m."

"He's slowing down!" One announced.

Dodger could feel it. And the glow he was creating with the crystal was fading. He felt his lungs starting to hitch, like something was stopping them. Like he was being frozen.

"Dan Spirit's advice is to go to bed early tonight, and when you wake up tomorrow, it's going to be sunny again, with highs in the low sixties—"

He was losing control of his muscles. The crystal slipped out of his hands. Dodger heard it shatter on the rocky floor.

The walls around him had completely lost color.

And now up ahead, he saw that the tunnel ended. There was a solid metal door. It was silver and sleek. There was no handle, no lock, only two black circles at chest height.

Dodger hit the door and leaned against it. The metal was warm. He pushed himself up, trying to find a gap at the edge of the door, anything, but the door was flickering in that freezing strobe light and his heavy breaths were slowing down and he could barely even move his neck and they had him, they had him.

A reflection caught his eye and Dodger saw a mirror image of his pursuers in one of the black circles that was down by his shoulder. The two alien agents, the freezing box flickering.

Dodger felt his body going rigid, no more feeling in his feet, his thoughts slowing. . . . There was no way out. . . .

Wait. . . .

Unless . . .

The reflection in that black circle . . . like crystal . . .

As if he was moving through two tons of wet clay, Dodger slid his hand over the black reflective disc. When his fingers touched the surface, it began to glow orange.

Maybe these discs opened it somehow . . .

Dodger tried to move his other hand, *dragged* it through the black-and-white world, time slowing down, stopping. . . .

His hand rested on the other disc. Both hands ignited orange.

And there was a flash.

A moment of blackness . . .

Dodger blinked. The strobe light was gone. His head was swimming, but he had feeling again in his body. He lurched forward, almost falling on his face, but caught his balance, and stood.

He looked behind him. There was the door. He was on the other side of it. Somehow, he had *used* the door.

And now he was in a room.

A vast room.

It was a spherical space cast in warm, fiery light. Its walls were made of some kind of metal that also seemed iridescent, like puddles around the city sometimes looked. Dodger was standing on a platform that ringed the room. Here and there, catwalks led out to the center of the room, to an inner ring that encircled a giant ball of crystal, maybe twenty feet tall, with a thousand angled faces It glowed with such intensity that it was nearly impossible to look at.

Wow, Dodger thought.

Waves of energy and warmth pulsed out of the crystal, and as it washed over him, Dodger had an eerie sensation of being called to. Summoned. But not *ordered*. It didn't feel like he had to approach the crystal. He wasn't being dragged, but he was being invited, and he felt strongly like he wanted to go to it, like a smaller magnet being drawn to a larger one. He remembered the crystal shard warming as he'd lowered into the mine shaft. Maybe it had sensed this pull, too.

Dodger started across one of the catwalks toward the center. Around him, he sensed that there were banks of flashing equipment along the perimeter of the room. There were other doors here and there, too. He perceived this from a state of total calm. As he neared the giant crystal, he felt its power humming in him. This place . . . he was at peace here, and felt sure that things would be fine. He didn't need to worry about those people chasing him anymore. He was safe here.

Except then a little electric buzzing made Dodger glance over his shoulder and he saw that One had just popped into the room. She stepped aside as Two also appeared. His strobe light machine was turned off. They both looked around, and One saw him and pointed, and they hurried toward him.

Dodger ran across the catwalk to the center of the space. As he arrived, he realized there was a figure standing nearby, a little silhouette eclipsing the sun-like glow of the crystal.

This person glanced at Dodger. He was wearing a yellow hard hat and an orange jumpsuit. He had smooth plastic skin and black goggles over his eyes. He was holding some kind of glowing clipboard. He did a little double take when he saw Dodger and then he turned to a little console that was mounted on the catwalk railing. There were two black discs there, too. Tucking the clipboard under his arm, the little man pressed his hands to the discs. They lit up orange, and so did he, and then the man winked out of sight completely.

Dodger heard footsteps on the catwalk behind him.

Only one thing to do, he felt sure of that. He ran over to the console and placed his much larger, human hands on the pads. They lit up, and so did he—

And he left the catwalk, and, it seemed, his body.

He found himself lost in an orange space of light. Beyond that light there seemed to be stars in all directions, above and below. In the distance, he saw something bright like a collection of suns all in a cluster, orange like this light he was in. It almost looked like a collection of these very crystals, but so much larger. They were strung together with vast beams of some kind of iridescent metal.

But the view into vast space was not the only view. There were also caves, it seemed, tunnels, as if he was in two places at once. This was familiar. Somehow this was Juliette, but also not.

Welcome, the crystal said, *to the Main Directory at Amplification Node 18.* Dodger felt like it wasn't technically speaking, but more presenting itself to him, as if his consciousness had interfaced with it. *Please choose function.*

Dodger became aware of options, again not actual words on a screen but a sense of things he could do inside this crystal. Was he actually inside it? He couldn't tell. Maybe his body was still back on that catwalk in that round cavern, in which case, One and

Two might grab him and yank him from that console at any moment.

He had to be quick. He scrolled through the option-feelings. They seemed to be: *Connectivity, Time Parameter Management, Transit.*

Dodger had no idea what these meant. And yet he did, or something. It was making his head hurt. But he felt sure that what he needed right now was Transit.

Transit, the crystal confirmed. *Sublocal, Local, or Upload for Macro.*

Dodger had no idea. *Local?* he thought. That made sense.

A kind of map appeared seemingly all around him. At first he couldn't even make sense of it, but then he saw that there were light points across landforms. It was a map of the United States, no wait, it was bigger than that, it was the continent, oceans, the world. Okay, it was the world, and all around it were these little orange dots.

Please select a destination node.

Dodger felt a kind of mind-blowing sense of possibility. Here, apparently, was travel to the far corners of the world. But what did it mean? That there were crystals like this one at all these locations worldwide? There were hundreds, no, thousands of points, maybe ten thousand, he . . . This was all too much. Dodger couldn't handle it.

I just need to get out of these caves, he thought to the interface.

Sublocal transit, the crystal confirmed. *Please select a Sublocal transit access point.*

Dodger now saw something like a map, except it was vertical as well as horizontal, a kind of schematic of Lucky Springs both above and below the surface. He saw little discs that seemed to represent doors like the one he'd entered the room through. He spied one that seemed like it would work and thought, *There.*

Commencing.

There was a rush, a strange pulling and stretching, and for a moment Dodger lost track of everything, no thoughts even, just a kind of nothing, and there was a sound like the ocean through a seashell, a vastness that seemed to spread and exist between each of his billions of molecules. . . .

And then he was himself again.

And he was in the regular old dark.

And he was falling on his face.

He landed on a dirt floor, and immediately vomited. Sour liquid splattered on the rocks.

Dodger looked up and saw that he was in another tunnel, similar to the one he'd been in while fleeing from One and Two, only this one was lit with weak lightbulbs strung along the ceiling. He got to his knees and turned to see another metal door with the black crystal ovals. He was outside of that cavern now, the place where he'd interfaced.

Dodger tried to piece together the flotsam in his brain from the last minute. It was as if giant feelings of disorientation and then understanding had flooded over him in successive waves that had now left him pummeled and lying on a beach. First, he'd uploaded himself into a giant crystal. Then he'd seen a view of space, or something. And then a "local" map of the entire planet (and that made him wonder, what would he have seen if he'd said "Macro"?), and then a map of this mine system, from which he'd picked this door to exit by. Based on that map, this tunnel he was now in should be part of Vee's mine tour and lead him right back up to her shop. The lights on the ceiling seemed to confirm this. But so did something else.

Dodger stood up, stumbled forward on rubbery legs, and slammed into an iron-barred gate. It was made of damp rusted bars. Dodger saw that there was a sign on it, but he couldn't read it from this side. Probably put up by that mining company Vee had mentioned, to keep tour people away from the door.

Dodger shook the gate as hard as he could, but it didn't budge. He was trapped. His only way out was to go back through the door behind him, but what about One and Two? They would be here any moment, wouldn't they?

He turned back to the gate and rattled it again. "HELP!" he shouted. His voice reverberated up the tunnel. There was no reply—

Except now footsteps. And a light, rounding the corner and falling on him.

It was them. They'd already figured out where he'd gone and—

"Francis?"

The light stopped. Behind it was a large hulk of a man.

Harry.

"Dad," said Dodger blankly.

Harry stepped up to the bars. He was breathing hard. "What are you doing in there?"

Dodger saw Harry gaze past him, to the metal door. He aimed the flashlight at it.

"Dad," said Dodger, feeling a nervous spike inside at what his dad might be thinking. "Can you get me out?"

Harry turned his attention to the lock. "It's pretty rusty, hold on . . ." He reared back and slammed it with the flashlight. The flashlight casing cracked, but the lock held. Harry reared back and hit it again. This time the flashlight shattered, the bulb popping, but the lock also came free, thudding to the ground.

Dodger pushed against the gate, felt it being pulled as well, and then it was open, and he stumbled out, right into his dad's chest.

"Oh, hey," said Harry awkwardly. His hands fell on Dodger's shoulders and he moved him a step back, gently.

It was an odd feeling. Dodger almost flinched away from Harry's grip, but he was too tired, too completely wiped out.

"Are you okay?" Harry asked. He was talking quietly, almost like he was trying not to get caught, either.

"Fine," said Dodger.

Then he stumbled to his knees and barfed again. Whatever he'd done—"teleporting" was as good a word as any—had messed him up worse than any roller coaster.

Harry's hands slid under his arms and dragged him up. "Son, you . . . you're a mess."

Dodger wobbled on his feet but managed to stay up. Harry kept a hand on his shoulder.

"We should go," Dodger said, swallowing sour bile. They had to get out of here first, then Dodger could think about everything that had just happened—

"Sure," said Harry. He started up the tunnel. Dodger followed, and as he did his thoughts finally started to catch up with reality, and then there was one thought that immediately popped out of his mouth:

"I thought you were going to be at the casino?"

"Bah." Harry waved a dismissive hand. "Those tables were rigged, so I came and took the tour. As a result, two Royal Rip-offs in one day."

It was classic Harry Lane, Dodger thought, only he was overcome with a sudden and certain feeling:

Harry was lying.

Vee had been down in the mine with Dodger. Which meant Harry had found his way down into this mine on his own. Why would he do that? Had he seen Dodger go down into the mine shaft with Vee? Had he been *spying* on Dodger?

More than everything he'd learned just in the last few minutes, it was this newest revelation that struck Dodger. *Harry's lying to me. He knows something.* But what did Harry know?

As they followed a series of ascending zigzags up out of the mine, Dodger checked his pocket. His notebook was still there, the coordinates to Juliette inside. He glanced nervously over his shoulder. Why weren't those aliens after him right now? Maybe he'd lost them by using the crystal interface. Dodger wondered if his abilities had been a surprise to them, too. Maybe they needed to regroup before they came after him again. They would though—Dodger felt sure of it.

But still . . . if Dodger wasn't what the aliens had expected, what was he?

And yet, despite all that, Dodger found that he was worried as much about the strange figure in front of him as he was about those behind him in the dark.

Roswell, NM, July 6, 3:45 p.m.

The next afternoon, Dodger found himself gazing at the barren landscape of eastern New Mexico. Vast miles of brown plains, mountains in the distance, pure blue sky arcing overhead. They were approaching one of Dodger's dream places to visit, yet he wasn't excited. He'd spent the hours since Lucky Springs, including an evening in the southern canyon country of Utah and a mostly sleepless night in a Relaxation Depot in Farmington, NM, wondering when those aliens might appear again and expecting it to happen any moment.

He'd also been worrying about his dad.

Harry drove in silence. The radio was off.

There had been no talking. Barely any talking since the day before, since they'd walked out of the mine tunnel and back to their car and driven out of Lucky Springs. It was just Harry gazing out at the road, and Dodger just staring out the window, except for—

There it was again.

Dodger felt a tingling sensation and when he looked over, he found Harry looking at him. But then Harry's eyes immediately flicked away.

There had been at least five or six other moments like this since they'd left the mine.

What does he know? Dodger wondered again. What had brought him into that mine yesterday? Dodger had considered that Harry's story could be true. It was possible that he'd just gotten tired of blackjack and decided to come find Dodger, and then when he wasn't in the map room, he'd tried the mine.

But Dodger didn't think so. Not after the way Harry had stared at the radio back at Heavenly Frequencies. Dodger felt certain that he knew, or at least suspected, something. But what? Not that Dodger was actually being chased by aliens, or manipulating crystals, or teleporting. He couldn't suspect that, could he? If he really knew what was up, he'd have turned the car around by now, right?

Dodger was no longer sure. Not about his dad, or about the aliens and their plans, or even what he was. All he knew was that he had to get some answers. He had to get to Juliette. Yet that was a whole different problem. And Dodger wasn't even sure if his latest plan was going to get him there.

Because even though he had the Juliette coordinates in his pocket, when Harry had asked Dodger *where to next?* as they were leaving Lucky Springs, Dodger had said: "Roswell," which was hundreds of miles from Juliette's location. In fact, by heading for Roswell, they'd spent nearly an entire day driving in the wrong direction.

But Dodger had chosen Roswell for two reasons. The first had to do with the aliens. Dodger assumed they were watching him, and so if they saw him heading to Roswell instead of Juliette, he hoped they might assume that they'd intercepted him in the mine shaft before he'd had the chance to get the coordinates. And so maybe then they'd think he wasn't a threat and leave him alone, or at least sit back and wait to see what he'd do next.

The second reason had to do with his dad. If Harry really was starting to suspect that Dodger was somehow actually connected to real aliens, the trip to Roswell might ease his suspicions. After all, Roswell was probably the last place that actual aliens would show up. Dodger had also told Harry that Roswell's UFO museum might have vital information about Juliette, but judging from what he'd read online, finding any real alien information in Roswell was pretty unlikely.

But hopefully, all of this would buy Dodger enough time to figure out how to actually get to Juliette. Currently, he had no idea how he was going to make that happen. He was just stalling. Somehow he had to lose these aliens, and, if Roswell didn't seem to throw Harry off the trail, then . . . *You might have to ditch him, too.*

This thought caused a nervous flutter inside. He couldn't tell if it was fear or excitement or both. But how was he going to get to Juliette on his own? Hitchhike? Hide on the roof of somebody's RV? Steal a bike? And could he even do it? Could he really ditch out on his dad and try to make the journey to Juliette alone?

If I have to, he thought, trying to convince himself, *I will.*

"This place looks like another tourist trap," Harry mused. They had arrived on Main Street.

On one side of the street, Dodger saw the Visitors Welcome! Café, and on the other, Crash Site Gifts. The sidewalks were lined with black lampposts with frosted white tops. These globes had been decorated with giant black alien eyes. Ahead, a tall marquee with a small, golden flying saucer on top announced the International UFO Museum and Research Center. The streets were nearly empty in the searing heat.

Dodger was glad to see that Roswell lived up to its kitschy reputation, but also maybe a little disappointed by it, too. Roswell was the site of an alleged alien crash in 1947. There was ample evidence that the crash was actually an experimental weather balloon, and yet, there were also curious facts that didn't add up and had kept the story alive for decades. Either way, Harry's assessment of the shops and museum was probably right.

"I'm starving," said Harry as he swung the car into a public parking lot. "Maybe we should get lunch before the museum."

"Sure," Dodger replied. Lunch would kill time. Keep Harry's guard down. Yet it would also bring Dodger an hour closer to the moment when he needed to know what to do next.

They got out of the car. Dodger looked around. The parking lot was empty except for a large mobile home. The driver was sitting behind the wheel, reading a book. Dodger wasn't totally sure, but it looked like the white-bearded gentleman was wearing a hat made out of tinfoil. There were maybe antennae sticking out of it, too.

Dodger caught the man's eye, and the man seemed to flinch. It almost looked like he tried to duck, but then one of the antennae got caught on the rear-view mirror, and since the tinfoil helmet seemed to be attached with a chin strap, the man proceeded to start yanking his head, trying to get free. He clutched at the hat. Dodger wondered if he should be worried about the man. Finally, he clawed the chin strap off. He looked at Dodger again, breathless, and then slid slowly out of sight behind the dashboard, leaving the hat hanging there. Dodger guessed that, in Roswell, a man driving an RV and wearing a tinfoil hat and acting odd was fairly normal.

They headed up the sidewalk. "Wow," said Harry, checking his watch. "We sure are a long way away from Seattle, huh?"

"Mmm," Dodger grunted.

Suddenly a hand fell on Dodger's head, ruffling his hat. Dodger flinched.

"Sorry," said Harry, snatching his hand back. "Didn't mean to embarrass you."

"No, it's . . ." Dodger trailed off. He hadn't been embarrassed, really. Just surprised. He couldn't remember the last time Harry had done that.

"Well, anyway, I was going to say that this has been fun," said Harry.

"Yeah." It had? Dodger also couldn't remember a

single time that Harry seemed to be having fun.

"I'm glad we got this time."

"Mmm." Dodger glanced at his dad. Harry's hands were shoved in his pockets. He was walking slightly hunched, gazing at the ground. Dodger didn't know what to make of it, but it was freaking him out.

Main Street was bathed in sun, the air burned dry. In between the storefronts catering to alien enthusiasts, the other businesses looked a little run-down. Some stores were vacant. The museum was beyond the next intersection.

"How about here?" Harry pointed. They were passing a Denny's on the corner.

"Okay." Dodger actually didn't feel like eating anymore. The head rubbing, the statement about having a good time . . . There was definitely something weird going on with Harry. As they walked into the restaurant, Dodger felt a nervous alarm ringing inside. He felt like he was being walked into the room where the mob hit was going to take place. Something was about to happen, he could feel it.

They sat in a brown booth. Looked over the menus. Ordered beverages. Then food. Harry ordered a breakfast that somehow managed to include french toast, home fries, and biscuits and gravy. Dodger ordered the Super Mega Pancake Slam. The whole time, there was no eye contact or conversation. The waitress returned with coffee for Harry and a chocolate milk shake for Dodger.

"Jeez," Harry finally said after sipping his coffee. "There's another alien gift shop." Harry nodded toward the store across the street, the Extra Tee-rrestrial Shirt Company.

"Mmm," Dodger grunted.

"You seem like you're feeling better," said Harry. "You know, other than that stomach bug yesterday."

That was how Dodger had explained his post–teleportation barfing.

"Yeah," he said.

"And no bloody noses," Harry continued, "or those headaches that would get bad. Unless you haven't told me."

"Oh, um, no," Dodger said.

"I—" Harry's eyes flashed back out the window. "I worried about those, you know."

"Okay," said Dodger, thinking, *you did?*

"It had to have an effect, is what I mean." Harry picked up his coffee, but then put it back down without drinking. "On your schoolwork, and other stuff. It makes sense . . . you can't exactly do your best when you're feeling ill."

"Guess," said Dodger. Inside, he was knotting up. There was a metallic taste in the back of his mouth that even his milk shake couldn't erase.

"Point is, you seem better." Harry nodded. "Like this trip has helped. Getting away from it all for a few days. It seems like you've been figuring some things out, maybe?"

Dodger shrugged. Some things? Like how to interface with crystals? What was Harry getting at? Dodger felt his nerves winding tighter. "Sure."

"I was thinking that when we get back we can try to make . . . more of an effort with everything."

"Oh." *What "everything"?* And when they got back? The thought sent a chill through Dodger, and he realized that he'd been so focused on finding Juliette that he'd never really even considered the idea of going home. But what if, after all this, after all he'd learned, they just turned around and in three days he was back in his old room with his old life? The thought was nearly unbearable. . . . And worst of all, he'd have to live with the certainty that there was something different about him, something he had come so close to finding but would never know.

"Listen," said Harry, his eyes darting around the restaurant, out the window, everywhere but at Dodger. "There's something I want to talk about, you know, father-son. Since we're out here, together, with all this time . . ."

Dodger's heart was racing. Something was coming, but what?

Yet Harry didn't seem quite ready to reveal it. "But, I mean, you might have things, too. Is there anything, um, on your mind? That you want to talk to me about?"

"Um . . ." said Dodger.

Their food arrived. Dodger felt like he'd been saved. He dumped syrup on his pancakes and shoved a huge bite in his mouth. Maybe it was the burst of sugar, but Dodger had a wild thought: *Tell him.* Not just about the events of the last couple days, but . . . maybe he should tell his dad about everything. The months of radio station, or how even before that, his whole life, really, he'd *never* felt right, how it wasn't just the headaches, or the clumsiness, but more like a gnawing, deathly scary feeling of emptiness . . . of pointlessness. Because how could there be a point when you always felt different, always felt alone, and didn't know why? If he couldn't trust his dad with it, who could he trust?

But did he trust Harry? Did Harry even really want to know? Dodger had always felt like he didn't. He'd never understood and he was never going to. These were the roles they'd always played . . . except here was his dad, changing his role, asking Dodger. *Tell him. . . .*

But no, no! What about the part where Dodger was hoping that when he found Juliette, he might find a new home, a new life? How did you explain that to your own dad?

"Dodger?" Harry asked. He was looking at Dodger with something like real worry again. . . .

Dodger couldn't take this. Everything was welling up inside. Suddenly, he felt a hitch at the back of his throat, almost like he was about to cry. What was happening to him? He had to get out of here.

"I—I um, forgot my meBox," Dodger mumbled, sliding out of the booth. He'd get some air, some space to think, to breathe. "It's in my suitcase. I— I need it for the museum."

"Oh." Harry seemed startled. "Um, well, I . . . sure." He pulled out his keys. "Hurry back, though, before your food gets cold."

Dodger snatched the large key ring and hurried down the aisle. He burst out the front door into the warm sun and half-ran back to the car. Once he was there, he sat on the back bumper and tried to calm down. He barely understood this feeling. Like he was scared and yet deeply sad at the same time. But about what? Was he scared about telling his father what was really going on? Or was he scared about what Harry might tell him? What *was* all of this? He wished he still had the crystal shard. Something to connect with and feel some kind of certainty.

Dodger popped the back gate and spied his backpack at the top of the pile. He considered just taking it to the curb, hailing a cab, and going. Vanishing, just like that.

He grabbed his pack by the strap and yanked it out, but doing so caused the unsteady arrangement of bags to shift. They toppled out of the car, an avalanche of gear crashing to the pavement. Something cracked hard, and there was a little tinkle of broken pieces.

Dodger slammed his backpack to the ground in frustration. *You probably just broke your meBox, too, you idiot,* he scolded himself, but who even cared!

He looked around the empty parking lot, wondering if anyone had witnessed his tantrum, but there was no one around. Even that RV was now empty. Dodger picked up his backpack and fished out his meBox. He shoved it in his pocket, thinking he could at least take some pictures in the museum.

He grabbed the tent and a sleeping bag and hurled them back into the car. He picked up his dad's suitcase and heard the shuffle of whatever he'd broken. He placed it on the ground and zipped it open to see what he'd messed up now.

"Franny, everything okay?" Dodger looked over his shoulder to see Harry approaching, walking quickly.

"Fine!" Dodger called. He flipped open Harry's suitcase.

Harry's footsteps were getting closer. Hurrying. "Franny, wait!"

Dodger looked inside.

Everything was no longer fine.

"Hey, what are you doing in there?" Harry was right behind him.

Dodger lurched to his feet and spun around, his face red. He felt woozy and barely stayed upright. Inside, it felt like shelves were overturning, floors falling through.

Harry's eyes grew wide, his mouth hanging half-open. Dodger had never seen that expression before: like he'd been caught.

"What are you doing with this?" Dodger asked, holding Sid and R2's lunch box radio. His fingers were shaking. His voice felt hoarse, a clump of cotton. His heart was pounding.

Harry's jaw moved up and down before he finally spoke: "I—I went back for it. Listen, Dodger, just come back inside with me. I can explain. This is what I wanted to talk to you about."

And Dodger suddenly saw a different version of his dad over these last few days: Harry sneaking back to get the radio, sneaking down into the mine after him . . . all those glances . . .

"You've been spying on me," said Dodger.

"No, not spying, Franny," Harry stammered. "I'm your father. I'm trying to protect you. . . . I . . ." He trailed off. Glanced at the sky. Peeled off his red baseball cap and wiped at his forehead. With each little move Harry made, Dodger felt himself winding tighter.

"Look," said Harry. "I—I thought this would be the right thing to do, coming out here on this trip. Thought it might help you to figure things out, thought we could talk, but I haven't known. . . ." He glanced back up to the sky. "I haven't known where to start."

"What are you talking about?" Dodger took a step back. He wanted to run, but he was frozen in place because he was suddenly having this giant, time-stopping realization that something big was about to happen, something that had been about to happen for a while, something *huge* that maybe Dodger had even been expecting for a long time, without ever realizing it.

"Franny, listen." Harry started bending the rim of his hat with both hands. "We have to *talk*. I've been trying to find a way this whole trip. . . . But then, you'd been acting better, and so I wanted to give you space, so that maybe you would come to it on your own, but then yesterday . . . someone was after you, weren't they? And I realized that you're not going to be safe, but I didn't know what to do. . . . I . . . haven't known what to do for a long time."

"Dad!" Dodger screamed. Who *was* this stammering person? And what did he mean—

"Sorry, I—" Harry's face seemed to quiver, like there were fault lines giving way beneath it. He sucked in a huge breath of air, checked in with the sky one last time. . . .

Dodger felt time slowing to a stop, his body freezing. No alien box required. What was about to—

"Franny," said Harry. "I *know*. About the radio voice in your head and the feelings you've been having."

"What?" Dodger whispered. His dad hadn't just said that. There was no way.

But there was his dad wringing his hat and looking at him. "I've been trying to find a way to tell you," Harry went on. "I mean, we don't understand all of it, your mother and I, but enough. . . . And there's things you don't know, Dodger. Things we've wanted to tell you forever."

Dodger's heart was slamming against his ribs. His hands shook. It was hard to make words. All the gears spinning, nothing lining up. "Tell . . . me . . . what?"

"That—" Harry gazed up at the sky. He put his hands out like he was making the sides of a box, crafting a space in which to place what he said next: "The reason these things are happening to you."

"The reason?" Dodger croaked.

"You—you don't remember . . ." Harry said. "I mean, we thought that was good. The therapists we took you to afterward, they told us that because you were so young, you wouldn't even remember it. You seemed okay. And there were no scars, or any of those things you read about, so we . . . we just wanted you to be normal. And then even when you weren't . . . I mean, *lots* of kids withdraw. Lots of kids have a hard time making friends or doing activities. All the books say it's well within normal. There was no reason to think it had anything to do with the . . ." Harry trailed off, looking anywhere but at Dodger.

"The *what*?" Dodger whispered.

Suddenly Harry's breath hitched. He wiped tears from his eyes. Dodger had never seen anything like it, and it made what Harry was saying even worse. "The abduction," he continued quietly. "It happened when you were two. We were living in California then, and . . . I woke up, middle of the night and, just thought the clock was wrong, but Sophie got up to check on you and . . ." His voice halted again. "You were gone, Son. There'd been some kind of sixteen-minute gap. We had the police, the FBI, everyone, but there was no sign of a break-in. It was impossible. No leads, like you'd just vanished from us. And there was nothing I could do. Nothing."

Dodger just stared. *Abducted.*

"Then, eight days later, the longest eight days you could imagine, it was about five a.m., maybe the first sleep any of us had gotten since you were taken, and we heard crying, and there you were, back in your room, right where you'd been. It was like waking up from a nightmare. Like that week had been some strange alternate reality. You were with us again. And you were fine. Fine . . ."

"Why didn't you tell me?" Dodger shouted, the words erupting out of him. He felt like some wild creature was running around in his head.

Harry threw up his hands. "How could we tell anyone? No one was going to believe us. The FBI suggested a cover story—so we could say *something*—about an aunt who had a breakdown and ran off with you, briefly, how she couldn't have kids of her own, that kind of thing. We got the family to buy it, or at least go along with it. Just to put it behind us. I mean, it didn't even seem real after a while, because you were okay, you were fine, we—"

Dodger started trembling. "I had a right to know."

Harry shook his head. "We thought about it a million times, probably every day, but the timing never seemed right, and what good would it have done you?

You've got to understand how we felt. . . . We've never been the same, but we thought you could be. We thought if you never knew, you could be normal."

Dodger blinked. Then he hurled the radio at Harry. "Well, I'm not normal!"

Harry barely deflected it with his forearm, sending it skidding across the pavement.

"Nothing about me is normal!" Dodger shouted.

And he grabbed his backpack and ran.

"Franny, wait!"

"Stay away from me!" Dodger tore out of the parking lot, down Main Street, past the Denny's, across the intersection.

He looked back, but Harry hadn't followed. Dodger ran on until he reached the shade beneath the UFO Museum marquee. There, he fell against the wall, breathless, thoughtless, choking on tears.

He looked down at his hands. He hadn't been switched at birth. He wasn't some magical being from another home. He . . . he was just a lab rat. Everyone's lab rat. Taken and . . . changed? It sounded like it. Then returned and . . . watched. Mourned. Lost to everyone, even himself. Until now, and . . . He stared vacantly. What now? What exactly was he supposed to do now? What exactly was he supposed to do, ever?

A flash caught his eye and he looked up. A car had just passed, catching the sun—no, it hadn't been that.

The flash had come from across the street.

Standing there on the far sidewalk were two people. They were dressed in particularly loud floral outfits. The sun reflected brilliantly off the pale, plastic-looking skin of their faces and arms, and even more brightly off the silver box that the male was holding, which had begun to pulse with silver strobe light.

They'd found him. The world began to flicker and drain of color around One and Two, a sphere of strobe light growing, its light enveloping the buildings, the street. People near them stiffened and stopped moving. A car passed through the spreading wave, slowing almost to a stop before lurching free. The next car didn't escape. The entire street was coming to a halt.

Run! Dodger thought to himself, but he didn't move. What was the point? They were just here to collect him again, wasn't that it? Back to pick up their little lab rat, their malfunctioning abductee. Heck, they'd probably take him back to Juliette, where he'd been trying to go anyway, to fix his circuits and get him shipshape! Maybe by the time they were done, there'd be no more weirdness. Maybe they could just wipe his memories clean and stick him back home in Washington. Or he could just ask them to make him someone else completely. Maybe that was what he wanted. Just to let them take all this away, all these painful memories . . .

The black-and-white had reached the near curb.

"Francis! Hey!"

It took Dodger a moment to realize the voice was directed at him. A girl had appeared near him. About his age, wearing glasses, her brown hair in a braid. Her face was red and gleaming with sweat, and she was out of breath. She looked normal enough, maybe a little high-strung. Dodger knew the type from school. Always on top of everything. Always raising their hands and always disappointed to get Dodger as a partner on a project.

"You're Francis . . ." she was saying. "Right?"

"What?"

"The FAD."

Dodger knew he understood the words, but he still peered at her. "I—I go by Dodger."

"Huh?" she asked.

"It's from an old cartoon," Dodger stammered. "You know, Duck Dodgers in the twenty-fourth-and-a-half century. It was a parody of Buck Rogers—"

She cut him off. "Okay, fine. Dodger. I'm Haley." Her hand fell to his arm. "I'm the other fellowship winner. You need to come with me."

"You . . ."

279

She pulled at him. "Now!"

Dodger yanked his arm free. "Let go of me!"

"Come on, Dodger!" She glanced across the street. "It's a Missing Time Field."

"I've seen it before," said Dodger, not meaning to sound defensive but maybe he did because where did she get off knowing more about what was happening to him than *he* did? "Have *you* seen it?"

Haley frowned at him. "Yes." She glanced worriedly at the advancing light. "Now, come with me if you want to get to Juliette."

Dodger looked at her. Looked back at One and Two, who had started to hurry across the street toward them.

"Tick-tock!" the girl, Haley, shouted.

17

Roswell, NM, July 6, 4:18 p.m.

"Fine," said Dodger. "I'll go."

Haley nodded. "Here." She reached up and pressed hard against the skin behind his left ear.

"Ow!" Dodger flinched away at a stinging pain. He reached for the spot—

"Don't," said Haley. "It's a field disruptor. It will keep the missing time from affecting you."

"Oh. Sweet," said Dodger. He thought that was pretty cool.

"Yeah, well, it can't keep them from grabbing us. Come on, this way. We have to hurry!" She yanked him toward the glass double doors and into the museum.

Dodger looked back and saw One and Two getting close, the light spreading even faster. Missing time, so that's what it was. Hadn't his dad just said something about that . . . sixteen missing minutes? When they'd taken him, as a baby, so long ago? Suddenly Dodger felt a pang of regret for being so hard on Harry. He glanced up the street, wondering if Harry was still at the car, or—

"Come *on!*" Haley dragged him through the entryway.

"Welcome to the museum," said an elderly volunteer behind the counter, "Admission is fr—" Her mouth stuck open, her body beginning to drain of color.

"Faster!" Haley urged.

They sprinted into the exhibit hall, a tall, hollow room with display booths along each side, separated by Peg-Board walls. Dodger saw blurry photos of things that could be flying saucers or clouds, framed letters and newspaper reports, a display of old radios. The exhibits were already flickering, color bleeding out. "Where are we going?" he called to Haley.

Haley didn't answer, just dragged him to the middle of the hall. Before them was a small replica flying saucer, made of what looked like crinkled tinfoil and papier-mâché, and an inexplicable life-size plastic horse covered in old newspaper pages.

Dodger saw Haley gazing frantically around. "Now what?"

"He's supposed to be here," she said. "He said all I had to do was get you in here and he'd have an exit strategy."

"Who said that?" Dodger asked.

"Long story," said Haley, head still whipping about.

"Well, what's the exit strategy?"

"He didn't say!" Haley shouted. "Ugh! He never says enough."

Dodger looked around. There were other patrons in here, some looking at them oddly, others just gazing at the exhibits.

And all of them beginning to freeze in place.

"Uh-oh," Haley breathed.

"What?" Dodger followed her gaze and saw a couple emerging from the back hallway. Not One and Two; this couple appeared elderly, the woman wearing a woven hat, the man a mesh baseball cap, both with white hair, hunched over, pastel shirts and starched pants . . . but both with the tiny black goggles and porcelain skin.

"No need to hurry, young lady," said the male agent in a grandfatherly voice.

"Not good," said Haley. "Come on!" She spun

around, yanking on Dodger's arm, but then he saw her eyes widen.

"Just relax, kids."

Dodger whirled to see One and Two entering the hall from the front. The entire room had faded to flickering black and white.

"What now?" Dodger asked.

"I don't know!" said Haley.

Dodger looked around wildly. There was another exit from the exhibit hall, on the far side. "There!" Now he took Haley's arm and started darting between the frozen people.

"Ow!" Suddenly Haley yanked back on Dodger's arm. He turned to see her arched to the left, her shoulder in the clutches of another black-goggled, pastel-wearing agent, this one in a white panama hat. His fingers were retreating from behind her ear.

And the color was draining out of Haley. Her body freezing in black and white.

Dodger was about to turn when there was a wicked sting behind his ear.

"There we are."

Another agent. Right behind him. It was One. "Nice to see you again," she whispered.

Dodger tried to move, but it was already too late. He looked down and saw his legs losing color, his hands, the feeling going with it.

Haley was a statue now. Behind her, the world was still, except for the agents—

And that little papier-mâché UFO. It was wiggling. Now it shot straight up into the air as if it had been launched.

Dodger saw a circular hole in the floor beneath where the UFO had been. And then he saw a giant man spring from it, dressed in black.

The agents spun. It was Two who was closest. He advanced, but the giant man went right at him. He met Two with a kick to the sternum that sent him flying.

Three others—there seemed to be six agents total—went after him. This guy was fast. A roundhouse kick, a lightning punch. He knocked the alien in the panama hat aside and frozen Haley fell into his arms. He pressed a finger behind her ear then dropped her and lunged toward Dodger.

With the little control he had left, Dodger tried to lurch to his side, to throw One off balance. All he managed to do was turn them a few degrees, but this allowed the large man to land a kick to One's shoulder. She flew back.

There was a sting as the man pressed a new field disruptor behind Dodger's ear. He felt his body seeming to come back to life. Haley was getting up from the ground, too.

"I'm the Alto," the man said to Dodger. "This way." He ran back to the hole in the floor.

Dodger grabbed Haley by the elbow. "Let's go," he said.

They staggered to the hole. Dodger saw a stepladder below it. He dropped to the floor and slid into the hole. The Alto was fending off another attack from Two as Dodger slipped out of sight. He landed on the concrete floor of a basement hallway.

Haley half climbed, half fell down beside him, stumbling woozily.

The Alto dropped down. He made a motion for them to follow him and ran down the hall. At the far end, a set of concrete steps ended at a trapdoor. The Alto pushed this open and jumped up into daylight.

They emerged on the sidewalk, just beside the museum. The world was colorless, flickering, the people paused in midstride, the cars still, silent, like toys that a child had carefully set up but then left to play with something else. The sun was colorless. There was no wind, nothing.

"Now what?" Dodger asked.

"Fun," said the Alto, jogging out into the middle of the street. He ran his finger back and forth on the face of his watch.

Dodger heard a screeching of tires and a long black sedan lurched around the corner. It swerved between the frozen cars and pedestrians, the Alto clearly steering it with his finger. He brought it to a skidding stop right in front of them. Dodger saw a hula girl bobbing enthusiastically in the window.

The Alto jumped in. Haley slipped in front. Dodger opened the back door but paused. "Come on," shouted Haley.

"Where are we going?" he asked, though he thought he knew.

"Juliette," said Haley. "You know its location, don't you?"

"I do . . ." said Dodger, but he didn't get into the car yet. He'd been looking back up the street toward the Denny's, and now he saw that there, among the few people paused walking this way and that was Harry, caught in midrun. He'd probably been coming after Dodger, to try to apologize, to explain more, to help him.

"What is it?" Haley asked, following his gaze.

He looked at Harry. Back at the purring car beside him.

"We need to move," urged the Alto.

Dodger sighed to himself, and felt a new kind of emptiness inside. "I'm going to go," he said quietly, not knowing if he wished his dad could hear him or not. The confusion returned. *Lied to me my whole life. Made me feel like I was a failure when he was really just*

*trying to get over what had happened to me . . . and then
. . . Brought me out on this trip hoping we'd figure something out. He wanted to find Juliette, too, not that he knew
what it was. . . .*

But right now, if Dodger really did want to get to
Juliette, his frozen father wasn't going to be able to get
him there. These people were.

He slid into the backseat and slammed the door.
"Punch it!" he shouted.

"I don't follow," said the Alto blankly. In the rearview mirror, Dodger saw him looking up, almost like
he was trying to find a thought inside his head.

"It means go!" said Haley.

"Ah, affirmative." He gunned the sedan forward.

They hurtled down the flickering street. Ahead
was a blurry barrier, like looking out from beneath
the surface of a pool. The Alto crushed the gas pedal
and the sedan hurtled through the barrier, out of the
sphere of missing time. The car convulsed, fishtailed
wildly, then the Alto regained control and they sped
away, out of Roswell and across the golden desert.

chapter

Suza Raines was getting suspicious. As she slapped at her alarm clock, she wondered: *Am I the only one who hates getting up in the morning?* She sighed and slipped out of bed without looking at the clock. For a moment she thought: *Put on your glasses, dummy,* but then stopped. She didn't wear glasses. Never had.

Fifteen minutes later she was out on the front porch and realized that she was up earlier than usual, because there were Mr. Davis and MacDougals. Mr. Davis was literally *in* the road, sitting on his knees and rubbing his head.

How did I end up out here so early? Suza thought.

She got on her bike and rode off.

"Hey wait—" Mr. Davis called to her.

As Suza started down the hill, a strange thought passed through her mind: *Next time I take it— Next time I take it— Next time I take it— Next time I take it—*

But as soon as the thought arrived, the rush of wind swept it away, and Suza coasted on to a perfectly normal day.

Juliette, AZ, April 25, 6:43 a.m.

Suza Raines was getting suspicious. She'd been lying awake for minutes in the deep blue silence, staring at the ceiling. Outside she could hear the birds chirping in their pre-sunrise frenzy. Through her wall, she could hear those short, yucky snores that Angie always made.

What am I waiting for? she thought. Because she was waiting for something. Why else would she be awake *before* her alarm clock?

The numbers on my clock will be wrong, she thought. *All the numbers will be wrong.*

Suza put on her glasses, then turned and saw that the red digits looked like a line of symbols instead. Her thoughts went on predicting in a way that didn't surprise her: *The music will be wrong, too. And I know why. It's because something's wrong with this day. And there's something I need to do to stop it.* She couldn't remember— Wait, there was something.

The metal key, she thought. *When did I see it?*

On this same day, she thought to herself. *One of the other times that it happened.*

This day had happened before?

Yes, I already know that, she reminded herself. *I've been repeating this day over and over. That's why I keep thinking that I have to take it. The key.*

But how could this day be repeating? How was that possible?

I already know that, too. Because of them. The ones who brought me here.

Brought her here? That thought caused a cold tremor.

Yes, I've been told that I live here, like, programmed to think that, but deep down inside I know that I don't. I was brought here, and those people in the other room . . . they're not my real parents.

Lying in her bed, fists clenched beneath the covers, Suza began to leak tears from the corners of her eyes. It was all true! She had finally figured it out. She had finally *remembered.*

How long have I been gone?

Months, maybe more, she thought to herself. *I don't really know, because every time this day starts over, I can't quite remember, but part of me does. I'm one of only a few who have been able to resist their control, and . . .*

We have a plan.

That's right. That was it. The plan! They'd been piecing it together for months. *And my part in the plan is to get that piece of metal and take it to the observatory like AJ told me. I have to do it secretly, before they know that I'm malfunctioning and try to reset me. I have to do it while I remember—*

But even though these thoughts were such a huge relief, they also felt like too much. It was too much to comprehend, too much to do . . .

I have to, quick, now, now now—

Suza sobbed, because now she could see them. Steph. Her mom. Amber, her home. Oh, she missed them so much.

Come on, Suza! she thought to herself, trying to fight the tide of sadness. If she could just do this . . . *I'll get to see them. I have to move, have to GO! Now!*

Suddenly Suza's alarm clock blared to life with that weird, ancient-sounding music.

"No!" Suza screamed. The sound tore through her sanity. It was too much! She couldn't do it. "I CAN'T! I CAN'T! MOOMM!!!!"

There was a thump from beyond the wall, as her dad or Angie was startled awake.

SUZA, a voice spoke up in her head. CALM DOWN AND STOP THIS N—

But Suza drowned it out with her screaming. "MOMMMM!"

Now a searing pain erupted behind her left ear, but even that couldn't stop her.

"MOMMMM!"

Her bedroom door burst open. Suza looked up to see Angie in her blue robe—followed by four small men in orange jumpsuits, yellow hard hats, and black boots and goggles. They converged on her bed, their smooth faces leaning over her.

"NO!!! MOM!!! MOM!!!"

And then everything washed away in orange light once more.

THREE

Gila National Forest, NM, July 6, 8:36 p.m.

Haley watched the boy named Dodger through the rearview mirror. He was slouched, his head lolled back against the seat, eyes closed.

She wanted to give him time to adjust. After all, she'd needed some. The first night after she'd left her parents, on the journey west across Arkansas and Oklahoma, she'd felt like a dry fried thing lying in the road. The smushed version of her former self. She'd spent hours going back and forth about whether leaving had been the right thing to do, whether it could possibly have been a good idea to strike out on her own with this strange man in black, until her thoughts were reduced to a low, broken hum.

She'd wondered about her parents, wondered what they were doing. Had they headed west, like she'd told them? How were they holding up? *They're a mess, you know they are,* she'd thought bitterly to herself. And that was all her fault.

Sometime after dawn, she'd actually slept, a bunch as it turned out, almost until noon. Despite the questions and regret, there was also a kind of stern calm that had settled over her. There was no more lying, no more trying to figure out where the story would lead next. Now, she knew: The Alto had access to the purchase records of the other fellowship winner's debit card. He was heading south and east. By late morning of the 6th, the Alto had guessed that Roswell was his destination.

Now they had him, and he looked much like she had: smushed.

Haley turned to the Alto. He was driving, motionless. This guy never had a scratch or an itch or needed to change his seating position or anything. In the nearly forty-eight hours since they'd left Fort Bluff, he'd only slept two hours, each one at dawn in a rest area. He'd lain on his side on the long vinyl front seat and immediately fallen asleep, like someone had shut off a switch, while Haley had gone to get snacks. His alarm had gone off exactly sixty minutes later and off they went again.

Haley had asked him how he could survive like that.

"The mind can be trained," the Alto had replied.

And yet the Alto's mind seemed to be his least reliable part.

"What took you so long, back in the museum?" Haley asked him now.

The Alto shrugged. "Nothing. I was in position; I just wanted to wait until the moment of maximum surprise."

"Yeah, well that was super fun," Haley muttered. "I thought you said the agents wouldn't try another public Missing Time Field like that. You said it was too risky for them."

The Alto shrugged. "That was before they failed in their attempts to get the two of you separately. And besides, Roswell is an exception. Because of the town's notoriety in connection with UFO's, nobody's going to believe reports of a Missing Time Event *there*. Can't cry wolf too many times, right, Holly?" The Alto reached out and flicked the tiny smiling hula girl on the dashboard. She bobbed in agreement, her tan grass skirt ruffling.

Haley looked at the doll, then back at the Alto. He'd done this a couple times before, conferring with the plastic doll and then flicking her, as if her springy bouncing was an actual response. "You know that's weird, right?"

"What?"

"Talking to a hula doll."

"Holly is my copilot," said the Alto in what seemed to be complete seriousness.

"You don't spend enough time with real people."

"Real people?" said the Alto. "I've seen real people these days. It seems to me that a hollow plastic doll isn't much different."

"Well, that's cynical."

"Or just experience," said the Alto. "Anyway, it was risky to try an MT Field in the middle of broad daylight, even if it was in Roswell. But worth it to try to get both of you at once, and because we're obviously getting close." Upon saying this, the Alto reached to his wrist and fidgeted with the charm bracelet.

Haley glanced up at the darkening sky. The sun had set behind a line of rock mountains, spraying golden beams across the purple. "So they'll come again."

"Without question. That is, if they can find us."

Haley watched the high country pass by. Crumbly rock hills dotted with yellow grass. Dry valleys strewn with boulders, deep in shadows. Stands of pine trees here and there. A rickety fence ran alongside the road: low posts with barbed wire strung between. They saw a herd of brown cows standing there chewing at the tough grass. They gazed at Haley forlornly with their wet, brown eyes. In the distance, giant white windmills lined a bare spiny ridge, spinning slowly. All of this beneath a sweeping, cloudless sky. It was a vast country, beautiful and stark. It filled her with a sense of space, of grandeur, and limitless potential, but also, it was lonely.

Haley got out her tracking map. She'd written Dodger's coordinates down in the right margin. She ran her fingers in from the left and the top so that they met at the blank spot where Juliette was supposedly located. Currently they were on a small road winding through the Gila National Forest in western New Mexico. It was about eight more hours to the coordinates. The question remained though: what to do when they got there.

They'd compared notes once they were out of Roswell, Haley telling Dodger about the Missing Time Events, the mining company, and how something was being put in the ground at each of these sites. Also that people were being taken from each town.

Dodger had told Haley and the Alto about the radio station he could hear from Juliette, and about the orange crystal. He'd explained the strange cavern beneath Lucky Springs, with the doors and the giant orb of crystal, and together they'd decided that there was only one explanation: There must be one of these spherical rooms—Dodger thought it was called an amplification node, which led Haley to wonder *what* exactly was being amplified—beneath each missing time town. What were the aliens going to do with these nodes once they had been installed? And why were they taking the abductees?

"And how can you *talk* to this orange rock?" Haley had asked. "Or hear this radio?"

"I don't want to talk about it," Dodger had said, before laying his head back and exiting the conversation.

For the moment, they were still heading to the Juliette coordinates, with no further plan.

Haley looked at the GPS on the Alto's dashboard. "Wouldn't it have been faster to take the highway?" Interstate 40 was north of them.

"Affirmative," said the Alto, "but that's where they'd be expecting us to go."

Haley looked around the boundless countryside. "Yeah, but out here we're so exposed."

"Again: *if* they find us."

Haley checked the rearview mirror again. "What do you think his deal is?" she asked the Alto quietly.

The Alto was silent for a moment. "He's been through a lot," he replied. "I'm sure he'll tell us when he's ready."

Haley nodded. "You sound like you can relate."

"So do you," the Alto replied. A moment passed with only the humming of tires on the road, before he spoke again. "When I was younger, all I wanted to do was get out and see everything there was to see. I thought I could push the boundaries of the world without consequence, but I was wrong."

"What do you mean?" Haley asked.

"Every experience, every journey changes you," said the Alto. "It's good, but it's risky, too."

"Risky how?"

"If you change too much, you'll no longer be what you were. There's a balance. Go too far and you become a foreigner even to yourself."

"I don't see how that's possible," said Haley, but the idea had caused a nervous flash inside her. She wondered: Who would she be after this adventure?

"It happens one choice at a time," said the Alto. "So gradually that you don't even know until you look back. One day you're in high school and dreaming of getting away from home, the next you are enlisting in special forces, then next running guns for rebels in . . . in . . ." The Alto gazed up into his eyebrows again, searching his head. "Then you take the job after that, going farther, and then the next one that sounds the most amazing yet. You agree to have your identity changed, because of course you can't be

303

discovered. Then you agree to have your parents' identities removed for their own safety. You agree to have certain operations wiped from your memory, again, and again, until you have a hard time remembering what you tried to keep."

"New map," said Haley quietly.

"What's that?" the Alto asked.

"Nothing, just, I kinda know what you're talking about," said Haley. "Well, the thirteen-year-old version." She thought about what the Alto had said. How it had happened one choice at a time, a step-by-step process that had led to his current situation. And she wondered: Had her choices so far, lying to her parents, leaving them . . . had those been the first steps on her journey to becoming someone whose best friend was a hula doll?

After a few miles of silent driving, the sky cooling to black, Haley asked, "So, how do you go far, but not too far?"

The Alto shrugged. "You're asking the wrong amnesiac. I'm not sure you have a choice. Some of it's just how you're programmed."

"Programmed? What is that supposed to mean?"

"I mean," said the Alto, "that when it comes to the big choices in life, even if you did your life over again, you'd probably still make the same decisions, because that's who you are."

"So," said Haley, "does that mean that we would end up out here every time?"

"Perhaps."

Haley wondered about that. It was comforting in a way: Like, maybe Haley hadn't needed to worry about how she *didn't* get those other fellowships, because this was where she was destined to end up anyway. Maybe the wilds of New Mexico were on her map, just like Thorny Mountain was on Maddy's or the JCF was Bradley's.

"Where are we?" Dodger spoke up from the back.

"Almost to Arizona," said the Alto.

Dodger sat up. Haley saw him rubbing his forehead. She reached down to the supply of food on the floor and turned around with a clear plastic container that was all steamed up. "Dinner?" she asked. "Well, breakfast, actually. Pancakes, from a truck stop. You know, breakfast served all day."

Dodger just looked at the box.

Maybe pancakes weren't his thing. "I had no idea what you'd want to eat," said Haley, backpedaling, "but I remembered that after I escaped from those agents, not to mention meeting mister man-in-black here, I was like zombie hungry. And I mean, nothing says *brraainns* like pancakes!" Haley almost threw a hand over her mouth. She couldn't believe this ridiculous stream coming out! What was with her?

Dodger was eyeing her. Haley noticed that he had a sort of piercing gaze. Not like action-hero-piercing, more like he was literally trying to figure out what her deal was, like she was speaking a foreign language. "Sorry," she said quickly. "I just, um, thought pancakes were sorta easy. You know, comfort food. There are eggs in there, too."

Dodger took the box. "Thanks," he mumbled, his expression blank. Haley was about to chalk this up as further evidence that he thought she was weird, but then she reminded herself that he was still recovering from the escape. She turned back around and heard Dodger take a couple bites. When he spoke again, quietly, it was in a zombie's low guttural growl. *"Pannncakesss . . ."*

Haley laughed and felt a little stir. "It's nice to have someone around other than Mr. Serious," she said, cocking a thumb at the Alto.

She heard Dodger chuckle a little at this, but then she heard the Alto sigh, and found him rubbing that bracelet again. "Christine . . ." he said quietly to himself, and then shook his head.

"What?" Haley asked.

"Nothing," said the Alto.

"Okay . . ." said Haley.

"So," Dodger asked between bites, "you're like, a Man in Black, or what?"

The Alto flicked the plastic hula doll on his dashboard. "Remember the Men in Black, Holly? Those were good times." He cocked his head toward Dodger. "I am a person for hire. I am adept at certain things."

"So you do, like, secret missions and stuff?"

"Affirmative."

"What's the coolest place you've ever gone for a mission?"

"I don't remember most of them, but I think I was in Antarctica, and that was neat. Another time I might have briefly been on the International Space Station."

Haley peered at him. "Come on, really?"

"Oh, and Mall of America was pretty cool," the Alto added.

Haley just shook her head. "We need to make a plan. What are we going to do when we get to Juliette?" She turned to the Alto. "What did Alex Keller think we should do?"

"She said that she would be in touch with more information," said the Alto. "But first, she had to get her and her dad off the grid, to assure that the aliens didn't come after them, too."

"She's going to call you?" Haley asked.

"Affirmative," said the Alto. "I gave her the sequence of prepaid phones that I am using, a new one each day. Hopefully we will hear from her soon."

"I wonder if they got her," said Haley, glancing out into the twilight.

"She didn't sound like someone trained in avoiding alien encounters," said the Alto. "And I believe her dad may be a bit of a crank."

"Okay," said Haley, turning back to Dodger. "So, if I'm understanding this right, and if Juliette's not on any map, then it's not even going to *be* there when we get there, right? And how is that possible again?"

"It's in a time loop, stuck repeating a day in 1994," said Dodger. "At least, I think."

"The whole town," said Haley, trying to picture it. "And so the people inside . . . they don't know what's happening to them?"

"I don't think so," said Dodger. "At least, their radio DJ seems to have no idea."

"That would make sense with testing trial protocol," said the Alto.

"What do you mean?" Haley asked.

"Well, when you are running tests, experiments, you want everything to be the same each time except for the variables you're testing."

"Okay," said Haley, thinking of science class, "so, the people are the test subjects, and the test is . . . the day? And they have to keep repeating it."

"More like the people are the rats, and Juliette is the maze," said Dodger.

"Okay, so the people are being brought there, then run through different tests. Since the day is always the same, they can see how the tests work. But," Haley wondered aloud. "What are the aliens testing? And what does it have to do with putting chunks of that crystal underground all over the country?"

"All over the world," said Dodger. "That's what it looked like on the map I saw."

"They must be setting up to do something on a global scale," said the Alto.

Haley tried to imagine it: going to bed each night thinking the next day would come, all the plans and hopes, only to wake up and start all over again. And to not even know it? Was there a worse nightmare than to have the possibility taken from your life?

Haley's thoughts were interrupted. She noticed the Alto whispering to himself, a word, over and over. "Bliss . . ." And he was fiddling with that bracelet.

"What?" Haley asked again.

"Hmm?" The Alto seemed to shake out of a trance.

"You just said something," said Haley. "It sounded like 'Bliss.'" She peered at him, but the Alto's face remained its usual blank, his eyes on the road.

"Bliss . . . Bliss . . ." He seemed to be running the word over his tongue, as if he was trying to get to know it. "It's—something, familiar to me. I'm not sure what."

"You knew about the sun-falling-to-earth thing the other night, too," said Haley suspiciously. "What exactly is it that you know about all this stuff?"

The Alto shrugged. "I don't know anything . . . at least as far as I know."

Haley frowned at him. "You know that's a ridiculous answer, right?"

"Hey, sometimes it's hard to know what you know," said Dodger.

Haley looked from one to the other. "Is this a boy thing?"

"Maybe," said Dodger, and he finally smiled. "Sorry."

Haley looked away, surprised by a thought she'd just had. There was no time for considering whether this Dodger character was cute or not.

Then she heard that jangle from beside her again. When she turned to see the Alto fiddling with his bracelet yet again, she held out her hand and said, "Okay, that's it. Hand it over."

"What?" said the Alto.

"The bracelet. Give it. Now."

The Alto glanced at her, frowning. Haley figured he would refuse, but then he sighed and slipped the chain off his wrist. "I don't know where I got it," he said as he handed it to Haley.

Haley turned the bracelet over in her fingers. The

chain was a tarnished silver color. Five little charm pendants hung off it. They were oblong, flat polished discs of a silver-gray stone. Each had a crude shape etched into it. On the first disc was a rounded circle, possibly the letter C or a crescent moon. The next one showed three vertical lines, slightly wavy, the middle line the shortest and the right-most line the tallest. The next charm had what looked like IX, either letters or Roman Numerals. The fourth had a little sun and a line like the horizon, and there were two little vertical lines above the sun. And the last charm had a symbol that Haley couldn't decipher. It looked sort of like a yin-yang.

Haley looked at the Alto. "Did you make these?"

He shrugged. "I don't know. Maybe? Or someone gave them to me . . . Christine . . . no. Charlene."

Haley considered the symbols. "You keep saying 'C' names. Someone you're trying to remember." She held up the crescent shape. "Maybe this C is to remember her name."

The Alto nodded. "That is what it feels like.

When I look at that C, I feel a hollow place where the name should be, like a puzzle with a missing piece. Sometimes I even think I can see her face, but . . . I can't be sure."

"And . . ." said Haley. She held up the symbol with the little sun. "Is this the 'night sun descending?' Like we saw the other night?"

"I believe so," said the Alto. "Those are the only two I have figured out."

"Why would you be wearing a symbol for those crystals falling to earth?" Haley wondered aloud. "Unless . . . You know something about all this."

"I . . . I'm not sure," said the Alto. "I mean, yes, I do.

"About a year and a half ago, I woke up in a hospital in Phoenix. I literally had no memory of where I'd been. Everything before that is this big blank. I mean, I remember snippets of earlier jobs, and most of my childhood, but whatever I was doing right before I woke up in Phoenix has been . . . erased. But then I found this bracelet, sewn into the cuff of my pants. Wherever I'd been, I smuggled it out."

"So how did you end up with us?" Haley asked.

"Well, since then I've been taking odd jobs for hire, run-of-the-mill black-ops stuff, trying to piece things together, until this job posted."

Haley raised an eyebrow. "Posted? What, is there

like a job board for mercenaries?"

The Alto smiled. "Of course. But it's on a site whose server can only be accessed from about twenty computers in the entire country. I was at the one in the basement of a preschool in Mississippi when I saw Keller's post looking for help. Usually there are multiple bids for a black ops job. But nobody wanted this one. And when I read about the missing time and Juliette, it felt right."

Haley looked back at the bracelet. "So, you've got the falling crystals. And someone's name that begins with C. And no idea about these other three?"

"No. I don't even know what puzzles those pieces are missing from yet, so to speak."

"Do you think the aliens took your memories?" Dodger asked.

The Alto looked up into his brow. "That is the most likely scenario . . . right, Holly?" He reached out and flicked the doll. Holly bounced vigorously, her spring squeaking in the lingering silence.

Haley sensed that the Alto had shared enough for the moment. She handed back the bracelet. "Okay," she continued. "Well, so, anyway, let's assume Juliette is a lab . . . for testing whatever they plan to do globally. If we're going to free those people, and the planet, then we're going to have to get in there."

"Free them?" said the Alto. "That's a different

mission than you were talking about two days ago. What happened to just getting the story?"

Haley's motor had started to whir, and her thoughts surprised her. "Well, it's bigger than that now, isn't it? Whatever this is, it's dangerous . . . to everyone. I mean, if they're installing this technology all over the world, what if the goal is to have us all repeating the same day?"

"That may be, but stopping them it is a good deal more dangerous to us," said the Alto.

Haley didn't like that thought, and yet she snapped right back at him. "Is that a reason not to do it?"

And now the Alto smiled. "Of course not. Danger is always preferable."

Until it's too dangerous, Haley thought to herself, her insides twisting. *Are you sure you want to do this?* The doubt demon had a good point. She'd gone from trying to uncover a possible alien conspiracy to trying to stop one.

"What do you think?" she asked Dodger.

He sighed. "I just wanted to get to Juliette . . . but, I mean, sure. I guess. We could save the world, too."

Haley nodded. It wasn't a very enthusiastic response, but hopefully Dodger would come around.

"So, if I understand this correctly," said the Alto, "our new mission parameters are to get into Juliette and somehow disrupt the time loop program."

"Yes," said Haley. "Freeing Juliette should be the key to exposing the rest of the plot. Which brings us right back where we started. First, we need a way in. I don't suppose they'll be a door with a welcome mat when we get there."

"A door . . ." said Dodger. "Oh . . . wait." He sat up, like a light had gone off in his brain. "I think I could get in there, and maybe get us all in."

"How?"

"When I was underneath Lucky Springs, in that room I told you about with the giant crystal, I kind of interfaced with it."

"Interfaced?" Haley asked.

"Yeah, like, I uploaded into it, but the point is, I had the option to travel to a bunch of places. And I think one of them was caves beneath Juliette. So, I think if I had wanted, I could have beamed myself to Juliette right then. How far is it to go back to Lucky Springs?"

Haley decided to leave her pile of questions aside for the moment, most of which concerned how Dodger could have *uploaded* himself into a rock. Instead, she pulled out her Tracking Map. "Too far," she said, "but if you're right and there's one of these rocks beneath each abducted town, then . . ." She ran her fingers over her map again. "Here!" she said. "Mesa Top, Arizona. It's the closest abductee town to us. Southwest of here, not really on the way to Juliette but a lot closer than Lucky Springs. They had a Missing Time Event about ten years ago, and they have a UCA mine. What if we go there?"

"If I were those agents," said the Alto, "I would not expect that."

Haley looked back at Dodger. "Yeah," he said.

"Okay, then. That's the new plan. Should we try to get there before dawn? When no one's awake?"

"Affirmative." The Alto plugged Mesa Top into his GPS. "We should stop in a couple hours for me to engage in sleep, then we can be there by four a.m."

Haley sank back into her seat. Outside, the stars had begun to bejewel the dark in earnest. Beneath her excitement for the new plan, she also felt fresh worry. This was yet another decision they were making *not* to go back. *One choice at a time,* the Alto had said . . . but again, this felt like the choice they *had* to make.

And she had new questions now, too, beyond what was happening in Juliette and around the globe. Haley now found herself wondering: Who were these aliens? And where were they from?

Haley looked up at the stars and wondered how

far you had to go to get those answers, and she wondered what she would do with the part of herself that, despite these dangerous choices she'd already made, was still yearning to find out.

Apache National Forest, AZ, July 7, 12:36 a.m.

Later, in the unknown void of dark, Dodger awoke to find the car silent and still. He sat up. The front seat was empty . . . no, not empty. The Alto was curled on his side, asleep. There was a timer perched on the dashboard, which read 39 minutes, 40 seconds, and was counting down. Dodger wondered where Haley was. The windows were all fogged.

He grabbed the blanket that the Alto had provided him with and got out of the car. The air was cool and sweet-smelling. The car was parked in an inky patch beneath a cluster of pine trees. Beyond that was a wide, barren slope and then distant folds of desert hills sketched in silver. Here and there were dome shapes, little cinder cones from long-ago volcanic activity. Dodger saw a lump a little ways from the trees, like a person sitting.

He headed across the slope. Tiny, sharp-edged volcanic rocks crunched beneath his feet. He saw that Haley was wrapped in a blanket, knees pulled up. And he heard a sniffle, like crying.

Dodger wondered if he should leave her alone, but then her head snapped around, probably at the sound of his footfalls. Dodger saw her wiping quickly at her nose and eyes.

"Hey," he said. "Mind if I sit?"

"No," said Haley, her voice hoarse.

Dodger dropped down beside her but immediately jumped up. "Ow." The volcanic rocks were like needles.

"Here," said Haley. She scooted over, making room on a pad of grass and dirt, a little island in the cinders.

"Thanks." Dodger sat beside her and looked up. "Wow."

"Yeah," said Haley. "I have never seen so many stars. And the Milky Way—it's usually just a smudge, but here it's, like, feathery."

Dodger followed the brushed edges of the galaxy, stretching up from the horizon and bowing overhead.

"We're at a pretty high elevation," he said. "That's why things are so clear. Well, that and"—he swept his hand around—"middle of nowhere."

"I can't even pick out the constellations," said Haley.

Dodger gazed at the sky. One of his favorite maps at home was of the night sky. Haley was right. The constellations were irrelevant with all these other stars.

"It's just crazy," Haley was saying. "I mean, there are really aliens, which means . . . How many other worlds do you think are out there? There could be hundreds, *millions*. That's so many, and like, compared to that, we're just a little speck. Isn't that freaky?"

Dodger hadn't really thought about it. "I don't know—why would that be freaky?"

"Well, just because, like, it's not just stars and comets and stuff out there—it's, like, different ecosystems and different civilizations, and each one has its own customs and holidays and pets and favorite foods and . . . it's so much. I was thinking, at the beginning of this trip, about how the world was so big, with so many details, that there was no way you could see it all. But if there are alien worlds, too, that takes it to a whole other level. It's . . ."

Dodger heard her sniffle again, and a little clicking sound. He looked over and saw Haley blinking at tears again. "You okay?" he asked.

She huffed. "So stupid," she said, motioning to her leaking face. "I wanted to get out here, on this adventure, out in the big world."

"That's not stupid at all," said Dodger, realizing that he'd never thought of this trip as an *adventure*. He'd always thought of adventures as being more . . . fun. It occurred to him now that maybe this was what an explorer's life was actually like: lonely, full of tough choices, danger, and now and then a talk with a fellow adventurer by moonlight, in some desolate place. That last part didn't seem so bad, but the other facets had so far proven to be harder than Dodger could have predicted.

"Yeah, well," Haley was saying, "except now, thinking about how big the universe is, about all the possibility . . . it's making me miss home. I miss my silly little town of Green Haven, my house, my parents . . . and that stinks! I've been feeling so bad since I left them, I'm beginning to wonder if I was even made for all this. It's like I got stuck with a faulty heart."

Haley knocked on her chest with her fist. "Sorry, ma'am," she said in a male voice, "this ticker won't be able to handle the big adventures you had planned." She sniffled and wiped her nose on her sleeve.

Hearing Haley made Dodger feel a little guilty. "I don't think I've missed my dad yet," he said, except how many times had he pictured Harry frozen on

Main Street in Roswell? A hundred? Once a minute? So maybe that was missing him. "At least you got to call your parents and tell them what was happening," said Dodger.

"Would your dad have any idea about the missing time, or that kind of thing?" Haley asked.

"Oh, he'll have a pretty good idea of what happened," said Dodger. "At least, the alien part." Dodger glanced at Haley. He had been about to tell her more but then held it back. Haley caught him looking.

"What?" she asked.

She had a kind of clear gaze, he noticed, behind the starry reflections in her glasses. Her eyes seemed wide-open, taking you as you were. And they seemed to want the truth. Or maybe it felt like she could be trusted with the truth. Sheesh. It suddenly occurred to Dodger that Haley was maybe cute, too. He hadn't really noticed before now. And she also looked hurt and lonely out here, just like he was. *Tell her,* he thought. But normally, he didn't really tell anyone anything. . . . Then again, nothing was really normal anymore.

"It happened to us before," he said.

"What did?"

"The missing time. Well, to my dad. When I was really little I . . . I was abducted."

"Whoa," said Haley. "You mean by . . ." She glanced up. *"Them?"*

"Yeah," said Dodger. "I don't remember it, but I think I always sensed it, at least that something had happened. They didn't take me forever, like the people in Juliette. I was gone for eight days and then I got put back. I think that's why I can hear the radio and use the crystal and stuff. I think I've even been to Juliette. Like, they took me there. That's why the caverns looked familiar when I was uploaded."

Dodger felt like he'd uncorked himself and now he was pouring out into the night. He'd never said any of this. Never considered putting it into words. He half expected Haley to back away from him like he was actually an alien.

Instead, she rubbed his arm. "That's crazy, Dodger. I'm sorry."

Dodger nodded. "My parents never told me about the abduction. I had no idea until this afternoon."

"They were probably trying to protect you," said Haley.

"Maybe," said Dodger, "but my whole life I figured that they thought I was a screwup, that they were disappointed in me, and I already felt weird inside and that vibe from them only made me feel worse . . . but all that time they were actually feeling guilty about the abduction and worrying about if my weird behavior was because of the aliens. It's like we were going around in circles, over and over."

As the words came out of his mouth, Dodger was kind of amazed by what he was saying. It was almost like listening to someone else speaking.

"Ha," Haley chuckled.

"What?"

"Lines need to be straight," said Haley. "You said going in circles, and that's just something I'd been thinking when I was back with my family. It's not really the same, but sort of. They were driving me nuts. I didn't know how I was going to survive the whole trip with them."

"Ditto," said Dodger. "I just can't believe they didn't tell me. I mean, my dad had to know that if we came on this trip, we might run into aliens. Why do that if he didn't want me getting abducted again?"

"Maybe he was looking for answers," said Haley. "It sounds like your parents felt guilty and sad about the abduction, and they never really even knew exactly what had happened to you while you were gone. That's probably part of why they didn't tell you. Maybe your dad wanted to know more, so he could make it make sense to you."

Dodger thought about their conversation in the Denny's. How tortured Harry had seemed. And something was suddenly so obvious that he couldn't believe he'd never realized it before. "He wanted to find Juliette just as much as me."

"Probably," Haley agreed.

The thought stunned Dodger. All those hours he and Harry had spent in the car, not speaking . . . they'd both been secretly hoping for the same thing! Dodger almost laughed. Unbelievable. And Dodger probably knew what Harry was thinking right now, wherever he was: *He thinks they took me,* Dodger thought to himself. *He thinks he failed to keep me safe, again.*

Dodger felt his insides twist with guilt. He hadn't meant for that. When he'd decided to leave, he'd been angry, furious. And didn't he have every right to be? His entire life had been a lie! And yet his dad had been trying, had maybe been trying all along, but Dodger couldn't see it. . . . He rubbed his hands over his face. "I am an idiot."

"Here we are," said Haley, "two idiots. But at least we're two idiots who are about to save the planet from aliens. Right?"

Dodger laughed. He looked at her and they shared a smile and Dodger felt something kind of electric lighting up his nerves. "Right." He tried to think of something funny to say, something that would be easy to talk about instead of all the heavy business of their current predicament. "Seen any shooting stars out here?"

"No luck yet," said Haley, "but I haven't really been looking that hard."

They both looked up. Dodger tried to let his gaze go wide. "My aunt says it's a good omen not to see a shooting star," he said.

"How so?" Haley asked.

"Well, you're supposed to wish on a shooting star, so she said that if you *didn't* see one, that meant that all your wishes had been fulfilled. Like, you wouldn't see one unless you needed it. She's kind of a hippie. My dad can't stand her."

"Oh," said Haley. "That's kind of a cool theory, though. I mean, a different spin. Like the universe is looking out for you."

"I guess," said Dodger. "I think she just made it up so we wouldn't be disappointed." Then again, if Haley liked the idea, maybe he could, too. He looked around for something else to show her. "Check it out," he said, pointing to the horizon. "There's Mars."

Haley followed his finger to the little orange dot. "Oh, neat."

"I think," said Dodger, shifting around, "Jupiter is going to be coming up here somewhere soon—"

"Oh, hey!" Haley smacked Dodger's shoulder and pointed. "Over there! Shooting star!"

Dodger scanned the sky. And then he saw a little white light to the east, falling earthward.

Except then the light leveled out and started coming straight toward them. "Oh, crap," said Dodger.

"That's not a star, is it?" said Haley. "Come on! We have to get back to the car."

It was coming fast, so fast that Dodger could already make out multiple blinking lights on it. It stopped not far from them, its circular hull glinting in the starlight. Now a brilliant orange beam speared down from its belly, illuminating a patch of forest below. The craft darted a few hundred feet closer, the light scanning over the ground again.

"Come on," Haley whispered. She was in a crouch, tugging on his arm. "We need to hurry—"

"Hold on," said Dodger. He knew she was right. The ship would be here soon, too soon, he feared, for them to even make it to the car. And yet the closer it came, the more Dodger thought that he could *feel* the ship. There was crystal inside it, maybe the ship's power source. And after interfacing with the crystal beneath Lucky Springs, he knew what the magnetic connection felt like. He closed his eyes and he could almost sense the crystal out there, not just as energy and warmth—his body was starting to heat up—but also as intelligence.

In fact, he felt like there was only crystal in the ship. No actual aliens. He could practically picture the interior, a basketball-sized chunk of crystal floating among circuitry. Maybe this was a reconnaissance drone.

It was all Dodger could do not to call out to it, through his mind and the energy currents that connected them, and say, *I'm right here!* Except . . .

"Dodger . . ." Haley's voice was shaking. She yanked on his sweatshirt.

Right, no, despite that connection, he had to remember that he didn't *want* to be found, didn't want to end up in the clutches of those alien agents. The ship zipped closer to them, practically overhead—

"Wait." Dodger suddenly had an idea. If he could feel the crystal, could he instruct it not to find them? It felt possible. He had to try now—

Dodger closed his eyes, reaching out through magnetic energy, until he felt himself touching the warmth of the crystal with his mind, and he thought, *Turn right.*

He peered out of squinted eyes. The ship was still headed right for them. He tried again, harder, pushing all of his mental energy toward the crystal warmth. *Turn right.* And he added *Twenty degrees southeast.*

The ship jagged to the right, ever-so-slightly off its initial course, but far enough that, when the orange light speared down, it illuminated a stand of trees about fifty yards from Haley and Dodger, just south of where the Alto was parked.

Dodger reached out to the craft again. *Continue*

on present course. Somewhere beyond the crystal, he thought he could feel the presence of other forces, like repelling magnets, maybe the aliens who were controlling the ship remotely. They knew something had happened to the ship, maybe could even sense him, but they couldn't quite see him, just like he couldn't see them. Probably better not to linger, though. Dodger pulled back, into himself, and opened his eyes.

"Did you just do that?" Haley whispered.

"Yeah."

Haley was peering at him. "You interfaced again. And made the ship leave."

Dodger nodded.

"Wow," said Haley.

She helped him up. His legs felt rubbery. His head was throbbing. And he felt strangely alone, almost like he missed that connection to the crystal, like it maybe . . . completed him in some way.

They hurried back to the car and woke the Alto. As they pulled back onto the road, they watched the skies for the alien craft. There was a flash, far off. Dodger wondered if it was the UFO, but then he saw the lit silhouette of a tall thunderhead.

They drove on through the night, the car humming over empty roads. Gazing out into the starry dark, in the hollow aftermath of interfacing with the crystal, Dodger found himself sinking back into his head. He thought about what Haley had said, about missing home. After this long day and its revelations, he considered that maybe, for the first time that he could remember, he did, too.

chapter

20

Apache National Forest, AZ, July 7, 3:45 a.m.

At some point, Haley slipped into an uneasy sleep filled with plastic-faced agents and buzzing UFOs. When she woke, it was still night but with the faintest rim of blue on the horizon.

"How's it going?" she asked the Alto.

"Going," said the Alto. He was dead still. "We're on schedule to make Mesa Top in an hour."

"Cool," said Haley. She grabbed a bag of soy crisps from her stash on the floor, then turned back to see if Dodger was awake. He was, staring out the window.

He saw her looking. "Got any more pancakes?" he asked.

"Sorry, Cool Spa flavored soy crisps?"

"What does a Cool Spa taste like?" Dodger asked, taking the package.

"Basically like sour cream and onion," said Haley. She turned to the Alto. "Want any?"

The Alto shook his head. "No food required at this time."

Haley rolled her eyes. "Did you hear that, Holly?" she said, reaching out and flicking the doll. "Your chauffeur doesn't need food. Are we sure he's not a vampire?" She watched the doll bob in agreement. "That is pretty satisfying, actually."

"See?" said the Alto. Haley glanced over and thought she saw the slightest smile.

Haley got a bag of chips for herself and drank some of a now-flat soda. She leaned back in the worn vinyl seat, put her feet up on the dashboard, and watched the night pass. She'd grown kind of fond of this big old car. It smelled like rest areas now, gasoline, salt film and feet, and it didn't help that she'd been wearing the same thing without a shower now going on three hot days. But as a result, it maybe felt homey.

They were passing over high country, currently making wide, slow curves down from a plateau. The land dropped away to the left, down to flats that stretched all the way to the horizon. To the right, a ridgeline stretched away from the road, the eroded edge of the plateau. Knobby rock fingers stuck up out of the dark stands of pine. These rock spires glittered in the pearly combination of light from the stars and the sliver moon.

The ridge ran off to the east. Here and there, a few of the rock spires stuck up on their own, like monuments. Single ones, a double, and one set of three right beside one another, the middle one slightly shorter, the rightmost one the tallest. . . .

Wait a minute.

Haley felt a jolt. "Hey," she said to the Alto. "Look out there."

The Alto glanced in that direction. "What is it? UFO?"

"No, the rocks."

The Alto squinted. "What about the rocks?"

Haley grabbed the Alto's wrist. "Let me see the bracelet again."

The Alto flinched. "The—"

"Just let me see it!"

The Alto yanked his hand away, but then pulled off the bracelet and handed it over to Haley. She flipped through the charms to the one with three vertical lines. Looked back out the window . . .

"Stop the car!"

The Alto brought the car to a screeching halt on the dirt shoulder of the road. Haley jumped out and peered into the distance, then back at the charm.

"What is it?" the Alto asked, he and Dodger joining her.

Haley held out the charm for them to see, and pointed. "Tell me those three rock spires don't look *exactly* like the marks on this charm."

They both looked.

"Looks like a match to me," said Dodger.

The Alto stared out at the rocks. "Bliss . . ." he said faintly.

"This is part of it, isn't it?" Haley asked.

The Alto made his searching face. "I'm not sure, but, if it's on the charms, then she . . . she thought I should remember."

"Who?" Haley asked quickly, hoping the Alto might remember without even realizing it.

"Charlotte . . . C—" He shook his head and looked at the spires again. "Let's just go."

They jumped back in the car and the Alto sped onward. As they went, he tapped his GPS, zooming out from their route. "Looks like there's a road up ahead that heads in that direction. It's unmarked."

They reached the road a minute later. The Alto pulled over a few hundred feet up the hill from it. The road wasn't much more than a dirt track, but it was heading straight toward the fingers.

"Should we check it out?" Dodger asked.

"It will delay our arrival at Mesa Top," said the Alto.

"Yeah," said Haley, "but what if this is another clue about Juliette, or what the aliens are up to, something we need to know?"

She looked at the Alto. It was hard to be sure, but she thought he looked worried. "Are you scared of what you'll find?" she asked.

He didn't answer.

Then a light flashed in the rearview mirror. "Someone's coming," said the Alto. He switched off the car and the lights. "Duck," he said. "Just in case."

Haley heard the groan of a heavy engine approaching. Just as the lights arrived, there was a whine of brakes. A truck passed them, slowing down. It was white, the kind with the little cab and the short, square trailer. As it passed, Haley recited what was painted on its side.

"United Consolidated Amalgamations."

And then she watched as the truck turned onto the little dirt road. "We're going to follow that, right?"

"Affirmative," said the Alto. They watched as the taillights crossed a grassy field and disappeared into pine trees. Then, the Alto pulled onto the road and followed, lights off.

They entered the pines and began to curve back and forth up a gentle incline. Haley felt her nerves racheting tighter.

"I believe," said the Alto, "that I may have worked for those people."

"Wait, you mean the UCA?" Haley asked.

"I do."

They drove slowly, navigating only by the fuzzy predawn light, winding gently but steadily up into forest. Finally, the road left the pine trees. They passed between the rock fingers. Haley saw that they were made of stacked discs of rocks, like something Liam had piled quickly and carelessly. Ahead, the road passed over a steep grassy slope that seemed to end at the night sky.

The Alto stopped the car just below this edge. They got out. There were still faint dust clouds from the truck. They could hear it in the distance and climbed to the top of the ridge, onto a spine of crumbly rocks.

Below, Haley saw a wide, rounded bowl of land, as if someone had scooped out a giant spoonful of a hillside. It was over a mile across, with steep walls around it. She saw the headlights of the truck moving down the side from their perch. Beyond that, the slope flattened out in the middle, in a shadow garden of boulders and little scrub brush.

She looked back again, but the truck was gone. Like it had never been. *What truck?* She thought to herself. *There never was a truck. What are you even doing out here when you're supposed to be going to Mesa Top—*

"Hey." It was the Alto. Haley turned to him. "Did you just feel that?" he asked.

"What?" Haley asked blankly.

"That was the effect of the memory cloaking," said the Alto. "We came here to follow that truck."

"What truck?" said Dodger blankly.

"Look." He pointed back down the slope.

Truck? Haley thought. Oh, that's right, the truck! Haley looked back down and, sure enough, the truck was still there, farther down the steep road. That's right, the UCA truck, the reason they were here. . . .

"Wow," she said. "It was like my brain just went blank."

"Weird," Dodger agreed. "Memory cloaking?"

"Yes," said the Alto. He pointed at the bowl below them. "This area has been protected with a suggestive memory cloak. It makes you forget what you saw, or more accurately, you can't quite focus on what you need to. Your mind wanders."

Haley looked back into the space below them. At the truck . . . but then her gaze slipped up to the far ridgeline, to the fading stars . . . but this time she caught herself. "I felt it that time," she said. "I slipped right off the thought of the truck."

"You have to keep focusing on it," said the Alto.

He pointed at it again.

"Why can you do it?" Haley asked.

"I have been trained to subvert the cloak," said the Alto. "I don't remember the training, but I can feel it kicking in. There is a frequency transmitting here that affects the electrical pattern of your brain waves. The . . ." He searched above his eyes. "Yes, the aliens have a symbiotic relationship with electrical energy, as in that conductive orange rock of theirs. They can use it to control minds, in this case, things unseen, or unremembered. They likely used this same effect to make people forget Juliette when they first put it into the time loop."

"Did you just remember all that?" asked Haley.

"I had the pieces, but seeing this is helping it to come together."

"So," said Haley, "you're saying that there's something here that we can't see?"

"Keep watching the truck," said the Alto.

Haley found it again. The truck had stopped down where the walls of the bowl leveled out. It was paused there. . . . She could feel her brain sliding to other things, but she kept reminding herself: *Watch. The. Truck.*

Then a loud air horn sounded.

The truck began to drive forward.

"Keep watching . . ." the Alto ordered.

"Truck, truck, truck," Dodger repeated to himself.

And then suddenly things began to change. There was a shimmer and a rippling and Haley's vision seemed to swim, and now the truck was on a road, a road lit by lights, leading to . . .

A complex. There was a cluster of central buildings, but most impressive was the ring of giant white satellite dishes around them, aimed at the sky, little red and white lights blinking on their edges.

"Whoa, all of that just appeared out of *noo*-where," said Haley.

"It was always there, but your brain was being tricked to ignore it, until the truck began to go there. Then your brain had the bit of truth necessary to disprove the suggestion of the cloaking."

"Is this UCA's base of operations?" Dodger asked.

"Yes, for Project . . ." The Alto exhaled in relief. "Bliss. This is Project Bliss. I worked here. She did, too."

"The mystery girl?" Haley asked. The Alto nodded. "Okay, so what's Project Bliss?"

"Still working on it," said the Alto, searching up in his brow. "This is the base of operations for setting up those caverns Dodger saw, the . . ."

"Amplification nodes," said Dodger.

"Right," said the Alto. "This will be the control center. And . . ." The Alto stopped, and cocked his ear.

Haley heard it, too. A sound from back the way they'd come. An engine.

"Back to the car," said the Alto.

They ran for the sedan. Haley saw headlights bouncing in the trees. They'd barely reached the car when a vehicle emerged. Haley expected another white truck, but instead it was a long, white mobile home. It careened up the slope toward them, dust billowing behind it, and skidded to a stop. Dodger thought it looked familiar.

"Stop!" a voice shouted from inside.

There was a jostling. The mobile home rocked from side to side. The door popped open. A figure stumbled out into the dust cloud and marched toward them. It took a moment to make out his features in the dust and darkness. He was an old man with square glasses and a white beard. He was wearing sweatpants, a flannel shirt, and a half-moon-shaped helmet covered in tinfoil.

"Don't go any farther!" he shouted, pointing angrily at the Alto. "You've done enough!"

"Who are you?" the Alto called.

"I've seen you before," said Dodger. "You were in the parking lot at Roswell."

The man looked at Dodger, his face changing instantly from furious to composed, like he'd flipped a switch. "Yes, we were about to intercept you there, but then we were caught in a Missing Time Field." He looked back at the Alto and his anger returned. "Who do you *think* I am?" he shouted. "I'm your employer, Gavin Keller!"

Haley saw the Alto's shoulders slump. "Oh," he said.

Gavin marched forward. "You just step away, Mr. the Alto, and leave these children to me. You've got some nerve! Taking them off into the night and dropping off the face of the Earth!"

"Dad!" A young woman was emerging from the mobile home. "Dad, just settle down."

"I'm not going to settle down! I—I . . . This was not supposed to happen! None of this was supposed to happen!"

"What are you talking about?" Haley asked. She was already stunned that this was Gavin Keller. This haggardly dressed, wild-eyed old man in a tinfoil hat was the brains behind her fellowship? At least Alex Keller looked more normal. She was in a black shirt and jeans, smart glasses on. She looked younger, maybe in her twenties.

"I—" Gavin turned to Haley, and his wild, excitable gaze switched off again and he spoke calmly. "Excuse me, Haley, Dodger, my amazing fellowship winners. I hate to be meeting you under these circumstances. What you've discovered is unbelievable!

You should be commended. I—I never dreamed when I started this fellowship that you'd really uncover the truth behind extraterrestrial visitation."

"You didn't?" Haley asked. This disappointed her.

"Well, I *hoped*, of course," Gavin said, "but, I've spent half my life looking into all these theories and never gotten this far. Leave it to young minds unencumbered by assumptions. . . . But I was mainly just trying to put the money to good use, to awaken future generations to the great questions of our time—"

"Hold on," said Haley. "What money?"

Gavin threw his hands in the air. "All of this is my aunt Colleen's fault! She died last year and suddenly I inherited the royalties to a natural gas well on the family property in Colorado. I didn't even know it existed! Turns out it's worth a fortune, all in my name, and I don't want it! I've worked hard to build a life off the grid. I haven't paid taxes in years, not going to give a dime to those warlords in Washington. Everything I need I keep with me, in my house here. I'm a free man with a free mind, open to the possibilities of the universe."

"You live in your mobile home," said Haley.

"I see the world," said Gavin. "The road is my teacher, the horizon my muse!"

Haley made a note to herself to remember this the next time she started freaking out about getting out over the horizon. Ending up like the Alto was not an option, but neither was this.

"And so I thought," Gavin went on, "what better gift could I make of my money than to give youth that same chance I've had? But then YOU!" He pointed at the Alto. "Putting them in danger like this!"

"He's protecting us," said Haley.

"He is not!" shouted Gavin.

"Please keep your voice down," said the Alto.

"Keep my voice down? You have a lot of nerve—"

"Well then, can we talk about this somewhere else?" the Alto asked. Haley saw him glance worriedly back at the ridgeline.

"And give you a chance to take off again?" said Gavin. "Not a chance! You were instructed to get these two out of danger and back to their families! To the FBI, we told you! Do you know the legal trouble we're going to be in because of you? Children are missing because of my fellowship! There will be police, lawyers—all the vultures will be after me!"

"Dad . . ." Alex rubbed his arm. "He's a kind man," she said around him. "Really, he just wanted to do something good."

Haley tried to process what she'd just heard. She turned to the Alto. "You lied," she said. "You said it was too dangerous to turn around, that it was our *mission* to go to Juliette. That Keller wanted us to."

The Alto shrugged. "I didn't lie about the danger," he said to her. "Maybe about what Keller said, but it was my professional opinion that he was not acting in your best interests. Besides," said the Alto, fiddling at his bracelet. "I needed you, too."

"Best interests?" Keller shouted. "You've brought these children further into danger! Tell me how exactly you plan on getting out of this?"

"We were working on it," said the Alto.

Haley stared at him. She supposed she should be angry at him, and yet hadn't Gavin Keller gotten her in much more danger than the Alto had, sending her off to research things that had nearly led to her being abducted? And sure, she was "missing" now, but there were already kids like Suza missing for real.

"How did you find us up here?" the Alto was asking.

"Well," said Gavin proudly, "that was the work of my amazing daughter, who took off the entire summer to help me with this project. Alex?"

Alex had been watching the whole proceeding with a queasy expression. Haley thought she looked like she would rather have been somewhere far away. "More like keeping you out of trouble," said Alex, rolling her eyes. "I've been tracking your meBox's web updates," she said, looking at Dodger.

Dodger seemed shocked by this. "Huh? I couldn't

even get that thing to connect to Wi-Fi."

Alex shrugged. "It's been automatically posting your photos from an app called InstaMe! to your MymeBox page on the *Viva Value!* website. The pictures always include a map indicating where they were taken. All the pictures are black, though."

Dodger shook his head and reached into his pocket. He pulled out the meBox and stared at it. "Why couldn't he just get me an iPod?"

"Now, Haley, Dodger," said Gavin. "I want you both to get in the RV and we will take you to the authorities and put an end to this."

Haley looked from Gavin to the Alto. She felt a flash of longing at the thought: If she got in that RV, they could be back with their parents . . . but no, this wasn't really a choice. She glanced at Dodger and indicated the Alto with her eyes. Dodger nodded.

"We're not going with you," Haley said to Gavin. "We're on a mission to save the people of Juliette. We're the only ones who can do it. Thanks for your fellowship award, but we'll take it from here."

"You—" Gavin seemed to swallow a mouthful of words. "Well, that was an inspiring and brave thing you just said, Haley. I . . . but you!" He turned back to the Alto, as if he had to be mad at someone. "You are *not* getting paid for this." Back to Haley, calm again. "I must insist. We've been in touch with your parents,

we can get you to them and put an end to all this—"
Something distracted him and he whipped back to the
Alto. "What are you doing?"

Haley now noticed that the Alto had walked backward a few paces and was gazing over the edge of the
ridge. "I'm checking to be sure that all your shouting
hasn't attracted any attention."

This idea seemed to surprise Gavin. "Oh . . . and?"

The Alto turned back around. "I asked you to
keep it down," he said.

And then he started to run. His eyes caught
Haley's, and she knew she should be doing the same.

She'd barely turned when the UFO leaped over
the ridge like a pouncing cat.

"My gods!" Gavin exclaimed.

"Dad, come on!" Alex Keller shouted, running
toward the RV.

"The woods!" shouted the Alto. Haley grabbed
Dodger's arm and sprinted after him, past Gavin,
who was staring, awestruck, at the ship.

"They're really here!" he exclaimed. "They're
really—"

Zzap!

Gavin vanished in sizzling orange light.

Haley and Dodger followed the Alto toward the
trees. He vaulted over a giant fallen log. They all
ducked behind it and turned around.

Out in the grass, the Alto's sedan began to peel out.

Haley saw that the Alto was using his watch to control the car. It spun around and started racing down the road away from them.

"What are you doing?" Haley whispered.

"The Alto tapped rapidly at a holographic display on his watch. "Creating a diversion."

The UFO zipped after the car and out of sight.

"Nice," Haley said—

But then another craft darted over the ridge.

"Rats," said the Alto.

The second craft bobbed over the clearing, swaying back and forth. Its orange beam scanned the RV.

There was a light snap from beside them and the sound of breaths.

Alex Keller appeared, ducking beside them. "I told him," she said, panting, "just keep the money, buy a new RV or something, but no. . . . I was supposed to be doing a law internship in London this summer, but he was having a fit, so—"

"Sshh!" the Alto instructed.

"Stupid family," said Alex.

"Sorry," said Haley. "They make it hard." She wondered what it would be like to have a dad like that. But more importantly, she wondered how they were going to get out of this.

"What do we do?" she whispered to the Alto.

The Alto was looking around. "Working on it. . . ." Then his eyes seemed to pause on Dodger.

Haley turned and saw that Dodger's eyes were closed, and he was mumbling to himself.

"What are you doing?" Haley hissed.

Dodger half opened his eyes. "Trying to tell it to go away," he said. "Its orders are coming from close by, stronger than back in the mountains, maybe in that complex . . . but I think I can do it."

Dodger closed his eyes even harder. He put his fingers to his temples and kept mumbling. Haley thought it sounded like he was saying "Turn south thirty degrees" over and over.

She looked up. The craft paused, then started off away from them. It disappeared behind the trees.

"You're doing it," said Haley.

The craft jumped back overhead.

"Can't. . . ." Dodger winced. "The controllers are fighting back. They can sense that I'm here. It's hard. . . . Turn south." He tried again.

The craft jagged away, darted back, jagged away again.

"If I could just get a better handle on the energy," he said, still pushing.

Haley watched the ship bob back and forth over the empty clearing like a marionette. Something occurred to her. "Could you get a better handle on the energy if you got on board?"

Dodger squinted, still trying to keep his hold on the craft. "Well, definitely. That's where the crystal is."

"And," said Haley, "if you had better control, do you think you could *fly* it?"

Dodger considered this. "Maybe, yeah, I . . ." He trailed off and suddenly looked queasy. "Oh no. . . ."

"What?" Haley asked.

"I— there's . . . Hold on, need to stop it I—"

Suddenly Dodger's mouth snapped open, and his body lit up in neon orange light, and a voice blared out of him, as if he himself was a radio.

"—CAN ANYONE HEAR US, OVER! THIS IS A. J. LARSON AND I AM INSIDE THE TOWN OF JULIETTE, I REPEAT, I AM TRAPPED IN JULIETTE!"

Apache National Forest, AZ, July 7, 4:17 a.m.

The voice tore through Dodger before he could push it back. He knew how to keep the radio transmission at bay, but this was different. Someone had hacked into the crystal network and was blasting this broadcast.

"I REPEAT, MY NAME IS ADAM JOHN LARSON AND I AM SENDING THIS TRANSMISSION FROM THE TOWN OF JULIETTE, ARIZONA, AT EIGHT O'CLOCK MOUNTAIN STANDARD TIME."

Dodger managed to open his eyes. The shocked gaze he was getting from Haley made him pretty sure that this voice was blaring out of him into the night. He had to stop it, but he also wanted to hear it. He tried to split his mind in two, half holding the UFO at bay, and the other half listening to the signal.

"WE ARE CAPTIVES HERE, I REPEAT! IF ANYONE CAN HEAR US, PLEASE SEND HELP! MOST PEOPLE HERE DON'T SEEM TO UNDERSTAND, BUT SOME OF US ARE AWAKE! WE'RE AT THE OBSERVATORY IN JULIETTE AND WE HAVE A PLAN! WE'VE ISOLATED THE SOURCE CODE OF THE PROGRAM. . . . IT'S SOME KIND OF TIME LOOP."

Dodger found the voice in the warmth of the crystal transmission, almost like he could see its bright frequency among the others. He wanted to keep listening but wanted to make it quiet. . . .

"WE DON'T HAVE MUCH TIME! THEY ALWAYS FIND OUT, AND I THINK THEY RESET US EACH DAY!"

Dodger finally corralled the radio and quieted it. Stopped himself from glowing. In his head though, he heard the rest:

"WE ARE GOING TO TRY AGAIN TONIGHT TO DISRUPT THE TIME LOOP! IF YOU ARE OUT THERE, PLEASE SEND HELP TO THE SOURCE OF THIS SIGNAL IMMEDIATELY! WE DON'T KNOW HOW LONG WE CAN DISRUPT THE CODE—"

The transmission ended. The rest of the world flooded back in, just in time for Dodger to hear the Alto say:

"Watch out!" He was diving right at Dodger, grabbing Haley in the process, and the three of them tumbled backward and around the thick roots of a large tree.

The beam from the UFO zapped where they'd just been.

"Whoa!" said Alex, who'd barely avoided it.

"So can you commandeer the craft or not?" said the Alto, jumping to his feet.

"Right," said Dodger. He reached back through the energy. The others controlling it seemed to have momentarily disappeared. Maybe they'd been busy trying to quell that transmission from Juliette. *Land in the clearing,* Dodger commanded.

The craft began to lower but then yanked sharply back up. Dodger could feel that the controllers had returned. *Land!* He instructed it.

The craft jerked, then lowered, back up . . . *LAND!* Finally, it obeyed and started to drift down.

"I've got it," he said, jumping to his feet. "Come on, quick, before I lose my grip." He stumbled out of the woods into the clearing. Haley, the Alto, and Alex followed him.

Dodger emerged in the grass. The ship was above him, lowering. Dodger kept commanding it down. His head ached, and he could feel the warm blood running from his nose, tasted its salty tang in his mouth, but he kept pressing, holding on to the craft.

Haley put a hand on his shoulder. "You can do it," she said.

Dodger squeezed the light as hard as he could. The ship dropped down and settled on the grass.

Dodger approached slowly. *Open,* he thought to it. A section of the center sphere of the craft slid open. Dodger could see the orange crystal glow inside as well as the blinking of electronics. He stepped up onto the ring-shaped edge of the craft and peered in the door. A labyrinth of machinery surrounded a circular space only a few feet across. In the center of the space hovered the basketball-sized globe of the crystal.

He slid inside the warm space. He felt like his skin was tingling, hairs standing on end as he got close to the crystal. He placed his hands on it and the voice of the interface spoke to him: *Manual Override engaged.*

He turned back to the group. "I got it," he said, "I think."

Haley climbed in. The Alto followed.

"Dodger," said Haley. "That message. There's a resistance inside Juliette. If they can disrupt the time loop . . ."

"Then we want to be there when they do," said the Alto. He started flicking at his watch. I'll send the car to the coordinates. Hopefully it will continue to distract them."

Dodger nodded. "So, straight to Juliette then."

"What about me?" Alex was standing on the rim of the ship, looking into the cramped space. "And my dad?"

"Contact our parents," said Haley. "Tell them to head for Juliette."

"Your father will have been taken there," said the Alto.

"But where is it?" she asked.

Dodger took a hand from the crystal and slipped out his notebook. He flipped to the folded-down page and handed it to Haley. "Give her the page," he said. "I have them memorized."

Haley ripped out the page and passed it to Alex. "Get everybody there, our parents, the FBI, police, news crews, military, anyone who will listen. Post it on We Are the Missing, too."

"You got it," said Alex. She jumped off the side of the spaceship and hurried back to the RV.

"Okay," said Dodger. He closed his eyes and returned his free hand to the crystal. He felt himself slip into the orange light. He ordered the door to close.

Please select destination, the interface said.

Take us to Juliette, said Dodger.

Access to Juliette is not possible, said the interface. *The next scheduled maintenance and transit gap into the temporal loop is scheduled to occur in three hundred fourteen hours.*

Take us to Juliette's location, he thought instead, thinking the coordinates.

Commencing.

Dodger felt a lurch. The craft was moving. Inside the interface though, he could feel the other intelligences becoming aware of his presence. The ones who'd been operating this ship, and he even thought he could feel One and Two. They would have to hurry.

Time to coordinates 35° 23' W 113° 49' N: twelve minutes.

Dodger slid back through the energy and returned to his body just as the ship shot off over the hills, going instantly from a standstill to hundreds of miles an hour. Dodger was thrown back, right into Haley.

"Sorry," he said, getting to his feet. "We'll be there in twelve minutes."

"That's okay," she said. "Nicely done."

Dodger looked around. "Where's the Alto?" he asked, but then he saw that the Alto had curled himself on the floor in the front curve of the circle of space.

"He said he needed ten minutes of sleep to make up for waking early before," said Haley. She sat down on the narrow space of floor, leaning against the strange, glassy machinery. "I wish there was a view out of this thing."

"Let me check." Dodger reconnected with the interface. *Is there a way to see out of the craft?*

Please select optical assistance or transparent mode.

Let's try transparent mode.

Commencing.

Dodger was pulling out of the interface when he heard a gasp. He opened his eyes and saw Haley gazing around in wonder. The craft around them was . . . gone. It was as if they were floating over the predawn world, the black ground, the purple-to-blue sky, the last stars fading with the brightening horizon. For a second Dodger worried they would fall, but he could still feel the invisible ship beneath his feet.

They were traveling incredibly fast, little clusters of lights sliding by below, highways now and then.

Haley laughed to herself.

"What?" said Dodger.

"We are traveling in a SPACEship!" said Haley. "I mean, just take a second to think about that!"

"Yeah," said Dodger. "That is pretty cool."

"Sorry," said Haley, "This shouldn't be funny. I know in ten minutes we're going to be facing who-knows-what, but just in case this is my last moment with my memories, at least I spent it in a freakin'

SPACESHIP!" Haley laughed more.

Dodger reached out and took Haley's hand. She looked at him. He pulled back lightning fast, thinking, *What are you doing?* but Haley smiled. "That's okay," she said, and took it back.

Dodger squeezed. *Flying on a spaceship,* he thought, and added, *with a cool girl.* For all the things he'd imagined happening when he'd left Port Salmon, most of them bad at best, this . . . this he had never expected.

"Ooh, hey," he said, having a pretty silly idea. He focused on the hand that was still on the crystal, and rummaged around in the energy interface for a minute. There it was. . . .

Music burst around them. It was KJPR, playing a poppy country song.

Let's get up in my pickup truck and rooo-o-o-ollllll,

This made Haley's eyes pop. "I know this song!" She cracked up. "My parents were listening to it on the drive."

She pretended to have a mic and started singing along, bopping her head from side to side.

"'Cause you and me we gotta gooo-o-o-oo."

Dodger watched her and tried keep himself from kind of freaking out. He looked at the sleeping earth far below where he was standing. At the sky becoming turquoise, and at Haley, and he wondered at how, all the way out here, he had stumbled into this amazing moment.

And he could barely enjoy it because his nerves were ringing and he was already sad because it was going to end, wasn't it? They'd be in Juliette in moments and then what? *Who cares!* he shouted at himself. *Stop thinking about that and think about right now!*

Yes, he should do that.

"Take it, Dodger!" Haley called. She tossed him the imaginary microphone.

Dodger caught it. He couldn't karaoke, never knew the words to songs, but wait—actually, he'd heard this song a hundred times or more over the last year on the radio in his head.

He sang: *"Baby baby we can roo-o-o-olll on and on."*

Yes! He did know it.

And they shouted the next lines together:

"And I don't mind, if you need time,

'Cause we got all niiiight,

Till the break of daw-aw-wnnn."

A guitar solo kicked in. Dodger and Haley shared a gaze, both breathing hard. Dodger noticed that Haley had dirt all over her forehead. A tangle of her hair was caught in the arm of her glasses. Her eyes were bloodshot. She looked awesome. Like a partner on a far off adventure. . . .

And then she smiled at him. "New map," she said.

"Huh?" said Dodger.

Haley took a little step toward him. And another.

Oh no! thought Dodger.

Another step. They were less than a foot apart. She looked up at him—

And suddenly brought the imaginary mic up between them, just as the singer returned with a triumphant scream that Haley perfectly mimicked:

"Awwwright!" Haley cracked up.

Dodger laughed and also felt like he was short-circuiting. He had no idea what to do next. It was like there were giant flashes and beeps going off in his head, saying *Warning! Warning! Craft has been target locked!* Dodger wondered if that meant he should just lean toward Haley and ki—

Wait.

Or that message was real.

Target locked! The interface was shouting at him. *Repeat: Craft has been target locked!*

"Dodger, what is it?" Haley asked. She must have seen his face.

Now Dodger caught a flash out of the corner of his eye. He glanced behind them.

And he saw the other spacecraft that was now in pursuit and that had just fired a burst of blue light at them.

"Crap!" Dodger threw both hands on the crystal and shouted *Bank hard left!*

Would you like to initiate evasive action maneuvers? the interface asked.

Yes! Dodger shouted.

Commencing.

The ship yawned hard left into a steep dive. The blue burst of energy narrowly sailed past the right side of the ship.

"What's going on?" asked the Alto, sitting up. He saw there was no visible floor beneath him and jumped before getting his bearings.

"We're being chased!" Haley shouted.

Dodger glanced behind them. The sun had crested the horizon, a brilliant pale ball of yellow. Their silver pursuer reflected the light. Another blue shot burst from it.

Target lock! announced the interface.

Take evasive action! Dodger shouted.

The ship bowed into a nearly vertical climb up, then flipped left, somersaulting upside down and back into a dive straight toward the earth as the shot sliced just above them.

The craft flattened out. Dodger thought he might barf.

Juliette location reached, the interface informed him.

Dodger saw a wide, flat plateau beneath them,

the ground all reddish dirt and rocks. *Like Mars,* he thought. There were grass hills around the perimeter. A snowcapped peak rose in the distance, sparkling in the dawn sun.

"We've reached Juliette!" he shouted.

"No town yet!" Haley replied, looking around.

Dodger wondered what to do. Should they stay in the area and just try to keep avoiding the fire from their pursuer? Should they take off and try to shake the other ship?

"Dodger, another shot!" Haley shouted.

Dodger spotted the next blue energy burst headed toward them. He ducked back into the interface. *Take*—he started to say—

But then there was a blast and a wicked shimmy of vibration. Dodger was thrown clear of the crystal. Giant orange sparks jumped around the ship. The exterior flashed in and out, the transparent mode malfunctioning. There was a whining sound that steadily lowered in pitch.

And the ship started to fall from the sky.

Dodger clambered back to his feet and slapped his hands on the crystal. *Pull up!* he shouted to it.

Primary antigravity thrusters have been damaged.

Dodger pulled back as the ship slowed, still rocking from side to side, and fell toward the barren desert.

He found Haley's wide eyes. "We're going down."

0001

Juliette

Juliette, AZ, April 25, 6:55 a.m.

Suza Raines was getting suspicious. Why wasn't her alarm clock working? She rolled over and smacked it, but no radio played. The time appeared as a series of incomplete digital bars. She leaned down out of her bed and fished through her jeans for her broken-band watch, but then remembered she didn't have one.

"Ah well," she said out loud, "just a normal day."

Up and dressed, Suza found the kitchen empty. This was a lucky break. It was probably early enough to go down to the One Horse and see AJ . . .

"Nah," she announced to the quiet kitchen. "I'll just have a muffin."

After wolfing down the dry item, she said 'bye to her dad, grabbed her backpack, threw on her denim jacket, and headed outside. She looked down at her bike. Everything was in place, exactly where it should be. Suza raced to school, arriving just in time.

Juliette, AZ, April 25, 12:43 p.m.

"Pass it!" Suza shouted, racing across the outfield as cheers sounded behind her. In front of her, poor Wilson Daly was struggling to pull the kickball out from beneath a row of bushes. Behind her, Stacey Evans was rounding second, her pigtails flopping. Now Wilson emerged from the bushes and threw the pink ball wildly, way over Suza's head.

She chased after it. The ball bounced up against an orange plastic fence at the back corner of the school field. Suza bent to pick up the ball. When she stood, she found a small man in a yellow hard hat, orange jumpsuit, and goggles looking at her out of a round hole in the grass, just on the other side of the fence.

"Hi!" Suza said brightly.

The little man seemed to gaze quizzically at her.

Suza grabbed the ball and sprinted off.

Juliette, AZ, April 25, 3:16 p.m.

Suza slung her backpack over her shoulder and headed down the hall along with the rest of her seventh grade class. As they reached the double doors, they passed Principal Howard looming in the middle of the hall. He smiled at them all, his arms folded over his gray suit. When he saw Suza, he smiled even wider.

"Well, Suza, you had a nice day," he said.

"Yup."

"Good. I'm so pleased."

"Me too."

"Excellent. Have a normal evening."

Suza smiled and walked out into the sunny afternoon.

Juliette, AZ, April 25, 7:43 p.m.

Suza stuffed her cleats into her backpack and picked up her bike. The sun had dropped behind Mount Randall for the day, and Juliette had become an evening world of blues and grays. Nearby, the radio blared from an open car window.

"—is asking everyone to be inside and off the roads before these snow squalls arrive."

Suza hopped on her bike and pedaled hard through the dusk, through the neighborhoods full of kids at play and the lingering aroma of charcoal and burgers. The orange streetlights were beginning to flick on. Suza started winding up the hill toward home. She was just passing a brown sign that read "Foster Observatory and Museum—"

When she veered left. *Go!* she thought to herself. *Go now!* She leaned over her handlebars and pedaled as hard as she could up the steep winding road toward the white tower.

SUZA! Stop what you're doing NOW! You—

"Shut up!" she hissed at the voice in her head.

A horrible burning sensation ignited behind her left ear. Suza wobbled on her bike, almost spilling onto the pavement, but gritted her teeth and hung on. *Next time I take it! Shut up shut up shut up!*

"Suza!" The front door of a nearby house flew open. A man she'd never seen before sprinted out of the house, barefoot, holding a remote control. "Suza, wait!"

"Suza!" A woman careened out, running straight toward Suza, a casserole dish still balanced in one hand, pointing a spatula at her with the other. "Stop, young lady!"

"No!" Suza shouted. She pedaled as hard as she could, felt a brush of fingers on her jacket, but sped past them.

Car engines roared to life. Headlights stabbing out of driveways. "Suza!" More doors were opening, men and women running out, some in socks, bathrobes, and all after her.

SUZA! You will go back to your home!

"No I won't!" Suza shouted.

She reached the observatory parking lot, her legs burning and her lungs about to explode, and jumped her bike onto the sidewalk. She sped straight for the observatory dome, which was beside a flat, stone building. The top of the observatory was slowly rotating with a low hum.

Tires squealed as cars raced into the parking lot.

The spot behind Suza's ear burned once more, sending pain shooting through the back of her head and down her shoulder. She veered and toppled off her bike, rolling across the pine needles.

It's over, Suza! Stop this now and return—

She heard car doors opening, the shouts of approaching voices, feet slapping the pavement. *Keep going,* she thought over the pain, and lunged to her feet. *You can't let up now.* It had been such a long day of hiding her thoughts, from that moment when she'd woken up to find that all the hidden thoughts in her brain finally seemed to have assembled correctly, like they'd almost done so many times before: *This time you take it, to the observatory, but wait until night, until right before the curfew, when they least expect it.*

"Suza, stop!" someone called from behind. And

this time Suza almost did. She glanced over her shoulder to see her dad among the men and women chasing her. She saw Angie, even Principal Howard. But their eyes were cold, their faces blank, like they didn't even know her.

"Suze!" A door had opened at the observatory's base. AJ stood there, waving to her. Suza threw herself inside like a sprinter at the finish line. AJ slammed the door. Suza turned to watch him lower a thick wooden crossbar over it.

"I can't believe you made it," AJ said. "I just sent a transmission out on that radio frequency. I don't know if anyone will hear it. It was so hard to hide my thoughts all day today!"

"Me too!" said Suza, feeling a great relief to have finally made it up here after . . . how many tries? She couldn't remember.

"Suza!" a muffled voice screamed from outside.

"That sounds like your dad," AJ said, glancing worriedly at the door.

Suza took a step back. "He's not my dad." Yet even though Suza knew this, it was hard to hear his voice furious like that. Slapping at the throbbing area behind her ear, she almost started for the door. . . .

But AJ pulled her toward the center of the room, where the giant telescope pointed out its open slice of roof. "We're all under some control," AJ was saying, "repeating the same day. But there's a way to stop it."

"With this," Suza panted, holding up the metal piece that Mr. Davis had left on her bike that morning.

Relief flooded AJ's face. "Yes, that's it! These are the same symbols . . . check this out." He turned to one of his computer screens and pointed to streams of white characters passing horizontally across a blue background. "The telescope picks this up. It's some kind of electrical energy. I don't know how long it's taken me to isolate this. I've only had so little time each night before they catch and reset me."

"What is it?" Suza asked.

AJ tapped at his keyboard. "Code. The code for the program, I think, that's doing this to us. And so, watch what happens when I do . . . this."

AJ tapped a few commands and the screen changed. The scrolling symbols moved to the top of the screen and a message appeared:

TEMPORAL LOOP PARAMETERS ACCESSED.

CURRENT STATUS OF LOOP: ENGAGED.

ENTER CODE TO DISENGAGE.

Below this message, a set of five short lines appeared. The first line blinked, like a cursor was on it. "How many symbols are on that key?" AJ asked.

"Five," said Suza.

"Yes. The password for the program. Davis said he had access to some kind of interface. . . ."

There were clangs on the outside of the observatory dome now. It sounded like feet. Climbing.

"Let's try it," said AJ. Suza held out the piece for him to see. "If we drag the right symbols into the right spots . . . " He watched the stream of symbols passing by. "There." He clicked on the symbol and dragged the mouse, moving into the first blank line. Once all five were in place, he said, "Okay, here goes. . . ."

He hit Enter.

A high-pitched whine shrieked all around them, and then a deep hum seemed to come from everywhere: the walls, the floors. The ground shook, and for a moment, brilliant daylight flooded down through the open observatory top.

"Whoa!" Suza looked up and saw that it was no longer night, but instead there was blue sky, high clouds, and dawn sunshine. She heard confused shouting from outside.

"Did we do it?" asked Suza.

"I think we did!" said AJ. "Ooh, and look."

A message had appeared beneath the five symbols:

PROJECT BLISS CONTROL STATUS: ENGAGED.
ENTER CODE TO DISENGAGE.

Below that, a single line blinked.

Just then, there was another earsplitting whine, and the daylight began to fade out, turning back to darkness.

"They must have overridden my command!" said AJ.

"Is there another symbol on that key?" he asked, looking at the screen. "We just need one more."

Suza flipped it over in her fingers. The back side was blank. "No."

"Well," said AJ, "I guess we can try each different symbol . . . but there are so many. . . ."

There was a huge crash above them. A vacant-eyed townsperson had dropped down onto the metal catwalk that encircled the telescope. Another was hauling herself over the edge of the observatory dome.

Behind them, the door began to splinter.

Suza looked desperately back at the screen. "I don't know which one!"

"Um . . ." AJ grabbed a symbol and dragged it down, but when he hit Enter, the single space just went blank again. He went to get another.

The first townsperson crashed on top of him. "Ah!" AJ shouted.

"AJ!" Suza leaped back. She saw the next woman preparing to jump and realized it was Ms. Fells, her math teacher. And three more townspeople were crawling over the observatory rim.

AJ wrestled himself free of the man and jumped to his feet.

There was a crack behind her. Arms began to reach in through a hole in the door. A hand found the doorknob and twisted, grabbed Suza's arm, and raced for the double doors that led into the museum.

"But the code!" Suza shouted.

Two more bodies crashed down onto the floor.

"It's too late!" said AJ. Suza could feel tears springing from her eyes. This was their last shot, she knew it. "If we don't get out of here, they'll get us and reset us and that will be it, all over again!"

They raced through the double doors into the dark museum. AJ threw them shut and lowered a security bar just as bodies slammed into the doors from the other side.

AJ and Suza backed away from the shuddering doors. There were more thuds from the front doors of the museum. Then, an enormous thud on the ceiling.

"Now what?" Suza whispered.

"I don't know," said AJ.

Suddenly the pyramid-shaped skylight above them shattered, glass raining down, and a giant figure dropped through the opening.

22

35° 23' N 113° 49' W, AZ, July 7, 4:22 a.m.
Dodger watched the desert floor rising to meet them as the failing transparent mode flicked on and off.

All at once, the world around them began to dim. The bright morning sun vanished and the sky inked in to nighttime black. The craft shuddered, and reality itself seemed to swim.

In a moment it had become completely dark outside, but then daylight flashed back, almost like a rubber band had been snapped. It was morning again, but now lines were appearing on the desert beneath them, geometric shapes like buildings and roads, almost as if they were being sketched into existence. Starting as outlines and then filling in, a whole town appearing. And Dodger knew: Juliette.

"They did it!" Haley called.

And then the world began to change again. This time, Juliette stayed, but the sky turned dark again, the sun falling away and black consuming day. Stars, the moon. It was night again. Juliette at night.

"What happened?" asked Haley.

"I think," said Dodger, "they disrupted the time loop, but only for a second."

"So are we in the loop now?"

"I think so." Dodger looked behind them. "And I don't think that other ship made it in."

He gazed at the streetlight grid of the town below. It was amazing! It looked just like it did on the map he'd drawn, from the visions he'd had for years. Here was the place, Juliette, the place he'd been before.

"So now what?" asked Haley.

"Can we get to the observatory?" the Alto asked. "That is, before we hit the ground?"

"I'll try." They were still high enough that maybe he could change their landing location. He remembered his map and then looked for the ridge south of town. There was the white building. He sank into the interface. *Turn left, thirty degrees.*

The ship made a weak turn, shuddering as it did, its descent now aimed at the observatory. Dodger corrected slightly to the right, then left. They were getting low. . . .

The ship made it over the ridge and barely cleared the museum roof beside the observatory. *Land here,* Dodger instructed. The ship hit hard, thumping to a stop. Sparks flew around the cabin, and the invisible effect ceased. Dodger, Haley, and the Alto were thrown against the computer banks.

Open the hatch, Dodger instructed.

There was a weak whine, and the hatch only slid half open. Dodger reached for Haley, who was leaning against the wall, getting her bearings. "Let's go," he said.

They stumbled out onto the gravel roof.

"It's cold," said Haley, crossing her arms against the chill.

"It's April in the high desert," said Dodger.

"April 1994," said Haley.

"Yeah," said Dodger.

"But why is it night?"

"The loop must not be a full twenty-four hours long. Maybe people need less sleep when you're resetting their reality every day." He glanced at the Alto. "Maybe everybody's like him."

He was gazing around with a puzzled look.

"Them," he said softly, and pointed to the observatory. Three figures were perched on the lip of the rectangular opening in the dome. And they were looking right at Juliette's newest guests. "On the roof!" One of them shouted. The three started pointing emphatically. Dodger guessed they were alerting more people below.

Then they all just leaped from the observatory. Two of them plummeted into the gap between buildings. Only the third made it onto the museum roof. There was a wicked crack of breaking bone, but then the woman got up and started hobbling toward them, dragging her leg awkwardly behind her.

"They're all under the mind control," said the Alto.

"They're like zombies," said Haley.

The Alto stepped toward the approaching townsperson and dropped into a martial arts stance, legs apart and fists up. The townsperson just kept coming, until the Alto's boot struck her in the chin. Then she crumpled to the ground, out cold.

"Come on." The Alto took a quick look around and sprinted over to a little pyramid-shaped skylight. He kicked through it, again and again, clearing the glass. Dodger and Haley joined him.

"It's about a fifteen-foot drop," he said. "I'll go first and catch you." He fearlessly jumped down into the dark. There was a thud. "Okay, come on—oof!"

There was a sound of breaking wood. A grunt. A

squealing voice that sounded like a girl.

"Alto?" Haley whispered.

A moment of silence. "Okay," said the Alto.

"Here goes," said Haley. She jumped down.

"Dodger," said the Alto.

Dodger jumped, slamming into the Alto's chest. The Alto half-caught him with one arm, and then Dodger tumbled to the ground. "Ow!" said Dodger, landing hard. He saw Haley sitting on the floor, shaken up as well. "I thought you were going to catch us?"

Then he looked up to see that the Alto was holding someone in his other hand. A girl, about their age. He also had someone pinned beneath his boot. A man with a baseball hat and ponytail. There were chunks of a splintered chair nearby, like these two had tried to attack him.

"Sorry," said the Alto. "There were some distractions. These two aren't under the control, though."

"Suza?" Dodger saw that Haley was peering at the girl, who made a whimpering sound through the Alto's hand. "Let her go," said Haley.

The Alto released the girl. She stumbled forward, catching her breath, and turned to Haley. "How do you know my name?"

"I—" Haley stammered. "It's really you. I met your sister, Steph, in Amber."

Suza's eyes widened. Dodger couldn't tell if it was fear or sadness.

"I'm Haley. This is Dodger and he's the Alto. We're from outside Juliette. We're here to free you." Haley fished in her pocket and held something out to Suza. Dodger saw that it was a watch. "Here. Your sister gave me this."

"You . . ." Suza took the watch. "I did have this." She shuddered, and sniffled. "Did they say how long I'd been gone?"

"It's been six months," said Haley quietly.

"Oh," Suza whispered.

"I'm sorry," said Haley.

Dodger stood up, and as he did so, he focused on the furious beating of fists and feet against a set of double doors nearby. And also from other spots in the museum. "We probably shouldn't stay here," he said.

Suza glanced back at the door. "They're everywhere," she said.

"Can . . . you . . ." the man beneath the Alto's feet croaked.

"That's AJ," said Suza. "He's one of us."

The Alto removed his foot. AJ jumped to his feet, catching his breath.

"We heard your message," said Dodger.

"You did?" AJ said, sounding relieved. "And how

did you get in here? Was it during that flash of day-light?"

"Yeah," said Haley. "The town reappeared for a second. Just in time, actually. Our spaceship was going down."

"Your . . ." Suza said.

"Long story," said Haley.

"But it worked," AJ said, with relief. "Cool. So . . . you guys are here—now what?"

Dodger looked at Haley and the Alto.

"What about accessing that code again?" Haley asked. "And stopping the time loop permanently?"

AJ pointed a thumb toward the banging door. "The only way to do that is through the telescope. You guys didn't bring, like, the army or anything, did you?"

Dodger tried to think of what they could do next, only he was finding it hard to think. His brain felt like it was swimming, like his thoughts were dunking beneath big waves crashing over him. It was a familiar feeling. . . .

He glanced around the room. They were in an exhibit hall, carpeted and dark, with a few dim ceiling lights on. There were glass exhibit cases around the perimeter of the room, and a few displays in the middle. In the minimal lighting, Dodger saw collections of Native American artifacts, pioneer and gold rush items.

Something glinted in a case by the wall. Something . . .

Dodger started toward the case. Within a few steps, he could see why he was feeling a magnetic pull in this direction. The glass case held a boulder-sized chunk of the black crystal.

It ignited in orange, as if to greet him.

"We could— Whoa!" AJ said behind him.

Dodger reached the case and put his hands on the glass. He felt the electric warmth flow through him.

"What is he doing?" he heard AJ asking as they all walked over to him.

"He's connected to it," said Haley. Dodger felt her put a hand on his shoulder. "Hey," she said.

"Look," said Dodger. He pointed to the exhibit plaque.

Haley read aloud from the metallic plate:

"THIS RELATIVE OF MAGNETITE IS KNOWN TO BE AN EXCEPTIONAL CONDUCTOR OF LIGHT AND RADIO ENERGY. IT IS ONLY FOUND HERE IN JULIETTE AND HAS BEEN DETERMINED TO BE EXTRATERRESTRIAL IN ORIGIN. THE PLATEAU ON WHICH JULIETTE WAS BUILT IS BELIEVED TO HAVE BEEN THE SITE OF A METEOR STRIKE, THOUSANDS OF YEARS AGO.

THIS SAMPLE WAS FOUND DURING EXCAVATION FOR THE FOUNDATION OF THIS MUSEUM IN 1889. WHEN

SHOWN TO THE LOCAL NATIVE AMERICAN ELDERS,
THEY REFERRED TO THE ROCK AS PAHA'NE, WHICH
TRANSLATES ROUGHLY TO BEGINNING/END. THE
ELDERS BELIEVED THAT THE PAHA'NE FELL FROM THE
HEAVENS AND BROUGHT THE FIRST SPARK OF LIFE TO
THE EARTH."

"Paha'Ne," said Dodger, feeling like the word made sense to him. Again, that feeling of knowing, of being connected somehow to the crystal, like they shared some identity, but also . . . Dodger turned and gazed off into the museum.

"What is it?" Haley asked him.

"There's more," said Dodger. For as much connection as he felt to this chunk of rock, he realized that this was not the true source of the magnetic connection he was feeling. There was something . . . bigger. Way bigger. "It might be the source," he said.

"Dodger." Haley's brow knitted in thought. "When you interface with the rock . . . do you think you could access the time loop code in there?"

Dodger thought back to Lucky Springs. "Yeah, I think I could," he said. "One of my options was *time parameter management*."

Haley turned to Suza and AJ. "I'm guessing there are mines in town. Maybe old gold mines that are sealed off?"

"Yeah," said AJ. "Actually, there's an entrance on this hillside, not too far from here. Are you saying we need to go into the mines?"

Dodger nodded. "We need to find the source crystal, and from there I think I can turn off the time loop. And maybe the mind control, too." He looked at Haley. "You think?"

"I think," she said.

The museum door suddenly splintered, a hinge popping free.

"Whatever we're doing, we need to get out of here," said Suza.

"Okay, then, this way," said AJ. He jogged across the exhibit hall, leading them through a door and down a hallway lined with offices. A stairwell led down to a basement hallway cluttered with bookshelves and remnants of past exhibits. There was a door at the far end.

It was shuddering from the thuds of fists.

"Um," said AJ. "There's a window, in the supply closet." He backtracked to a door and fumbled his keys from his pocket.

Thunderous footsteps sounded from upstairs.

"They're inside," said the Alto.

"Okay . . ." AJ's fingers slipped, but then he got the door open. They filed inside and closed the door, trying to quiet their rapid breaths as, outside, townspeople clomped past.

The Alto moved to a frosted glass window and slowly slid it open. He peered outside. Dodger half expected to see him get yanked out of it by mind-controlled hands, but he ducked back in. "Clear."

They clambered out the window, hopping down to the steep, pine-needle-carpeted hillside.

"The path is that way," said AJ, pointing toward the end of the museum.

The Alto crouched and led the group, weaving between the thick pine trunks along the slope. Up the hill to their left, Dodger could hear townspeople milling around by the basement door.

They moved farther down the slope and emerged on a wide path.

"Maybe a hundred yards down," AJ whispered.

They hurried down the hill. Dodger could feel the pull strengthening and sense that, like a whale under the water's surface, there was something giant beneath his feet, its power beckoning him.

IT IS MORE THAN THAT, DODGER.

Dodger stumbled. A voice had spoken in his mind. It sounded older and female, and yet also not entirely human.

"Dodger," said Haley from behind him.

"I'm okay," said Dodger. He focused on keeping his feet moving—

You are connected to the Paha'ne in a deeper way than you know.

This time he sprawled onto his knees. *Who are you?* he thought back at it.

I am the Director of this facility, the voice replied, and our operation here on Earth.

Haley stopped and helped him up. "What happened?"

"Their leader," said Dodger. "She's in my head."

There was a thudding sound up ahead. Dodger and Haley ran down to see the Alto standing over two fallen townspeople by a hunched cave entrance. He slipped a headlamp on. "Ready?"

"Yeah," said Dodger.

The Alto made a sweeping motion. "After you."

Dodger led the way into the cool dark. It smelled like dust and old leather. He felt the close presence of rock again, and more than ever the proximity of crystal, drawing him forward now, almost like if he stopped moving, it would pull him along anyway.

Yes, said the Director. You feel the power. Power that is yours. I can show you.

No thanks, Dodger thought back, except, he wasn't entirely sure that was how he felt.

I know you think what you're doing is the right thing, but you don't have the whole context. I can show you the bigger picture.

Dodger could barely speak. He felt like he was floating inside his head, in an energy field without gravity, on the tide of the orange crystal.

I am not listening to you, he said. He expected to hear more from the Director, but the voice went quiet.

The descent was long, the air growing cooler as the tunnel sloped through the black, and Dodger felt like he wasn't just traveling into the center of the Earth, but into the center of the universe and existence and all things.

For all that had happened along the way, a new certainty had taken over inside Dodger. He realized that it wasn't just that he felt like he was being drawn down into this tunnel, he also felt certain that he *was* supposed to come here. After all, whatever was down here, it really was something he was meant to see, that he *had* to see. Its power was vibrating every atom in his body, like it was connected to the orbit of each electron. He was sweating from the current, and yet sweat and air and even breathing and his racing heartbeat all felt like things that were somewhere distant on the surface of the world, up with the night and the moon and even the aliens and their plot. Dodger was inside now, inside himself, inside the stars, inside *being*.

He was so lost in his head that even with the light of the Alto's headlamp coming over his shoulder, he would have walked right into the door if it hadn't been for Haley grabbing his shoulder.

"Thanks," Dodger whispered, his throat dry.

It was a door like the ones he'd seen in Lucky Springs: sleek metal with the two black crystal discs at chest height.

"I've seen this before," said Haley.

"Yeah, me, too." Dodger put one hand on the door. The crystal ignited. He felt his connection with the energy sharpen. "I can go through this door," he said. He searched around in the crystal energy, trying to determine how the door operated.

Dodger turned to the group. "Okay, I can bring you guys through. I need you to grab onto each other, like by the shoulders. Don't let go, though, or it'll break the conductivity."

"What does that mean?" asked AJ.

"I don't totally know," said Dodger. "Kind of like we're making an electric circuit. So hang on."

He turned back to the door and felt Haley put her hands on his shoulders.

"Ready," said the Alto from the back of the line.

Dodger placed his hand on the other black disc. Orange flooded his vision and he felt himself melt into the crystal energy, slipping through space and then popping back into reality on the other side. He stepped ahead as the others came through.

The orange light faded from Dodger's eyes and

he saw that they were standing on a small metal platform, surrounded by a railing.

Before them was a cavern beyond measure. It was giant, a vast geodesic structure with hundreds of triangular walls that resulted in a nearly spherical chamber. There were platforms made of iridescent alien metal ringing the sphere at different heights. Dodger counted eight in all. The centers of all the platforms were open, and in the center of the space was a massive glowing sphere of crystal, hundreds of feet across, like a tiny sun, a million-sided polygon of crystal faces.

The rock hovered in space. At its equator, catwalks extended out from what seemed to be the main platform of the cavern. The catwalks each ended right at the surface of the crystal, and there were little workstations with consoles like Dodger had seen in Lucky Springs.

The crystal was blinding, coating the room in a flickering orange light, and yet Dodger also thought he could see darkness inside it, the black void of space dotted by infinite stars.

"Dude," Haley said quietly.

Then there was a flash, and an entire spacecraft, an oval model much larger than the drone they'd flown in, appeared as if out of the crystal itself and glided slowly toward the far side of the cavern, where it landed on the main platform. There were other spacecraft parked there, too. Many were of this larger size, and a few were even more massive, with complicated curving shapes.

"Whoa . . ." AJ breathed. Dodger turned to see him glancing back and forth from the door behind them to the central crystal. "They use the rock to transport themselves through space," he said. "Like you did with that door. Is it like tuning the electromagnetic properties of the rock to certain frequencies? In that case, they could be transmitting almost like wireless data." He looked to Dodger for confirmation.

Dodger just shrugged. "When I do it, it's just by feel."

"How does it feel?" asked AJ.

"Fuzzy," said Dodger. "Like stretching. I don't know—it just kinda happens."

"That's very zen," said the Alto.

Dodger considered that he had maybe never felt zen about anything before, other than studying maps. It was a good description. He pointed toward the catwalks that led out to the crystal. "Anyway, we have to get to one of those consoles. Then I can access the main interface."

"Down here," said the Alto. He was starting down a staircase from their little landing. It dropped down through the platforms below. They moved quietly down the sets of stairs until they reached the main platform.

They started across it, weaving between other parked spacecraft. Dodger kept an eye out for townspeople or agents, but this part of the platform seemed to be empty. In the distance, he could see figures moving back and forth from the ship that had just landed.

"All those UFO buffs have been looking up," said AJ, "when they should have been looking underground."

An electronic voice suddenly broadcast throughout the cavern: "PARAMETERS FOR TEMPORAL LOOP REPETITION 9,867 ARE SET. ALL STUDY VARIATIONS ARE DUE IMMEDIATELY."

"We were right," said Haley. "About the testing. Changing the variables each day."

Dodger stopped beside the final craft. There was a catwalk just ahead, but there were three figures standing there, small people in the orange jumpsuits and yellow hard hats and black goggles.

"I hate those guys," said Suza.

Dodger felt weirdly defensive at hearing that, almost like someone he knew was being insulted. He almost said something but stopped himself. What was that about? Was it like because he was connected to the crystal, he was also connected to these aliens? That felt complicated.

"Now what?" Haley asked.

But just then the little group moved on, walking toward the far side of the platform, almost like they'd been called away.

"Okay." Dodger led the way onto the catwalk. It was made of grated metal. Dodger looked down and saw a long drop to the distant cavern floor. Suddenly the waist-high railings of the catwalk didn't seem high enough.

As they neared the crystal, Dodger could feel the hair on his arms starting to stand on end, felt his teeth almost vibrating in their sockets, his eyes watering. So much power. And at this point, he wasn't sure he could have turned around even if he'd wanted to.

They reached the catwalk's end. The light was overwhelming. Dodger moved to the console with the hand spots, like he'd seen in Lucky Springs.

Haley, Suza, AJ, and the Alto clustered around him, all tiny and drenched in neon light beside the enormous crystal. Dodger saw it gleaming in Haley's eyes as she looked at him.

"You can do it," she said to him.

It surprised Dodger. Did he look nervous? He didn't feel it, did he? Or maybe he was terrified. He couldn't tell. Too much humming energy.

"Okay," said Dodger, "let's see what's what."

He was about to put his hands on the pads when an urge struck him. He looked at his fingers, flexed them, then reached out, leaning over the railing and placing his hands directly on the Paha'Ne.

Light and energy consumed him. No more skin. Just warm current.

It was so vast, he felt like he could travel the universe in this crystal, and maybe he really could. Dodger the explorer. He felt the idea beckoning him. *Let's go,* he thought to himself. It would be so easy to slip out into the cosmos from here.

Hello, said the interface.

Dodger had to take a second to remember what he was looking for. He accessed the main menu. *Connectivity, Time Parameter Management, Transit.*

Time Parameter Management, he said.

Please enter password, said the interface.

A sort of menu appeared in front of him, lines of symbols. There seemed to be about fifty. And he sensed that he had to choose five of them. Maybe this was the code that Suza had mentioned.

Dodger pushed himself back toward the surface and, with great effort, slid into his body and pulled one hand away from the crystal. Like in the space-ship, he found himself in a kind of double reality, the interface still present but the real world around him again. Only this time, the power of the crystal was so strong that his view of the world was like through a curtain of orange light.

"You said you had a code?" He spoke aloud, but the words seemed distant to his own ears.

Suza held up a small rectangle of metal. "Here."

Dodger looked at the symbols carefully. When he felt like he had the series memorized, he returned both hands to the crystal. He referenced the menu of symbols and pointed his mind at each. When he'd suggested all five, there was a whir of motion in the interface.

TEMPORAL LOOP DISENGAGED.

Distantly, Dodger felt the floor, the entire cave complex, shudder, as once again Juliette reappeared in the present day. Dodger returned to the next item on the menu.

PROJECT BLISS CONTROL INTERFACE STATUS: ENGAGED.

ENTER CODE TO DISENGAGE.

Dodger sensed now that a single symbol was needed. The same bank of many symbols was available to him. Which one? He surfaced again, pulling a hand away.

"I need the sixth symbol," he said.

"That's the problem," said Suza. "We only have

the five! We were just going to try each one until we found the right one."

"Okay, that's what I'll do."

"It's going to take too long," whispered AJ worriedly.

"Let me see that," said Haley. She took the metal piece and ran her finger across the symbols. Her eyes snapped up to the Alto. "Your bracelet!" she said. "That symbol!"

The Alto slipped the bracelet off his wrist and handed it to Haley. She flicked to one of the charms and held it out beside the other symbols. "This one," said Haley, showing Dodger the charm. "Maybe this is it." She looked back at the Alto. "Why else would you have it?"

The Alto shrugged. Then he glanced over his shoulder. "I hope you're right."

Dodger followed his gaze. "Uh-oh."

They'd been found. A group was running out onto the catwalk. It was One, Two, and a couple of the other agents they'd seen in Roswell. Behind them were at least ten small people in orange jumpsuits and hard hats. "Stop right there!" One called.

"Hurry," said the Alto. "I'll cover you." He stepped in front of the group and dropped into his fighting stance.

Dodger studied the symbol carefully. "Okay." He

turned and slid back into the interface. In the medium of light, he found the code again. He searched the bank of symbols. There it was. . . .

FRANCIS.

The Director. Dodger quickly selected the symbol, moving it—

IT'S TIME FOR US TO TALK.

Dodger heard another voice, distantly, saying "Dodger, hurry—"

And then as if on a cosmic wind, energy seemed to snatch him, dragging him fully into the interface, body and all. Dodger saw orange, felt the full possibility of the universe, and traveled.

Juliette, AZ, April 25th, 8:36 p.m.

The Alto was a blur of attacking limbs, but there were too many of them. Two was crumpled on the catwalk, and a couple of the tiny aliens had been tossed over the side, but now the Alto was down. Two of the little workers were grabbing at AJ. Suza was fighting off another.

One was pushing through the fray, right toward Haley. She turned, a hand already on Dodger's arm, and placed the other on his shoulder, getting as close as she could to his glowing ear. "Dodger, hurry—" she started to say—

Only then she was yanked violently forward, and she was flying, moving and it felt like she was coming apart, like she was a dandelion blown in the wind, seeds carried off, up, out, and far, far away.

Approximately six hundred light-years east of Vega

"Hello, Dodger."

She was tall and weirdly slender, like a being made of tree branches. She seemed to have many fingers, flicking on the end of her reedy arms. Her skin was translucent, the vessels inside visible by their incandescent orange glow. Her brain was a neon tangle behind a foggy glass skull, and her eyes were voluminous, reflectionless, black.

Dodger looked down and saw that he was whole and standing on a metal floor. They were no longer in the interface. They were beyond it, standing on the deck of a starship, its walls and consoles made of the iridescent metal with its oily rainbow texture.

Dodger also saw that he was no longer merely himself. His insides were glowing orange in the feathery patterns of his blood vessels, as if he literally had crystal in his blood.

"Congratulations to you both for disabling Juliette's time loop. We will, however, have it up and running again in short order."

Dodger turned and was surprised to find Haley. She wasn't glowing. She was instead looking terrified. Dodger felt something more calm. Like his shock at being suddenly far out in space was tempered by a warm certainty from inside, like from his blood and cells and from his very genes. A feeling . . .

Like he was home.

He sensed that he was still connected to the interface. It was somewhere back behind his consciousness, and somewhere beyond that, very far from here, was Earth.

The Director stood to their side, and before the three of them was a floor-to-ceiling windowpane.

It looked out on the universe. And Dodger realized that he'd been wrong to envision the world by map, because no map, no re-creation or attempt at organization could ever adequately express or contain what they could now see.

Infinite stars, pulsing in a million colors like spilled canisters of glitter.

Spiraling galaxies like wild paintbrush strokes.

Effervescent undulating clouds of nebulae splashed and running down the page.

Front and center: a star, a pale blue thing, fatigued, at its end.

Closer, the enormous ruin of crystal chunks that Dodger had glimpsed from Lucky Springs. They were massive, fractured, and held together by thousand-mile-long metal spans. They glowed more strongly in their fissures than on their cooled surfaces, like late-evening embers of a campfire.

"It was once a planet," said the Director. "Called Paha'Ne. Our home."

"What happened?" said Dodger.

"For seven billion years we lived on it. Our species evolved in tandem with its crystal structure. Our consciousness was connected to it, held within it. We could travel through it. A symbiotic relationship where we maintained the crystal, kept it free of corrosive bacteria and predatory species, and it maintained us in return."

Dodger was reminded of those little fish that clung to sharks, or clown fish and anemones.

"Let me guess," said Haley. "You overpopulated and overused the resources?"

"Ha," said the Director, and she almost sounded offended. "We are not like humans in that respect. No, we faced a calamity that your young planet will, too, eventually. Our star expanded into a supergiant. We had to flee into space, and then we watched as our planet was scorched to the point where it fractured." The Director swept her many fingers toward the remnants. "You can see that we salvaged the planet as best we could, but for centuries now we have lived in our ships, orbiting the graveyard of our past."

Dodger felt a somber weight settle over him as he listened to this.

"In time," the Director continued, "we began a search for a new home. When our planet exploded, chunks of the Paha'Ne were thrown out into the wider universe. We tracked these remnants. Many ended up flying into other suns or getting sucked into black holes, but we were able to locate a precious few that landed on planets. As you can imagine, most were quite uninhabitable—gas giants, frozen wastelands. . . . One that was overrun with tiny creatures that cause terrible rashes, that kind of thing.

"In our search we found only three planets that had an atmosphere and geography that could sustain us."

"Earth was one of them," said Dodger.

"Yes, the best one, in fact. And so we began sending exploratory teams, a few decades ago, by your time. We determined that with a few alterations, we could make Earth a viable new home. And so we have endeavored to do so."

"And what about the humans?" Haley asked coldly. "Project Bliss? It's mind control. You're just turning us all into mindless slaves?"

"Well," said the Director, "there was an early movement among us to exterminate humanity entirely, much as you might fumigate a house before moving in, but we value the natural world, on a universal level, and so, unlike *your* explorers, might I add, we strive to preserve and protect the individual ecosystems and habitats of the places we have chosen to settle."

"You're environmentalist aliens," said Haley.

"You could say that. Plus, after our initial research into the human species, we determined that your race and ours only differ by a few chromosomes. Rather important ones, *obviously,* but our DNA is largely identical."

"People have most of the same DNA as mice," said Haley darkly.

"Lab rats," Dodger echoed, though he felt like he was saying it more for Haley than for himself.

"I suppose," said the Director. "But the more important point is that there are two problems with humans: First, you are bound and determined to wreck your *own* ecosystem. If you raise the carbon levels of your atmosphere as high as you are projected to, it will have irreversible effects on the temperature and sustainability of life on the planet, as well as interfere with our crystal tuning. That would be a problem for us, and for you.

"Second, you humans don't share well. We need to move at least five billion Paha'Ne onto your planet. I'm sure you can imagine the response your population would have to that."

"They might not like it," said Dodger. It was only after he'd spoken that he realized he'd said "they."

"'Might' is putting it lightly. Once, we tried to introduce ourselves to a remote group of humans in Alaska, and your military secretly fired nuclear weapons at our ships. That was a nuisance.

"So you see our dilemma," said the Director. "We need your planet, and we don't want to heartlessly exterminate you. So, instead we are in the process of setting up a network across your planet. In the meantime, we have been experimenting with a proper mind control program in Juliette. When it is complete and the system goes live, we will put the human race into a blissful state of life, going about their days unaware that anything is amiss. We would also keep you from screwing up your atmosphere any further, and most importantly, we would program you not to mind our presence. Actually, we thought we might move you all to select continents and then we'll live on the others. We do so love South America. You could have Australia all to yourselves. It would be, as you say, a win-win."

"You'd be making us slaves," Haley muttered.

"Nonsense," said the Director. "Aside from having you build a few large-scale crystal interfaces, we would not make you trained animals. We would just give you happy, trouble-free lives. It would be like living in a really nice zoo."

"But that's not life," said Haley. "There'd be no choice. No change."

"It's all relative," said the Director. "You'll *think* you have choice. Is it really that different? At any rate, we're nearly finished, and we can't have our Juliette plans discovered. But all that is not why I brought you out here, Dodger."

"Then why?" Dodger asked.

"Because all of us have watched you these past few weeks, and for years before that. You were one of our early rounds of experiments here in Juliette. Part of a special group that we selected for genetic trials. We merely turned on a gene or two—ones that are active inside us but dormant inside you—to see what would happen. At first, the only result we saw was that we inadvertently made you immune to the mind control program here in Juliette. Because of that, we returned you to your home. End of story . . . until these powers started activating inside you over this last year. My scientists think it was caused by your human condition of puberty. What a crazy state of affairs that is!" The Director made an electric sound like laughter.

"But my point is: As a result you have become something more than human. I suspect that you know this deep inside. Know that you are now as much one of us as you are one of them, if not more."

Dodger nodded. He did know this. He'd suspected all along that he was different, wondered if Juliette would feel like home, and if his growing powers were steps in a process of changing. It was all true, in a way, and it explained so much of what he'd felt. And yet, what did it mean for him now? What was he to do?

"That is why I brought you here," said the Director. "To give you a choice."

"What choice?" Dodger asked weakly.

"You're powerful, and, in effect, we can't control you without locking you up. That doesn't seem right to do to one of our own. So, in exchange for your cooperation on Earth, we would like to invite you to live with us. You may roam free among the Paha'Ne, travel our world, our other new homes. And Earth too, of course. We feel that you are something special. Something to be cherished. And we would treat you as such."

Cherished? Dodger had never dreamed of having a word like that associated with him. What should he do? He glanced over at Haley. Her expression was hard to read. Blank, serious. He really wanted to know what she was thinking. Now he felt her hand slip into his.

"And then there's Haley," said the Director.

"What about me?" said Haley coldly.

"Well, your spirit, for one. Here you are, a young girl all the way at the far end of the universe, and you didn't do it with an internal connection, like Dodger. You are here because of your irrepressible desire to see beyond the horizon, to discover the unknown, to live beyond your life. It is very impressive."

"I'd just been calling it selfish and headstrong," said Haley quietly, "but . . . thanks, I guess."

"You do your species justice, and that's why we'd like to extend the invitation to you, too." said the Director. "Well, and also because he likes you."

This made Dodger feel like he was blushing, though it might not be showing up, given that his insides were already glowing.

"How about it?" asked the Director. "You two could be our ambassadors from Earth. We could all learn so much from each other. And if you think this view is amazing"—the Director waved her hand at the vast scenery beyond the window—"just consider that this is the part of the universe we think of as our boring old hometown. So, what do you say, Dodger?"

Dodger had no idea what to say. He *had* been a lab rat, and yet he was also something unique in all the universe. He gazed out the window, at the glowing world, the vast reaches of space that would be open for him to explore, the maps he could create. He thought of the yearning he'd had all his life, to escape from the world that always seemed to fit him all wrong, to find a place that really felt like home, that felt . . . right.

He glanced over at Haley.

She was gazing out into space. "New map," she said with awe.

She pressed her hand harder into Dodger's.

"Would we be able to see our families?" she asked.

The Director seemed to sigh. "You could see them, and know that they are well, but . . . since they would be part of the worldwide interface, you would not be able to tell them about their condition. We could of course program it so that they didn't miss you, or, if you'd like, we could have you removed from their memories altogether, for everyone's ease."

"I've seen how that ends up," Haley muttered. "And what if we say no?"

"Well," said the Director, "I guess then you'll take your place among your fellow man. We'll have to insert you in Juliette until everything's ready, of course. And you, Dodger, we'd have to keep you here."

"Doesn't sound like much of a choice," said Haley.

"Everything's a choice," said the Director. "So, what do you say, my intrepid explorers?"

"I—" Dodger didn't know how to finish. Here it was. Something like what he'd always wanted . . .

And yet, he had to wonder if maybe those things he'd felt, about not fitting in, were really true anymore. Sure, things had seemed that way, so many times in his life. . . . They had even felt that way on this trip, but that was all before he'd learned the truth about his dad, who actually wanted the best for him but had as little idea as Dodger did of how to make that happen. They'd been doing the best they could, or the best they knew how. . . . Maybe it could be better now, if he went back. And if he left them, he'd be condemning them to a life under alien mind control. Of course, as the Director offered, he could *have* his parents' painful memories of Dodger and his abduction removed entirely, but he had to wonder . . . back on earth, back in Port Salmon, had he really tried his hardest to make the world fit him right, to fit into it better? Couldn't he try harder, especially given all that he now knew?

But maybe I'll try and fail, he thought. Maybe he'd never really get it right and his parents would never really get him. Maybe he would still have trouble making friends. He looked at Haley . . . or maybe, just maybe, it was possible to not only make friends but maybe more than friends . . . if he tried.

Haley squeezed his hand even tighter. As she did, Dodger felt something pinching into his palm.

"I'm sorry," Haley was saying with a deep sigh as she gazed out at Paha'Ne, "but I can't take your offer. I . . . I just can't."

Dodger sighed to himself. He joined her in gazing out at Paha'Ne. At the same time, in his mind, he reached back along the interface, searching. . . .

And then he said, "Well, I think it would be amazing."

"You do," said the Director. She sounded pleased. "Dodger, this is very exciting. Our child of the stars come home."

Dodger kept searching. . . . There it was. He took his hand from Haley's. Held it by his side. The bit of metal that Haley had given him was still there. . . . He turned his palm up and glanced down quickly at it.

"But I'm sorry," said Dodger, "I'm gonna go home."

He sank back, and in his mind, he suggested the symbol from the Alto's bracelet, which Haley had transferred to his hand, to the interface.

The Director clearly sensed it. "What—"

Command accepted, said the interface. *Project Bliss Control Interface Status: Disengaged.*

Wild lights and sirens began to sound around them, and Dodger turned, grabbed Haley by both hands, and flung himself backward into the crystal glow from which they'd come.

They hurtled through the orange blur of space and time, part of a torrent of charged particles, bodies and yet information.

The interface around them was alive with a frantic, repeating message:

PROJECT BLISS INTERFACE STATUS COMPROMISED!
ALL TEST SUBJECTS ARE WAKENING. DISCOVERY IS IMMINENT.
ALL PERSONNEL BOARD TRANSPORT IMMEDIATELY AND EXIT EARTH
TIMESPACE. REPEAT, ALL PERSONNEL ARE TO REPORT TO THE NEAREST
EXIT POINT AND LEAVE EARTH TIMESPACE.

There was a blur of ships and aliens, departing

from points all over the globe and joining the interface, back to Paha'Ne, with only two humans heading
in the other direction, back across the universe, back
to Earth and Juliette, which Dodger had just freed.

Juliette, AZ, July 7, 5:43 a.m.

In the third spiral arm of the Milky Way galaxy, on the planet Earth, on a high desert plateau, in the early morning, a town appeared where there had not been one for nearly twenty years.

In a moment, about twenty thousand people who'd been getting ready to go to bed on the twenty-fifth of April 1994 suddenly found July morning light streaming through their windows. They stumbled outside, trying to comprehend it all.

Amazingly, the phone and power lines still worked, though not the cable lines. There were a few people with bulky old personal computers, one of whom had an early internet application called the gopher. That, too, was useless.

Only two people in Juliette even had cell phones, and they were primitive things the size of shoe boxes and they wouldn't connect to the current satellites, either because the technology was different, or because their accounts had been in default for years.

Luckily for the just-returned and unaware time travelers, there was a capable young woman sitting atop a mobile home, parked a few miles above the plateau. She called the police, the news outlets, and the military. Everyone over the age of twenty with whom she spoke remembered Juliette—the memory cloaking had been removed when Project Bliss was disengaged—and didn't even realize that they hadn't remembered it moments before. Combined with the astonishing video that Alex shot of the town sketching itself into existence, which immediately went viral, there was a sudden rush from all points around the nation to get to Juliette. Within an hour, the first helicopters were buzzing the area, and a steady stream of news vans and military vehicles began arriving on a newly remembered highway leading north from Interstate 40.

They found the streets full of people stumbling around, some in their pajamas, trying to reconcile what had happened to them.

One group that would never understand what had happened was the myriad of desert creatures that, over the twenty years of Juliette's absence, had dug their dens and burrows in the empty sands of the plateau. These hundreds of creatures, including the entire population of a rare and as-of-yet-unclassified species of lizard similar to the Gila monster, were unfortunately squished when all the roads and foundations returned without warning. The human species, meanwhile, was suddenly safer than it had been in a long time.

Juliette, AZ, July 7, 6:23 a.m.

After their return from the interface, Haley and Dodger had sat somewhat stunned, on the catwalk with Suza and AJ and the Alto, watching spaceships fly overhead. Then they'd heard an ominous announcement that *Anti-Detection Doors* were about to close at all exits to the cave complex. Dodger had instructed them all to hold on to one another's shoulders again, and he'd beamed them out through a door that led to a sewer tunnel beneath Main Street. They'd popped out in the tunnel, and when Dodger had turned back to the silver door with the black discs, he had no longer been able to make them light up. The Paha'Ne had shut down the interface, at least for the moment.

And just as they stepped away from the door, there had been a tiny snapping sound, and the section of tunnel just above the door caved in, hiding it from view.

"We need to find a phone," Haley had said immediately.

"Mine is toast," the Alto had replied. "I think teleporting might have fried it."

They had climbed up out of a storm drain, finding themselves in an alley off Main Street. Suza had left to go home, and AJ had done the same.

The Alto had been standing there looking lost, when Haley handed him his bracelet back. "One more charm to figure out," she said. "IX."

The Alto had slipped the bracelet back on and nodded. "And the name . . . Charity," he said, then shook his head. "Nope." He looked at Haley and Dodger and made something resembling a smile. It made his face look comical. "Thanks to you both. She's here, I think. I just have to figure out where."

Haley wondered if they would hug or something. But the Alto just started out of the alley.

"Thanks," Haley called after him. "You know, for lying to us, and the rest of it."

The Alto turned. Now his face was serious. "Don't say good-bye. They might be back someday."

This sent an unexpected chill through Haley. "What happens then?"

"I'll be in touch." The Alto rounded the corner and was gone.

"Way to leave on a downer," said Dodger. "Let's find a phone."

"Yeah," Haley said heavily. She wondered if the Alto was right. They'd thwarted the Paha'Ne's plans, but . . . their planet was destroyed. They still needed a place to call home.

"Don't worry," said Dodger. "They'd know better than to mess with the Fellowship for Alien Detection again."

Haley shook her head. "If they do come back, we are going to need a catchier name."

Juliette, AZ, July 7, 7:04 a.m.

Suza Raines was getting suspicious. As she dropped her bike and walked up the steps, she had almost convinced herself that this was still her house, still her life. . . .

She was so nervous that she paused at the door. It would take a while to put together all the mixed-up memories in her mind, but anyone who'd lived the same day over and over in a town where she didn't even *actually* live, a town that had only recently been returned to reality and the memory of the rest of the world, was probably allowed some time to sort it all out. And Suza was planning on some serious mornings of sleeping in late to do so. But that didn't change what was about to happen right now. She considered turning around and coming home later—

The door opened. Matt stood there. "Hey, kiddo," he said, rubbing his head. "We—um, I'm not your dad, am I?"

"No," said Suza.

Matt nodded groggily. "Do you know where we are? And what day it is?"

Suza shrugged. "Arizona. It's July."

"Huh . . ." Matt stared blankly outside.

Suza pushed past him into the house.

She ran to the kitchen and picked up the phone, dialing with a trembling finger.

The phone rang. It rang again. Picked up.

"What?"

Suza heard the clucking of a chicken in the background, and her heart tried to lurch its way out of her throat. She couldn't breathe. The phone started to slip out of her hand, but she caught it with the other and managed to whisper, "Steph?"

It was silent on the other end. There was a light clicking sound. Then a slow breath. "Sis, is that you? Where are you?"

"Juliette," said Suza. "It's in Arizona. Turn on the news."

A hand cupped the phone. "MOM!" Then Steph returned.

"Stay there, kid," she said through her tears. "We're coming."

Juliette, AZ, July 7, 7:25 a.m.

Before long, the major news networks had set up shop, flown in their crane cameras and even erected a stage with a podium for speakers to inform the confused populace about relief efforts, and for the people to give their wild accounts to a rapt national audience.

No one had much information, and the crowd was getting restless, until two young people were spotted making their way around the back of the crowd in main street. They had planned to avoid detection. They'd tried calling their parents from a gas station pay phone, but neither the Richards nor Harry was answering. Dodger and Haley had shared worried glances about this but hoped it was that EMP effect of missing time.

"It might mean they're close," Haley had said. "Close enough to be affected."

"Or close enough to get grabbed. They could be in Paha'Ne by now."

They'd decided to find food and try their parents again. But then all at once the townspeople started turning toward them.

"That's them!"

"They're the ones!"

"We were chasing them!"

"We don't know why!"

"But they did something important!"

"Haley! Dodger!" a familiar voice echoed from the stage. Haley looked up to see AJ standing at the podium. "Come up here, you guys!"

The crowd parted, and Haley and Dodger walked forward in a daze. As they neared the podium, Haley took Dodger's hand. "You up for this?" she asked.

Dodger shrugged. "I don't know."

Haley sighed. "Me, too."

"Over here," said AJ, motioning Haley and Dodger to the podium. They stood, dirty and exhausted, facing the crowd. "Go for it," said AJ.

"Is it true you're the ones who discovered the town?" a reporter yelled. The microphones below swelled upward like a horde of snakes.

"Tell us how you found it!"

"We heard you found some kind of connection to United Consolidated Amalgamations!"

"Do you know where their offshore offices are located? We want to reach them for comment!"

"They're pretty far offshore," Dodger commented under his breath.

Haley wondered where to start. She squinted

against the bright spotlights aimed at her, staring out at the sea of people. She thought again, of that moment in school. "My summer will be . . ." she said quietly, remembering the blank page.

Haley had the answer for her snickering classmates now: *My summer will be a trip to the far reaches of inter-galactic space, where I will help save the rest of you from getting locked into permanent mind control by an invading alien race. How do you like THAT?*

She thought of all that time she'd spent imagining just what it would be like standing at the Daily Times Building, and how she would feel like she was exactly where she was supposed to be. Now, she looked out at where she had actually ended up, a place she had never expected, but maybe, as the Alto had said, the place she was meant to end up all along. Relief washed over her. She'd taken a huge risk, followed her Sixth Sense at the expense of the other things she'd wanted, and . . . it had worked! She had the story, one bigger than anything she would have accomplished in the JCF. Inside, the doubt demon was quiet.

"What was that about your summer?" an anxious reporter called.

In the back, crane cameras lifted slowly. Beyond those, satellite trucks beamed their images out across the world. Haley imagined herself on TV screens in Amber, Greenhaven, Thorny Mountain, even perhaps in the Hilton in Nairobi.

"Is it true that there were aliens?" someone called.

"What did they do to you?"

"Well . . ." Haley imagined the words coming from her lips. Starting all the way back at the beginning with the clocks . . . then about Suza, Graceland, Roswell, about Dodger and his fascinating connections, their adventure together, all the way to the distant shores of Paha'Ne.

And suddenly her mind started spinning ahead. What would be next from here? If she could pull this off, there was no limit to what she could do! She had that sense of infinity again, of the possibility that was everywhere, beckoning to her. . . .

But then the creature in her gut squirmed and she remembered more. Like how even though she'd gotten the story, she'd come *very* close to going too far *how* many times? Just because things had worked out didn't mean there hadn't been a few moments when she'd felt worse than she ever had. And that was some part of why, when she'd had the chance, for the biggest story of all, to live with aliens, she'd said no. *How did I turn that down?* she thought. But when she heard a voice from the crowd, she knew:

"Haley!"

Haley saw a line of heads bobbing through the crowd.

"Haley!"

"Dad!" Haley cried. The feeling was overwhelming. She stared as Allan pushed toward the stage, carrying Liam, Jill right behind them. There was also a burly man right behind them.

"Dad?" said Dodger from beside her.

"Francis!" Harry shouted.

Haley felt her eyes welling up. She glanced at Dodger. He was looking out at his dad barreling through the crowd, and he had a look that was kind of shell-shocked but also maybe thrilled.

Seeing them, Haley felt a certainty: From now on there was going to have to be a balance between those things she yearned for, and those things she needed: the things, like family and friends that kept her whole. Behind the podium, Haley took Dodger's hand again. "Let's go," she said.

"Were you aboard a UFO?" called a reporter.

"Come on, tell us what happened!"

Haley turned back to the hungry crowd, the cameras, all of it, and offered her most professional smile. "We're kinda tired, and our parents are here, so, you can read the whole story in our field reports. Call the Keller Foundation if you'd like to publish the article." Haley stepped away from the podium.

Reporters shouted for more, but Haley and Dodger headed straight for Harry, Allan, Jill, and Liam, who were just reaching the steps.

Haley jumped down the steps and the tears were coming and she threw herself into the mess of arms and hair and tears and family.

And out of the corner of her eye, she saw Dodger wrapped tight in a bear hug from Harry, his arms hugging right back.

After a minute of hugs and blubbering, Haley asked Dodger, "You hungry?"

Dodger's face cracked into a slight smile, and he spoke in a zombie's moan: *"Pancaaaakes,"* he said.

Juliette, AZ, July 7, 7:49 a.m.

Something had happened, Caroline Rialto knew that. But, standing in the parking lot of the Plan Nine Mercantile on Foster Avenue in Juliette, staring up at the sun, she couldn't quite put it together. She remembered working here at the grocery store, where she was a checkout clerk and spent day after day running people's bad food choices over an incessantly beeping scanner, hating the starchy collar of her puke-brown-and-white uniform, and working too many hours and on and on. . . .

But she also remembered being a technician at a strange mountain laboratory, where she worked surrounded by giant radar dishes.

In some memories she bagged people's groceries, asking if they wanted plastic around their meat products.

In other memories she did experiments in tuning some kind of crystal for a mass hypnosis of some kind.

Project Bliss, it had been called. *Don't miss our daily specials,* she said to her customers. She had a feeling that one was related to the other. Like, maybe she'd ended up here at Plan Nine after that job in the lab.

Or . . . because of it? Had she been *put* here?

Well, she'd have to figure it out later. Ever since night had become morning, and since, somehow, twenty years had passed, even though in Caroline's mind it had never *really* been 1994 . . . whatever, the point was it was slammed inside the grocery store. People apparently felt some strange need to eat in order to cope with change. And yet here she was, standing outside, almost like she was waiting for something.

Project Bliss. Don't miss our daily specials.

She looked back to the sky, trying to find the answers, but all she saw was the store's big sign, where the name was written as Plan IX.

She turned to head back into the grocery store, when a car careened into the parking lot, tires screeching.

It raced right toward her, a dusty black sedan. Caroline didn't move. Something about this car . . .

It skidded to a halt right in front of her. She peered in the window and saw a hula doll bobbing happily. She also saw that the driver's seat was empty.

"C-Caroline?" The voice had come from behind her.

Caroline turned to find a large man, dressed all in black, with short black hair and olive-colored skin.

She thought he looked scary.

She thought she knew him.

He was just staring at her, his brow working. He had a finger on his watch but now pulled it away and started fiddling with some kind of charm bracelet on his wrist.

It was a weird thing for a large man to be wearing.

Or maybe she had made it for him. Before he left.

Project Bliss. Don't miss—

"It's Caroline . . . isn't it?" the man whispered, like he wasn't really sure.

Her gaze locked on him. "Yeah?" she said. He smiled, looking so relieved, and then she remembered: "Theodore?"

The man's face scrunched. He fished inside his shirt with his thumb and produced a set of dog tags. He held them out to her.

Caroline stepped closer and looked at the name there:

THE ALTO

The alto? That was a weird name. . . . Except it was clear that letters had been scuffed and scraped by years of action.

Letters of a name she knew.

"Theodore Rialto."

Theodore smiled, as if hearing this was a great relief. "That's it." He held up a bracelet. "You gave me this, to remember, after I . . . escaped."

Caroline felt an overwhelming rush inside. She held out her left hand. "You gave me this, right before you left."

Theodore looked down at her hand. At the slender silver band with the diamond on her finger.

He pulled her into a long, crushing hug.

"You found it," she whispered. "After they caught us. You got out before they plugged us into the project. Before they wiped our minds."

"Well, almost," said Theodore.

"Why? Why did we do it. . . ." Caroline could feel the pieces jumbling around. "We . . . we thought . . ."

"We thought it was wrong, what they wanted to do," said Theodore. "We wanted to stop it."

"And you did it. You got the code into Juliette. You freed the town."

"I had help," said Theodore. "Kind of amazing help." He pulled back from her and checked his watch. "The military just got here. They're going to want to interview everyone. If we leave now, they'll never know we existed."

Caroline tore off her apron and rounded the car. "Aww," she said as she opened the door, "you kept Holly."

The Alto smiled. "She was my copilot."

The black sedan screeched out of the Plan Nine parking lot and off toward the wide horizon.

Juliette, AZ, July 7, 8:18 a.m.
The One Horse Diner was packed. Dodger had shoveled in about half of his pancakes and was now picking at them, feeling a little queasy from the sudden burst of real food.

"So, they're gone," said Harry from beside him.

"Mmm," said Dodger, but then he remembered that was his old answer to his dad's questions. "They got out once the time loop was busted," he added. "They could come back, though. They still need somewhere to live, and this is one of their possible places."

"And you got to see their home world," said Allan. "Really?" He sounded a little jealous.

"If it's any consolation," said Haley, "it had been mostly destroyed by a star that went super giant."

"No fair!" Liam added, "Our sun is boring."

Dodger laughed. "I can't believe you guys met up," he said to Harry.

"It was that Keller lady," said Harry. "She gave us these coordinates and we met up over in Flagstaff before we came out here. I'm just upset we didn't get here in time for me to give those E.T.'s a piece of my mind, and by my mind I mean my fist."

"Dad," Dodger groaned. He rolled his eyes at Haley.

But then he felt his dad's hand fall on his hat and ruffle it around on his head. "I'm just glad you're still here."

"Mmm," said Dodger, but he reminded himself again, and added, "Me, too."

"You'll tell me all about it, on the drive home?" Harry asked.

"Yeah," said Dodger. "I'll tell you about all of it."

Juliette, AZ, July 7, 8:20 a.m.

Haley checked her phone account from her mom's line. She had a text just moments old, from Abby.

OMG I'm watching you on the news! Abby had written. Haley felt a little rush, happy to hear from her friend, guilty for not being in touch for so long.

:), Haley replied.

You saved a town?!

Kinda.

WAIT . . . Abby wrote. *Who's the BOY?*

Haley blushed. She glanced over the table to where Dodger was sipping a chocolate milk shake and studying the menu.

Alien boy, Haley replied. *He's a friend. More when I'm back.*

Wait, is he CUTE? Can't tell from TV.

Haley rolled her eyes. *When I get back.*

Haley checked her email next, and found a message from Alex Keller. She read it to Dodger and the table:

Dear Haley & Dodger,

Congratulations on saving Juliette, and the planet! That's something you don't get to say in an email very often!

I wanted to apologize again for my father's behavior the other day, and let you know that I did retrieve him from Juliette and he is slowly adjusting to reality again. He can't wait to read about everything you found!

I just want to commend you both on your exceptional courage and perseverance. I look forward to publishing your reports, and no doubt to the storm of interest they will generate!

And, though this will probably be the last time my father ever tries to offer a fellowship of any kind, I did want to say, if you ever need help in your further adventures, do not hesitate to contact me!

Fond regards,
Alex

"Further adventures," Jill muttered.

Further adventures, Haley thought. *Not now, thanks.* She'd had quite enough adventure to last her awhile. She actually felt . . . full. Which was good, because though it hadn't come up yet, Haley knew there was going to be some discussion about the lies she'd told, the danger she'd put everyone in. She might be the first world-famous journalist to spend the majority of her summer grounded.

But still, she had to wonder: How long would this sense of satisfaction, of balance, last? Surely she hadn't heard the last of that yearning inside her, the one reminding her that, successful fellowship or not, she was still *on the clock*. There would be another big story, new map, and possibility. Who knew what might happen next, given how things had turned out here? What could be . . .

"Mom!" Liam was suddenly diving under the table.

"Honey, what are you doing?"

"I dropped my foot!" Liam shouted from under the table, referring to a blue lucky rabbit's foot he'd gotten somewhere in Texas. Once they were back in the car, Haley had every intention of pointing out that the severed and dyed foot of a cuddly creature was a completely gross thing to carry around for luck.

Liam's head slammed on the underside of the table, spilling coffees and juices.

"There it is!" He darted out into the aisle, causing the waitress to pirouette, a tray full of plates shaking precariously.

"Liam!" snapped Mom. "We are in a restaurant!"

Haley looked at Dodger and sighed. They shared a smile.

Watching Liam's antics, Haley knew what her further adventures would be: driving home with an annoying brother and a dad intent on family fun, this time with no field study to keep him on track. And maybe, at least for now, that could be kinda fun.

Acknowledgments

Some books happen more quickly than others. This one took nearly a decade. At many points, I thought this story would be taking up permanent residence in the desk drawer, and yet, here we are, and there is something so satisfying about that. From the first time I wrote the sentence "Suza Raines was getting suspicious," I knew I had something, but it took a long time to figure out how to tell this story just right. Luckily I found the support of key allies at key moments, who now deserve huge thanks.

First, thanks to Tui Sutherland, who read the original version of this manuscript and gave it that necessary vote of confidence that any writer needs to press onward. Next, to George Nicholson and Erica Rand Silverman at Sterling Lord, Literistic. You always believed in this story, and helped me stay true to its heart and resist the temptation to try to make it something it wasn't. And then of course to Jordan Brown, Kellie Celia, and Debbie Kovacs at Walden Pond Press, for welcoming this book into your amazing family. Jordan, your Jedi editorial skills helped me finally realize this story's potential, and Debbie, wow, I guess it was meant to be after all!

I'd also like to thank my family: my parents for driving me and my brother around the West when we were kids; and now Annie, Willow, and Elliott, who love to jump in the car with Dad and ride off in search of further adventures.